OUT OF CONTROL

NEW YORK TIMES BESTSELLING AUTHOR
K. BROMBERG

PRAISE FOR K. BROMBERG

"K. Bromberg always delivers intelligently written, emotionally intense, sensual romance..."
—*USA Today*

"K. Bromberg makes you believe in the power of true love."
—#1 *New York Times* bestselling author Audrey Carlan

"Always an absolute must-read."
—*New York Times* bestselling author Helena Hunting

"An irresistibly hot romance that stays with you long after you finish the book."
—#1 *New York Times* bestselling author Jennifer L. Armentrout

"Bromberg is a master at turning up the heat!"
—*New York Times* bestselling author Katy Evans

"Supercharged heat and full of heart. Bromberg aces it from the first page to the last."
—*New York Times* bestselling author Kylie Scott

ALSO WRITTEN BY K. BROMBERG

Driven Series
Driven
Fueled
Crashed
Raced
Aced

Driven Novels
Slow Burn
Sweet Ache
Hard Beat
Down Shift

The Player Duet
The Player
The Catch

Everyday Heroes
Cuffed
Combust
Cockpit
Control (Novella)

Wicked Ways
Resist
Reveal

Standalone
Faking It
Then You Happened
Flirting with 40
UnRaveled (Novella)
Sweet Cheeks
Sweet Rivalry (Novella)
Sweet Regret
What If (Part of Two More Days Anthology)

The Play Hard Series
Hard to Handle
Hard to Hold
Hard to Score
Hard to Lose
Hard to Love

The S.I.N. Series
Last Resort
On One Condition
Final Proposal

The Redemption Series
Until You

The Full Throttle Series
Off the Grid
On the Edge

Holiday Novellas
The Package
The Detour
Forever More

This is a work of fiction. Names, characters, organizations, places, events, and incidents are either products of the author's imagination or are used fictitiously.

Copyright © 2024 by K. Bromberg

All rights reserved.

No part of this book may be reproduced, or stored in a retrieval system, or transmitted in any form or by any means, electronic, mechanical, photocopying, recording, or otherwise, without express written permission of the publisher.

Published by JKB Publishing, LLC

ISBN: 978-1-942832-95-9

Editing by Marion Making Manuscripts
Formatting by Champagne Book Design
Printed in the United States of America

OUT OF CONTROL

PROLOGUE

Rossi
10 Years Ago

I DID IT.

I won the damn race just like I was told to.

It was tricky and it might be F3, but it's mega important, especially when the Gravitas F1 team owner is present at the track.

"A minute, Rossi?"

At the sound of his accented voice, I grip the sides of the table my ass is resting against to hide the adrenaline-laced nerves trembling through them. I quickly glance across the pits to where my dad is standing. Our eyes meet and hold for the briefest of moments before I look up to Atlas Stavros, the Gravitas team owner. The man I look up to. I strive to achieve all he has achieved. The undisputed iron fist when it comes to team decisions and the determiner of drivers' futures.

And with this victory today, no doubt he's about to decide mine.

I look at my teammate, pretty boy Cruz Navarro, and his trophied last name, and smirk.

Yep. That's right, Cruz-y boy. I'm getting the promotion over you. You may have the money, the legacy, but that last name of yours can't fix everything for you.

"Mr. Stavros. Sir. Great race, huh?"

Stavros studies me with an indiscernible focus followed by a slight nod. I don't get intimidated easily. In fact, I couldn't care less what anyone thinks of me, but this man has the potential to make or break my future.

"Mmm."

And that means what?

"I'm so glad I could bring home a win for the team today. All the guys worked hard and gave me a really great car to contend with and . . ." *I fought like a dog to impress you.*

"And what?" He narrows his eyes at me.

"And I deserve the promotion," I state. I won. I proved my worth. I deserve it. End of story.

"Let me tell you something," he says in a low, even tone as he leans in closer to me. I straighten my spine and wait for the praise, for the good news. It's what I deserve, after all. "You will never drive for me." His eyebrows lift. "Ever."

I jerk my head back. *What the fuck?* "I don't understand."

"If you don't kill yourself, you're going to kill someone else. You're out of control. A danger to everyone on the track. A liability I'm not willing to take on regardless of how much potential you might or might not have."

My mouth is dry. My temper is hot. My disbelief is all-consuming. My dad had stepped closer so he could hear our conversation, and now I wish to God he hadn't.

"*What?*" It's the only word I can form. Can process. Did he really just say that? There were two of us who were the shoo-ins for promotion. Two of us to pick from. "But I won. Cruz lost. I don't—"

"You heard me." Stavros's smile is cursory but his eyes are unforgiving. "That wasn't skill. That was a stunt. A way to get everyone to stop and stare. Well, they're looking all right, but for all the wrong reasons. And the fact that you think stunts over skill will impress me is all I need to know about you as both a man and a driver."

"Atlas . . . Mr. Stavros." I hate the desperation in my voice when I call after him as he turns to walk away.

But he stops.

And he looks back at me.

"Good luck to you. To your future." He looks me up and down, glances over to my father, and then back to me. "You're going to need it." *The fuck?*

I stare at him as he approaches Cruz and shakes his hand before patting him vigorously on the shoulder. And as the grin on Cruz's face brightens, my world darkens with the crushing blow of realization, of rejection—of criticism—from the one man in this industry I truly looked up to.

"You're out of control. A danger to everyone on the track. A liability I'm not willing to take no matter how much potential you do or don't have." Fuck that.

"Oliver?" my dad asks.

The lump in my throat feels like a boulder as I fight back the emotion I refuse to show. My pulse thunders in my ears. My stomach churns.

"It's fine," I grit out. "It's nothing." I turn my back on my dad as I start shoving my stuff into my duffel. Gloves. Headphones. Sweatshirt. *Stunts not skill.* I call bullshit.

I need to get out of here.

Cell phone.

Have to.

My fingers touch the glossy cover of the magazine under my bag, but my dad's hand is already there yanking it out of my reach.

"Hasn't this shit caused enough trouble?" he mutters, holding it up so I can see the cover image. A canvas on an easel, its stark colors akin to how I feel right now. Violent. Alone. Desperate.

"Give it to me," I beg, hating the sound of my own voice. If I don't get the fuck out of here, I'm going to lose it. And I can't. Not here. Not in front of *them*. I refuse to give the Navarros the fucking pleasure.

My dad holds the magazine higher and out of reach before making a show of dropping it into the waste bin with a thud. I bite back my protest. That fucker was expensive. It's not like I'm rolling in money. But it's not the money that has me reaching for it, that has me digging it out of the can in a frenzy, it's what's inside it.

My first love.

The one I'm not supposed to care about.

The one that grounds me and quiets my temper, my restlessness, and my inability to focus. The thing no one can quite understand with the exception of my nonna.

"I told you I didn't want to see that shit again. It's caused enough trouble for our family."

"Yep. Got it."

"Money. Time. Embarrassment. That's all it's caused. Maybe if you spent more time at the track, more dedication working on your reaction times, more time in the simulator—*fuck*," he grits out and shakes his head. "This is your calling. *This* is what you need."

"I forgot. Racing will toughen up the sissy out of me."

"I never said that," he says evenly.

"You didn't have to." We wage a visual war. One that I hate *and* love, which confuses me. His words, his anger, his disappointment from years ago still feels like yesterday. I've been crushed once today. *Do we really need to rehash this?* "Stavros is an asshole."

"Maybe, but he's the asshole who matters."

"I won the fucking race!" I shout, flinging my arms out. "Won it fair and square. How am I the asshole in all this?"

His stoic nod and unrelenting stare grates. "You won it but it was far from smooth. You impeded but got lucky you weren't penalized for it. You had the benefit of poor decision-making on the other teams' parts of when to box or what tires to use."

Acid pools on my tongue. The last thing I need is criticism from the one person on this track who's supposed to be on my side. "So you agree with Stavros?" *How could he even think that?*

My chest aches.

My heart feels heavy.

"I love you with all my heart, Oliver, but I think that *this*"—he points to the art magazine and everything it stands for—"is a hobby. I know that first-fucking-hand. Real drivers don't like art. You look weak enough already having Stavros pass you up. Don't make yourself look weaker by carrying this crap around. Do the shit that needs to be done. The stuff you can do to improve yourself," he says, pointing to the track behind us.

I chuckle to cover the pain of the knife he's twisting even more. "I forgot. You know all, huh?"

"I know more than you can imagine. Besides, I'm the one paying the price right now, aren't I?"

I grit my teeth. I fucked up. I know I did. And he's still pushing me here, still sending all his money my way to encourage this other dream of mine, while he's paying off the other debts I'm responsible for.

Guilt eats at me in a way I'm unfamiliar with.

In a way that tells me I don't have a choice but to race. But to get my family out of the hole I dug for them.

"Yeah. I know."

"*Oliver.*" He waits until I meet his eyes. "I would take on any burden possible to make you succeed. Don't feel guilty about it. This is my job as your parent, but you have to knock off this art shit. This—racing—is what you will succeed in. I can feel it deep in my bones. That's why I'm being hard on you."

"This is a longer shot than art will ever be."

"No. It's not." He says it so resolutely I almost believe him. "You're sixteen years old. No one has the right to take your dream away from you."

But you did.

He must see the thought in my eyes because he shakes his head as if it'll take away the truth behind it. "Fuck Stavros. You're talented, Oliver. Gifted."

I hear his words but don't want to listen to them. Don't want to believe them. "You don't know that. All you care about is having the right someday to brag that your son is an F1 driver."

His shrug communicates everything. "What I want is for you not to have to live paycheck to paycheck like we do. Working non-fucking-stop so that you can't ever be present to watch your kids grow up."

"You're here now, aren't you?" I ask like an ass. "*Present.*"

His chuckle is self-deprecating, and I know I've said the wrong thing. I know he's taken off work to be here. Know that there will be some odd job he'll have to pick up to make up the difference in income. Know how hard he's worked to give me this opportunity.

Know that I'm being a prick . . . but he just doesn't understand.

"Exactly. I am. And I need to get back to work." He yanks the magazine out of the trash bin and tucks it in his back pocket almost as if he's afraid I'm going to dig it out the minute he leaves. *I was.* "Like I said, fuck Stavros. Fuck him into next week for all I care. Us Rossis fight any way we can to stay afloat and get to the top. You keep working hard. You keep getting there by any means necessary. Someone will notice." He grabs the back of my neck and pulls me in to kiss the top of my head like I'm a little boy. I don't resist. I'm simply indifferent. "You're the only hope you have to not be . . . *us.*"

He says the single syllable like it's a curse. Like destitute is all we'll ever be.

And fuck, it feels like that more than ever right now. The guilt? It's like a lead coat weighing me down. Owning me. I'm the hope for my family to get out from under our financial struggles.

And I'll never be able to do that with art.

I know it. He knows it. The whole fucking world knows it. It is selfish for me to even want to, considering that debt is because of me.

Stay the course, Oliver. Don't give up.

"Prove him wrong," he says with a pat on the back. "That's our ticket out, son." He walks away, my magazine in his pocket and a sag to his shoulders. My animosity trails after him.

He just doesn't understand.

Hauling my duffel bag onto my shoulder, I turn back to the track. To something I'm decent at but that's already telling me I'm not good enough for it.

Stavros's laugh rings out.

I'll make it someday, you son of a bitch. And when I do, you'll beg me to drive for you. And even if you do, I'll never accept your request.

CHAPTER ONE

Rossi

"Hey. You—you're that guy," the drunk fuck in front of me says, his finger wagging in my face and his glassy eyes narrowing on me. He stumbles and chuckles because of it. "The racing guy."

"The hot one?" the blonde on his right arm says as she angles her head to the side and wobbles, no doubt affected by whatever was in the bottle she's carrying.

"Rossi." The wind picks up the dust and swirls it around us. It doesn't faze him. In fact, at this point in his drink fest, I don't think anything will by the way he clumsily snaps his fingers. "Right? F1? That Rossi guy."

I run a hand through my hair and smirk. "Nah. That's not me, man," I say, pulling my handkerchief up over my mouth, and grateful that my years of speaking English make my accent so slight it can be mistaken for American. "I get that all the time though."

"Dude. You're a dead ringer for him."

I nod. "Not the first time I've heard that." If we were in any other country than America, this lie wouldn't fly for shit.

"Can we take a picture with you anyway?" he asks.

I glance over my shoulder and then back to him. "Nah, man. My girl gets weirded out by it." *That and the last thing I need is you posting that shit on social media and people saying it's really me. Goodbye anonymity.* I'm all for being the center of attention during a race, but not here. Not when I need this escape as much as I currently do. "Have a good time though."

"Rock on, man." The guy throws a clenched fist up and the girl giggles.

I lift a fist up to copy him and then turn to wander among the endless stages. Each one plays a vastly different sound from the next. My head dizzies at several points when I'm being hit in one ear with EDM and the other with hip-hop.

Or maybe that's the alcohol.

Like it matters. I welcome the feeling. The rumble of the bass in my chest. The bumping against my shoulders from strangers as we jockey for positioning to watch the performances. The euphoric—and most likely quite intoxicated—vibe from the attendees.

They're just happy they're here.

As am I.

It's a different high than what I'm used to. The crowds chanting my name. The camera lens in my face anywhere I go. The fans desperate for a glimpse of me.

The high I typically get off on but that lately hasn't been satisfied.

There's a thrill in the anonymity here. In being packed in tight beside people and few looking twice at me. In getting to just be one of thousands in the crowd. In the freedom to live my best life without having to think of placing in the points or cardio regimens or any fucking thing beyond getting lost in the music.

There's no pressure to be Oliver Rossi, Formula 1 driver. No demand that I perform. No doubt over what the fuck I'm about to step into with my new team for the first race of the season, and zero media asking me how I think I'm going to fit in with my new team.

It's just me. Just the beat. Just myself to please and no one else to give a fuck about.

It's simply this music set ending and my curiosity urging me to move to another stage where another new artist awaits me.

I move with the throng of people as lasers from various other stages flash across the sky. Dust swirling in the moonless sky gives the appearance of smoke in the lasers, which adds to the laid-back atmosphere.

It's a cool illusion that makes me stop and stare while the crowd moves on. Maybe that's why I hear it. The commotion off to my right. The woman shouting. The man growling.

"Stop." I turn just in time to see her shrug out of some drunk fuck's grasp. "Just stop." She pushes against him and makes a disgruntled sound that's equal parts frustration and annoyance.

Lover's quarrel.

Seen way too many of those this weekend. Glad I'm single. Glad I don't have to put up with any of that shit. My mind drifts to Blair for a moment—my ex—but is then pulled back to the couple again.

To the woman who suddenly steps forward in a stream of light. *Wow.* She's stunning. At least from this distance she is but, with the addition of alcohol humming through my veins, I'll reserve judgment for when I'm closer. Or less buzzed.

But for now, she's the best view I have to look at. Dark hair is peeking out beneath a paisley scarf. Her face is painted dramatically in glitter and makeup reflecting off the lasers. Her lips are a bright pink, and her body is showcased with minuscule clothing. Her curves are accented—a white crocheted sweater-type thing over a bright red bikini top, denim shorts, and boots that go just over her knee.

"Jesus," I murmur. I can't take my eyes off her. It's as simple as that.

And maybe that's a good fucking thing because as she goes to walk away, the man beside her yanks her arm back, the force making her land squarely against him. Her yelp is smothered by his forced kiss.

Go for it, buddy.

But my thought dies quickly as she thrashes her head back and forth. As she struggles against him. She's not playing. She's terrified.

It's not my business. Not my situation. But no one acknowledges what's going on in front of them. *It's more like they're ignoring it.*

I cover the distance in seconds.

Chivalry isn't exactly my strong suit, but I know right from wrong, and something's most definitely wrong here.

I hesitate. *Does she know him? Does it really fucking matter? She said all she needs to say.* No.

His hands are still on her.

End of story.

I grab the back of his collar and yank him backward while my other fist connects with his cheek. There's nothing satisfying about the feel of it or the sound it makes. It's just a necessary means to an end. A way to make this fucker stop.

He collapses like a pussified bag of potatoes. *Figures.*

But that doesn't stop me. I land another punch. His lip splits and he's too stupid to shut his mouth.

"She was asking for it."

And another.

"Dressed like that."

I cock my fist back again, but there's a shriek.

"Stop!"

A hand pulling back on my bicep prevents me from landing another punch.

I try and shrug it off but turn and look into the eyes of the woman I'm defending. "Seriously?" I ask in a rage-filled haze. I miss the startled look on her face—eyes wide, lips shocked into an O. Her sudden hesitation. *Something's familiar about her.* "The guy had his hands all over you, and now you're telling me to stop?"

I shrug off her touch, cock back my fist, and deliver one more blow. Those words and that mouth more than deserve it. His head snaps back, prompting him to hold up both his hands in surrender.

Good.

The *fuck you* chuckle that falls from his lips as he rolls over onto his knees and begins to crawl away has me clenching my fist again though.

But a crowd is starting to form and the last thing I need is to be noticed. I don't need rubbish about Oliver Rossi splashed across the tabloids . . . no matter how true or how grandiose it may be.

I turn to check on the woman, to accept her gratitude, only to catch a glimpse of her as she hurries away.

And to think I expected some gratitude . . .

"Hey. Wait up," I shout as I jog the short distance toward her. "Are you okay? Are you—" I reach out, my hand hooking accidentally in her pashmina so that when she turns around, it falls off.

I'm met with a full head of dark hair that falls in waves down her back and a pair of amber eyes framed by thick lashes.

We stare at each other in shock.

"Navarro?" I ask. *What the fuck is she doing here?*

"Unbelievable," she says like a swear word as a half laugh falls from her mouth. "Fucking unbelievable."

She starts to take off again, pushing through people like the seas should part for her. *Figures.* I scramble after her and piss a few people off in the process as I barrel through them.

"Navarro. Wait." I grab her arm again to stop her. This time she spins on me, hands on her hips and just stares at me.

"What?" she snaps. "What do you want?"

I'm rarely surprised by people and yet . . . "Why the hostility? I just saved your ass."

She gives a part laugh, part snort. "Saved my ass?" There's something about the way she says it that makes me wonder if she even believes the false bravado she's exuding. "I didn't need saving. I didn't need you to—"

"Fine. Good. Glad to hear it," I say, but before the words are out, I see it. The tremble of her fingers as she clasps her hands together to steady them. Her pulse pounding just beneath her jawline. The shaky breath she draws in. The tears suddenly pooling in her eyes.

She's shaken up and trying to hide it.

Shit. I don't do good with emotions. And I definitely don't handle tears well.

"Good," she asserts with a nod and an unsteady shift of her feet. "Appreciate the help. Now I . . . I have a stage to get to."

"Nope. Not by yourself you don't." *What are you doing? You're not here to babysit.* In fact, just the opposite. *You're here to be selfish.* To use this time to do whatever the fuck you need to do to come to grips with losing her. But of course, what do I do? I move beside her and start walking despite her protesting groan.

"Why be nice? Why start acting like you care?"

"Why be nice? I think I already showed how nice I can be." I flex my hand. It's sore. That's what I get for plowing it into some prick's face. Let's just hope I didn't do any damage. Holding a steering wheel in g-force doesn't exactly bode well with a damaged hand.

She doesn't respond, but her footsteps pick up. Mine do the same. "Typical. I help, I'm the asshole. I don't help, I'm the asshole. Can't fucking win, can I?"

Sofia stops in her tracks, and I nearly run into her. Our bodies brush against one another's and fuck if I don't notice it. Warm skin. Subtle scent. Expressive eyes.

"Look. I said thank you." She shakes her hands as if to rid the trembling from them. "It's just . . . I need even footing, okay?"

"Even footing?" *I'm fucking lost.*

"Yes. Even footing. I'm not supposed to like you or look your way. It's just easier not to like you."

"Not to like me? What do you know about me other than I was quick to defend you when no one else—"

"My brother has warned me about you, okay?" she virtually shouts, throwing her hands up in exasperation.

I scoff. *Warned her about me? Who hasn't been warned about me* is the bigger question. "Cruz for the win, huh?" I say sarcastically, referring to her brother—and my new teammate.

Guess I know where I stand in his eyes. Can't say that it bothers me.

"No, it's just . . ." She exhales loudly as music starts up again to the far right of us. She turns in its direction and looks into the darkness for a moment.

I stare at her profile. *Christ.* I always considered Cruz's little sister to be gorgeous from afar—*I've never thought of her for anything more than the view*—but I am definitely struck by her right now. She's . . . stunning with the alluring curve of her neck, the fullness of her lips, and her delicate features. But there's something about her that seems to be calling to me in this moment.

"Just what?" *How are you going to follow up that confession, huh?*

She turns back to face me and simply studies me. "Just nothing. You didn't see me. I didn't see you. What just happened never happened and we'll be better for it. Sound good?" she asks, and her voice cracks on the last word.

Vulnerable.

That's what she is. That's what's calling me to stay with my feet rooted in place rather than bail like I normally do at the first sign of complication. She always appears to be so confident, so composed and sure of herself. And while I see some of her fire there, I also see the vulnerability that's calling on everything *I'm usually not* to protect her.

What the actual fuck?

This is not me.

And yet . . . *damn.*

"Yep. Sounds perfect," I say.

"Nice seeing you, then." She swallows forcibly.

I chuckle at her comment when we both remain in place, staring at each other like a game of chicken.

She's still unsure of herself.

The surefire way to get her feet back on solid ground—and for me to avoid being this bullshit version of myself who actually cares—is to be *me*. An asshole. Something I've been practicing my whole life.

"Nice seeing me? You don't really think that, and yet you're still standing here." I chuckle and lean in closer so she can hear what I'm saying. "Still trying to figure out why you want me to stay by your side, why you find me attractive and can't walk away, when you've been told to feel nothing for me, huh?"

"That's such a bullshit lie." The roll of her eyes says I'm right.

"No, it's not."

"Watch me." She finally gets the gumption to walk away.

And I do watch her, although what I focus on, what I admire, is the sway of her ass. No man in his right mind wouldn't look. But those seconds pass and I'm left thinking about that prick's hands on her.

And fucking hell, *I follow*.

I'm already cursing myself as I fall into step beside her. There's just something about her.

"Stop following me," she says.

"I'm not. We're both headed to the same stage. You heading to see BENT?" I ask of the popular band, completely oblivious to when and where they play other than it being sometime tonight.

"You just made it clear why my brother was right—why I shouldn't like you."

"Why? Because I like BENT? That's weird. You'd think it would be over something way more important like my character or my—"

"You're not funny and you're still following me. *Why?*"

I scrub a hand through my hair and scan the crowd in front of us. I don't think she'll buy *fuck if I know* as an answer even though it's the truth. "You've been drinking, Navarro."

"It's Sofia."

"We all have. There's no judgment there. Is it so bad if I want to make sure you're okay and get to where you want to go?"

"I'm fine. I assure you."

"Looked like it a moment ago. In case you didn't know, guys like to take advantage of women in situations like this. Happens all the time."

"Go away, Rossi." She turns her back to me.

Is she here with someone? Fuck. Was she here with the prick?

"Who was the asshole anyway?" I ask.

"No one I know. A random guy I just met who started following me. You know, kind of like you," she mutters but refuses to look at me.

"Watch your step there, Bellissima. I'm the one who has to fight women off me. Not the other way around."

"God, you're so . . . *you*," she says. *Like that could be the worst thing in the world.*

"Exactly. Wealthy. One of the top in his sport. Talented. Athletic. Good-looking—"

"Full of himself. A manwhore."

"At least I can handle myself."

"*And* an asshole." She smiles, and there's more of that trademark confidence back in her eyes and demeanor. My job is done here.

"And yet, you still want me."

"I, what?" she shrieks incredulously.

"You heard me. You want me. It's okay, everyone does. It's something I've had to learn to deal with."

"Oh my God," she says with a slight shake of her head as if she's trying to process the truth. "You're being serious, aren't you?"

I shrug. "It's okay to admit you do."

"No. I don't. What I *want* is for you to . . . Look. I'm a big girl. I can handle myself."

"Clearly." I glance back to where we came from—where there's a trail of blood from a busted nose—and I lift my eyebrows while fighting my grin. "Maybe you should lay off the drinking."

"Maybe you shouldn't tell me what to do. And maybe us girls have to drink to deal with guys. Ever think of that?"

I fight my smile. "Nope. Never."

"Now that that's settled. Vincent Jennings is about to take the stage so that I can swoon over him." *Lucky man.* "So this is the part where we go back to pretending like we never saw each other here."

"Just like that?"

"Just like that." She nods resolutely.

"And what if another guy tries to take advantage of you? Is that what you want?"

She looks at me, a seductive grin crawling over those lips of hers. "God, yes." She throws her head back and groans . . . and the sound makes my balls ache. "What's so wrong with that? Not that jerk back there per se, but a man I *want*? A man I can taste by just looking at him? There's nothing wrong with wanting to get lost in someone for a while. So leave me be so I can do just that." She lifts her eyebrows as if to ask if I'm going to question her.

Well . . . shit.

And this time when she starts to walk away, I let her.

Her words could be for shock value.

They could be the truth.

Either one is hotter than hell and just made me sit up and take more notice of Sofia Navarro. *She's* . . .

A good girl.

Comes from a well-known family.

Has a streak of rebellion I can relate to, appreciate, and admire.

Is completely off limits.

All of which motivate me through the crowd until I see her.

And that's where I stay all night long. With BENT on stage at my back and Sofia Navarro a few rows away in front of me.

CHAPTER TWO

Sofia

MY BROTHER HAS WARNED ME ABOUT YOU.

The comment's a constant refrain in my mind. Too bad my visceral reaction to his presence doesn't heed that warning.

Then again, when has it ever? No matter where Oliver Rossi is in the paddock, I always seem to spot him. *Always*. He's like that dark shadow you know you shouldn't look for but can't help finding . . . and then can't look away from.

Dark hair. Broad shoulders. An air of indifference. An edge to him that's equal parts arrogance and irresistible.

And that damn shadow has been following me nonstop.

"Hey, your stalker's back," Lilith says as she lifts her chin over my shoulder.

"Great," I mutter. Why do I like the fact that he's here? Why did my stomach just flutter?

Just like he was watching me last night. Yeah, I saw him standing there during BENT's performance with his back to the stage and his eyes on me. There was something so damn sexy about him watching me, clenching his jaw every time a guy approached me. I've never been one for the overprotective boyfriend type, but Rossi gave it an all-new face last night and I liked it.

Did I let him know it? Of course not.

Did I even show gratitude to him for saving my ass? Not as much as

I should have. Especially when he was the only one in a crowd of people who stopped to help me when that prick assumed a courteous smile and a bit too much alcohol meant he could take without asking.

Truth be told? I was a wreck. My confidence was shaken, my sense of security stripped, and the last thing I needed was for someone I knew in my everyday life to see it. For that person—Rossi—to say something to my brother, who isn't thrilled that I'm here. For him to treat me like Sofia Navarro when I came here to get lost in this festival and be anyone but her.

The woman responsible for keeping her family from imploding.

The woman who everyone seems to need all the time.

The woman who is Cruz Navarro's little sister.

Just simply Sofia from Spain. That's the only person I want to be this weekend.

So I acted like nothing happened. *Even footing*. Isn't that what I called it? I just needed things to be status quo—where I'm not supposed to like him, where I'm supposed to think he's a problematic person. That way I could settle my nerves and pretend that creep who touched me didn't exist and my confidence wasn't shaken.

But Rossi followed me. Watched out for me. He was a quiet presence in a sea of people and after what happened, that somehow made me feel safe.

It was a weird feeling. A new one to me. I've always noticed Oliver Rossi in the paddock or garages, and last night I loved that he noticed me. *Was watching out for me.*

Maybe that's what prompted my parting words to him last night. The shit I said about getting lost in someone. I don't know. I'm not immune to having a good time.

Or to being attracted to Oliver Rossi—if the buzz I feel knowing he's here is any indication.

I glance over my shoulder. There he is—*again*—across the sparsely crowded space. He's in the shadows, his back against a retaining wall atop a grassy hill with a beer bottle raised halfway to his lips . . . and his eyes are locked on me.

Adrenaline hums. And yes, my pulse beats a bit faster.

"He wants you. *Bad*," Lilith murmurs as another stage in the distance starts its set. A dull throb of techno echoes over the distance and hits us.

I glance at my watch and pretend not to care.

"He can want me all he wants. That doesn't mean he can have me." I shrug and take a sip of my own drink.

"Um, hello? Have you looked closely at him? Why the hell not?"

"Because . . . because he's him."

She throws her head back and laughs. "I don't try to pretend that I know anything about your world. Not your esteemed family. Not the crazy-ass world of racing. Not anything in your realm . . . but that?" She lifts her eyebrows, referring to Rossi. "*That* I could get to know more about if you know what I'm saying."

Great. Lovely. *Same.* "He's just . . ."

"He's just what? Gorgeous? Sexy? Mysterious? Possessive?" She raises her hand. "Sign me up."

"The problem is he knows it."

"Can't fault a man for knowing what he is. And can't fault a woman for appreciating it."

I can still feel his eyes on me. *Still love knowing they are.* "Huh." It's all I say in response. It garners a sarcastic chuckle from her.

"You do realize you two are the same, right? Too gorgeous for your own good. Intense. *Here together.*"

"You forgot one thing."

"What's that?"

"That he's a total player and unabashed fuckboy."

"And your point? What's the harm in some fun? You're here. He's here. You have a common understanding of the life he leads . . ."

"I think this is the part where I bow out to get another drink."

"Make him buy it for you," she suggests and nudges me with her elbow.

"I can buy my own drink, thank you very much."

"Where's the fun in that, Sof?" she whines.

"I'm not helpless."

"No one said you were," she states, but that unsettled feeling, that twist of my stomach in fear from last night returns briefly, causing me to roll my shoulders. His hands on me. That forced kiss. The shakiness after . . .

"Look, the man is used to women falling at his feet. Can't say I wouldn't exactly fault any of them for it . . . but I will not be one of them."

"Ahhh, so you are interested then," she states.

"Whatever." I roll my eyes. *What would it be like to be with a man like him?*

No, Sofia. He's as off limits as off limits can be.

"You are. Admit it."

"Interested would be fine if we left here and never saw each other again. But that's not possible. He's my brother's teammate. He's—"

"He's who you're going to sleep with before this weekend's over."

I bark out a laugh despite the slow simmering ache forming at the apex of my thighs. "You're crazy."

"Exactly. And you would be if you didn't." She taps her plastic cocktail cup against mine. "You're about to jump off the deep end—at least that's what you're saying."

"I am. This time, I'm going to do it." A dozen false starts and losses of bravado don't mean I won't stick to it this time.

Lilith eyes me and nods. "I believe you." She smiles in encouragement. "And since I believe you, since I know you're about to jump feet first into making your gallery a reality, I also know that this weekend, *this festival*, is supposed to be your time to have a moment . . . so have one."

"How about I sleep with anybody but him?"

"You can." She smirks and looks over my shoulder, no doubt at Rossi. "But you won't. He's so your type. And you've never been big on the whole taking a stranger home for the night thing so he's perfect. Kind of a stranger. Kind of not. And if he really is a fuckboy, then at least you know he knows how to do it right."

"Glad you have it all planned out." She's crazy. And so damn right it's ridiculous.

"I do. You can thank me later for the mind-blowing sex."

"You're being ridiculous."

"On that note . . ." Lilith looks to the left of us and smiles. I follow her gaze and spot the guy she's been talking with online. The one who came to the festival more for her than for the music.

"Go," I say.

"I'm not leaving you. I'd rather hang with—"

"I don't need a babysitter, Lil. Besides, you want to watch Stella Ferguson perform, and I want to watch DJ Skillz. I'm fine being on my own. You know me."

"Yes. The wanderer." She eyes me.

I didn't say anything to her about last night. About what happened with the jerk and why I met Rossi. If I had, Momma Lilith wouldn't leave my side for the rest of the weekend. She'd forgo her fun for my sake and say something about how we only get to hang out a few times a year, so she doesn't mind.

"I can stay," she says. "We only get to see each other a few times every—"

"Go." I laugh at my mind reading skills. "I'm fine. I promise."

She pulls me in for a quick hug and then wiggles her hips. "Don't wait up for me. I might be . . . *otherwise* occupied with Zach."

"I hope you are. Just text—"

"So you know I'm good and safe. Of course, I will." She reaches down and squeezes my hand. "I'd tell you to wait up for me but don't. And uh . . ." She takes a few steps back. "Make him work for it."

"I'm not sleeping with him."

She snorts. "Whatever you say."

"I'm not," I assert.

"You'll fight it. You'll flirt. You'll get turned on by his reaction—or lack thereof. And then, girl, you're going to cave." She draws the last word out with a dramatic flair.

"You're such an asshole." I laugh.

"Perhaps. But you still love me."

"I do." I push her playfully. "Now go."

"Going." She weaves her way through the crowd that's slowly gathering. "Make him work," she sings out before throwing her head back, laughing, and then jumping into Zach's arms.

I watch them for a few moments, happy for my friend and wondering how my evening *will* unfold.

I'd like to say nothing is going to happen on principle. On the fact that the last thing I want to do is prove Lilith right. But if I prove her right, what does that net me? Who gets the short end of the stick in that deal?

Me.

Not her.

I glance over the space in front of the smaller stage where I'm standing and purposely overlook Rossi.

But he's there.

In the shadows.

I can feel him. *It's almost . . . tangible.*

God, it's been forever since I had the kind of sex that leaves you breathless and wanting more.

Maybe it's time to clear the cobwebs out.

He's so your type.

"No, he's not," I mutter to myself while I replay every second I spent with him last night and pretend like I didn't notice how damn sexy he is.

He's perfect. Kind of a stranger. Kind of not.

Get out of my head, Lilith.

And yet I risk a quick glance his way. My nipples tighten at the sight of him.

You'll see him again, Sof. It doesn't matter how good the sex might be, you'll have to see the man time and again. In front of your brother and dad. With women most likely hanging all over him.

Ugh. I can crave him all I want but I can't have him.

I won't cave.

Can't.

Now if I can just make every erogenous zone in my body believe it.

CHAPTER THREE

Sofia

THIS SMALLER STAGE HAS A MIX OF PEOPLE, BUT THE MUSIC HITS hard and the beat feeds my soul.

If I have my way, there will be so many changes for me in the coming weeks, that this freedom—this ability to get lost in the music—is exactly what I need. And I do just that, let myself get lost in the familiar beat, my head back, my hips swinging, and the freedom of knowing no one needs anything from me.

Rossi's nowhere to be found. Not that I'm complaining one bit. He probably found someone else to follow around, to watch from afar, and to . . . turn on by doing so.

It's more proof that he's a player and when I didn't play, he moved on. Good to know. Better now than after I made a mistake.

Oh my God. What am I thinking? I've let Lilith get in my head that sleeping with Rossi was preordained before this trip ended.

Was it?

My laugh at my own ludicrousness is smothered by the DJ transitioning the song from one with a pulsating electronic beat to something more bluesy with an edge to it.

But this time when I close my eyes and lift my head to the sky, when I try to escape in the music, Rossi invades my thoughts. Front and fucking center. Is he dancing with someone else right now? Kissing her? Paying her all of his attention?

Why am I thinking this?

And why does the thought of him with someone else have jealousy firing in my veins?

I stiffen when a body presses up against me from behind. It's not a rarity at this festival to be body to body as you push past one person to get where you need to go.

But I wait.

And the person doesn't push past.

A set of strong hands rest on my hips and begin to encourage me to move.

Case of mistaken identity.

I whirl around to make the most of an awkward situation. To say *Sorry, wrong ass* or something like that, but my breath catches when I come face to face with Rossi.

I open my mouth to say something, anything, but am blindsided by the intensity in his eyes. His expression is impassive but his eyes? They say everything.

Need. Desire. Want. Greed.

The moment is fleeting but I'm a confused mass of mixed emotions that have no business being there. I'm jealous because of my own thoughts. Mad at him because I thought them. Then there's pure unadulterated lust that I feel from his hands touching me, the look he's giving me, and my curiosity he's piqued over what his kiss tastes like.

And there's the plain truth of the matter. That he's him and I'm me and while our worlds intermingle, we do not mix.

My ego's hurt in the most superficial, asinine way, but I hold tight to it and use it like it's a protective armor.

I jab a finger into his chest. "You."

"Me?" He lifts his eyebrows while cuffing my wrists in his hands.

"Yeah. You." *Brilliant, Sofia.* This is the part where you tell him that you're mad at him for your overactive imagination and admit that you were thinking about him. *Cuz that's going to do you a lot of good.*

"Yeah," he murmurs and while it may be low, its timbre rumbles in his chest and into where he's holding my hands against it so that I can feel it. "*Me.*"

Still holding my wrists, he brings our hands down and moves them behind my back, effectively handcuffing me and pressing our bodies against each other.

I'm aware of every long, hard inch of him against me. Of the way he starts moving to the beat. How his eyes never leave mine. Of the hiss of his breath when I begin to rock my hips from side to side.

We move together throughout the song. Him leading and me following. My hands locked behind me so that my world narrows to just him.

It's a heady feeling to be in a crowd of people and feel like it's just the two of us.

Rossi leans in, the warmth of his breath feathering over my lips, and I prepare myself for what I've been telling myself I don't want but so damn do—his kiss. My nipples harden and chills chase over my body despite the warm night air.

I wait for it, eyes closed and anticipation like a drug.

"Don't look now, Sofia, but you do in fact want me."

My eyes flutter open as disbelief laced with that crazy mix of emotions courses through me.

But he's still there, lips so damn close, curving up in a taunting smile.

Head games.

He's playing them. My own head is too. And now it's time to take control back. I came here to lose myself. To feel good. To relish in the moment.

I lean in and see the widening of his eyes as he thinks I'm going to kiss him. I don't. I put my lips to his ear and whisper, "In your fucking dreams, Rossi."

And then I turn on my heel and out of his grasp, losing myself in the crowd.

But not before I hear his laugh.

Not before I see the shock register in it too.

CHAPTER FOUR

Rossi

I THINK ABOUT HER.

More than I fucking should, I think about her. The way her body felt against mine. The way her lips parted when she threw her head back. The scent of the festival on her skin. The seduction in her voice when she virtually told me to fuck off.

She's a contradiction in every sense of the word, and it's intoxicating in a way I've never experienced before.

Forty-something hours since I first saw her, first realized I wanted her, and I can't stop thinking about her.

And I fucking love that I do.

No doubt that has something to do with why I've followed her around like a lost fucking puppy dog—or a stalker. Both can be true.

Christ, Rossi. She's your fucking teammate's sister. Off limits.

I've made no attempt to hide that I'm following her. Even after her colorful send-off last night, I still walked at a distance behind her to make sure she got back to her rental okay.

It's like I can't stay away. I don't think I want to.

And the same goes for tonight. It wasn't hard to find where she was. She likes the DJ sets with their bombastic beats more than the live musicians. She likes to buy water from the stand in the VIP tent that's to the far right because she chats with the lady running the booth about her children. And she likes to rest with her friend on the top of the grassy hill to the left of the booth between sets or just to meet up and talk a million miles a minute in that high-pitched tone that women do when they get together.

Every time I lose her, that's how I find her.

You are so fucked in the head. Forty-ish hours and you've watched the damn woman enough to know where to find her in this massive sea of people.

Not another one. I grit my teeth and roll my shoulders as yet another man approaches her.

I watch them chat as my hand tightens on my beer bottle. She laughs and puts her hand on his arm.

I clench my jaw.

The music starts up again, yet another song in an endless stream that's played here. They both sway to the beat from their place on the fringe of the crowd. It's innocent enough—*at first*—but the minute the fucker does what I'd do if I were him, move in closer, hands on her hips, his body against hers, every muscle in my body tenses.

"Grrr," I say to no one in particular.

Every second of their interaction is like a snapshot of time unfolding before me between the pulse of the lasers lighting the sky.

As his hands cling to her hips, with her back pressed against his front, she raises her hands to the sky.

He whispers something in her ear, and when she smiles, my stomach twists.

And as she runs her hands down the front of her body, her neck, her breasts, her hips, making every part of me want, she looks across the distance, locks eyes with me, and smirks.

My balls draw up. Ache.

These two nights have been like a long, extended foreplay. A taunt and a temptation that's right in front of me, that's tangible, but that I haven't touched. And this, her smirk, her hands touching herself like I want to, is just one more douse of kerosene on a low, smoldering flame.

She knows I'm here.

She's playing the game.

And that makes me want to drag her against me and take from her lips even more.

I chuckle. How can I not? And then I do something that every part of me rages against—I make a show of pushing off the wall, of nodding at her so she knows I see her, and of walking away.

The startled look on her face is all I need to see. Game fucking on.

And as much as I want to look again, to see if her head is craning after me, I don't.

Instead, I wander the grounds, moving from stage to stage. I'm physically there, but my mind is on Sofia and all the reasons I shouldn't act on what I know I'm going to act on.

It's not like I've ever cared what's right or wrong before. Why start now?

I hear her before I see her. The soft purr of the engine as it comes to a stop followed shortly thereafter by her murmured thank you that cuts through the early morning silence. Then there's the door on the rideshare slamming closed and then the click of her boots on the pavement as she draws near.

"You may have been dancing with him, but you know you were dancing for me."

She yelps as I step out of the shadows and then just as quickly chuckles while lifting her eyebrows. "You're here. How charming that you know where I'm staying."

"Someone has to make sure you get home safe every night."

Her head jostles at the revelation. There's surprise there but she locks that shit down quickly as if I didn't already see it. "And you took it upon yourself to assume I wanted that person to be you?"

My smirk is my only response. The fact that she's standing here, squaring off with me when she can walk through her door is answer enough.

"What if I had brought him home with me right now?"

"You wouldn't have."

"So sure of yourself, huh?"

I step closer and love that her breath hitches and her pupils widen. Yeah. The attraction? The desire? It's most definitely mutual. "When that whole show was for me? You can deny it all you want, Bellissima, but you know it, I know it, and I sure as fuck am certain that he knew it."

"You don't know what you're talking about." She steps even closer, to add challenge to her words. My body goes into overdrive, my restraint not far behind.

"I don't? Now, why would you say that?" *Jesus. Her lips were made to be kissed.*

"Because simply put, I'm a game to you, Rossi. A trophy to be won. A mark to be made. A pawn to be played with."

"And I'm an escape for you, no? The good time you want but never allow yourself to have? The freedom to go a little wild, to chalk that wild up to being at a festival so that you can walk on it without worrying what anyone will think."

"That's not—"

"It seems we both have reasons for wanting this," I murmur.

"What are you escaping from?" she asks, head tilted to the side, eyes wide.

And fuck if those words aren't a punch to my gut. To the reason I booked the last-minute flight here as a means to escape for a bit and clear my head.

To grieve.

"Rules and expectations," I lie and deflect. It's way easier than explaining shit I don't want to explain. Feelings I'd rather not feel. "I'm not one for either."

"So I've noticed."

I smirk. "Just like I've noticed you want me."

"I don't want you," she whispers.

Her breath is thready and goosebumps chase over her skin. I lean in closer and cup the side of her face so that my thumb can trace over her bottom lip.

"Keep telling yourself that," I murmur.

"I came here to be anyone but Sofia Navarro. I'm not her this weekend. Not at all. So it doesn't matter who you think she is, when tonight, right now, I'm simply Sofia from Spain."

"Perfect. Sofia Navarro wouldn't dare act on the way she watches me around the paddock. The quiet stares. The hardening of her nipples. The forced swallows to deny I turn her on. No. That Sofia? She'd run and hide behind her big brother who'd protect her from me."

"That's not true—"

I push my thumb against her lips to stop her lie. "But it is true. Deep down you're thinking how damn bad you want me and imagining how good I'd feel."

"Rossi." My name has never sounded sexier.

"For the record," I whisper and brush my lips over my thumb and her lips. "I'd feel fucking fantastic."

She takes a step back, but I can see that she's at war. Her body against her mind. Her desire against her reason. Her sense battling against her foolishness.

She drives me fucking mad in every imaginable way—and I've never wanted anybody more.

I chuckle when she doesn't move, this battle already won and she hasn't even realized it yet.

"Call him, Bellissima. The guy you were dancing with earlier. Call him to prove to yourself that you don't want me."

I hold her stare, waiting for her to be who she wants to be—Simply Sofia from Spain. In charge. In control. The one to initiate.

Three.

Two.

One.

She fists her hand in my shirt and pulls me down to her eye level.

"Took you long enough," I say and smirk.

CHAPTER FIVE

Sofia

ROSSI STARES AT ME, HIS EYES DARING ME TO STOP AND BEGGING me to initiate whatever this madness is between us.

My brother's warnings are long forgotten. My sensibility is riding shotgun with it. Every protest I should wage dies an unceremonious death as I stare at the man I've hoped I'd have from the first minute I saw him this weekend.

Make him work for it.

Thanks, Lilith, because that seems really comical about now.

"Rossi . . . I—"

"Simply Sofia from Spain." The timbre of his voice ghosts over my skin like a feather—building anticipation. Daring me. "Just give me one night."

My chest constricts at the words. At the empty promise in them. At the unspoken allure to them. "That's all there can be," I whisper. "After tonight, I'm no longer this woman. I'm no longer—*her*. I can't be." How could he ever understand?

But he nods. His eyes meet mine with a quiet comprehension that both unnerves me and emboldens me.

"Then be her tonight."

"But what about—"

"Worry about tomorrow, tomorrow."

Our breaths mingle in the small space between us, thick with desire and uncertainty. The ache of wanting him, of needing him, overwhelms any rational thought.

"We shouldn't for so many reasons," I add.

He laughs. It's so quiet but I hear every sound. "You're talking entirely too much, Sofia." He brushes my hair back off my forehead. "You chased after me. What are you going to do about it?" He leans in and brushes his mouth to mine, this time without his thumb in the way. It's the gentlest brush of lips. A moment of calm amid our turbulent desire. "Because I know what I want."

"What's that?" I challenge as my body aches.

"Sweet Sofia, if I tell you, then I just might scare you away." He chuckles.

I hold tight to my bravado, to my desire, and lean my lips close to his ear. "Then show me."

I turn on my heel and head to the house at our backs. I add an extra swish to my hips, knowing Lilith isn't coming back tonight and I won't be walking inside alone.

The minute the door is unlocked and pushed open, Rossi has me spun around so that both his lips and his hands can feast on me and my body.

"I wasn't walking away this time. There was no choice in the matter. There never has been," he says, each sentence accentuated by another kiss that overwhelms my senses. "I'm going to fuck you, Sofia. I'm going to let you walk on that wild side. And we're going to enjoy every goddamn second."

He slams the door at his back and then cups both sides of my face as he dips his head down for another kiss.

One packed with urgency and need. With desire and fervor.

The world around us fades away. There's only Rossi, only this moment of raw intensity that consumes us both. His hands on my skin. His fingertips skimming ever so lightly over me has chills racing down my spine, igniting a fire deep within me that threatens to consume everything in its path.

I welcome its burn.

How can something I've been told is so wrong feel so incredibly right?

He leans back and chuckles. "I guess dreams do come true," he murmurs.

In your fucking dreams, Rossi.

Leave it to him to make right now about proving a point. "Fuck you," I whisper without any heat.

"That's the plan," he says and then slants his lips over mine yet again.

We move down the hallway in fumbles and laughter, but never quite breaking from each other's touch. It's as if we've wanted each other forever and now that we have each other, we're not letting go.

But we haven't. It's been me staring after him in the garage. Him staring at me at this festival. And yet . . . there's an intensity to our lust-driven frenzy that makes this feel like so much more.

We stop midstride, my fingers are threaded through his hair, and his smile is spreading against my lips.

"The bed, Bellissima, or the wall is going to get tested."

"As long as it's good and hard, I don't care where it happens."

"Oh, it's hard all right." He chuckles and then I smother the sound with my own kiss.

Our bodies move together, as if drawn by an unseen force. His step forward is my step back. His head tilt to the left is mine to the right. His moan is my groan.

His heart races a thundering staccato beneath my fingers, a wild, erratic beat that matches my own.

I pull my cropped T-shirt over my head as he does the same to his.

I'm rewarded with a guttural groan as he takes in my bare breasts and the tightened buds of my nipples.

"Christ, woman." He dips and closes his lips around one. I'm assaulted with the warmth of his tongue and the adeptness of the pleasing pressure he adds as he sucks.

He looks up at me, amber eyes heavy with desire, one hand cupping one breast, and his lips releasing the suction on my other. My body convulses involuntarily as the sensation creates a mainline straight to my core. "What does it for you, sweet Sofia? What's your thing? Do you like your nipples sucked? Your pussy finger fucked? Your clit licked? Your ass played with? My cock hitting that perfect spot inside?" He moves to the other nipple and draws it into his mouth, his tongue circling around it. If he keeps that up, I just might come right now. "What is it that gets you off?"

"How about all of the above?" I chuckle. Then moan.

He slides one hand up my bare back and the other one inside the waistband of his now unzipped jeans. His growl echoes as he frees his cock and strokes it. It's my turn to admire now. It's my mouth that's watering at the sight of its beauty.

I shove his pants down even farther and encircle his cock with my hand. It's silky smooth and incredibly hard, and all I can think about is having him in me. Pleasing me. Teasing me. Owning me.

I'm not a casual sex kind of girl. My sex life is active enough, but I don't think I've ever wanted a man more.

It's the whole package of him. The strong shoulders. The trim waist. The corded muscles beneath. The thick cock framed by strong thighs. His rough, cut jaw and his kissable lips.

The forbidden.

And I already know about his dirty mouth.

Oliver Rossi is most definitely an incredible package in all senses of the word.

"I love your eyes on me, but Bellissima, I want them on me while I'm in you." He lifts his eyebrows and then his lips find mine again. It's with a renewed hunger and an edge of desperation.

I feel both too and within seconds, we're landing squarely on the middle of my bed. His mouth is on me—my lips, my neck, my ear, my breasts. He's everywhere and nowhere long enough.

I'm all for foreplay. I'm the queen of wanting it. I spoke too soon, saying I want all of the above because right now I don't care about that. Right now I just want him filling me. Pushing into me with a punishing pace until I detonate in the best kind of way.

His hand delves beneath the lace of my skirt for the first time, and I buck my hips, wanting his touch there. Needing it there.

"Fuck," he groans as he slides my panties down my legs. "They're soaked." He holds them up so I can see the unmistakable dark patch. His smirk is cocky as he shifts to his knees between my thighs.

"You *were* dancing for me, weren't you?"

"Or maybe they're soaked because of him," I taunt but his flash of a smile says he doesn't buy the lie I'm trying to sell. I'm okay with it because his hands slide up the outside of my thighs and push my skirt up to my waist.

His hissed inhale when he sees my bare pussy is one of appreciation. With his teeth sinking into his bottom lip and his eyelids heavy with desire, he rolls a condom on his cock.

His eyes remain fixed on his fingers as they slide between my slit and part me. As they dip into my well, the unmistakable sound of him pushing into me, and the slickness of my arousal filling the room.

He watches me with a dedication I can appreciate and with motions that make my body sing.

My back arches as he thrusts his fingers deeper. My head falls to the side as he moves them around. My gasp falls out as his thumb adds friction to my clit with whatever skilled machinations he's doing that are utter bliss. They're like a palpable current charging through every part of me.

His biceps bulge with the action. The tendons in his neck are taut. His lips fall lax as his eyes take in what he's doing to me.

The arousal dripping everywhere.

The pink of my swollen pussy.

The tensing of my thighs.

"You like that?" he murmurs as he pants with the motion. "I can't decide what I want more. To taste you or to fuck you."

"Rossi. You. This." He switches the angle of his fingers. I don't know what it is about them but . . . "*God.*" I draw the word out as my world turns black, then white, and then as the orgasm hits me like a tidal wave of pleasure, a gush of water soaks the bed beneath me.

My eyes shock open as Rossi kneels between my thighs, his own now wet, and before I can process what just happened or *how* it happened, he grabs my thighs with a bruising grip and pushes into me.

His groan fills the room. It's feral and intoxicating and the only thing I can really focus on as my muscles pulse around him, squeeze him, and welcome the incredible fullness of him being inside me.

His hips jerk as he restrains himself but God, is he gorgeous. His head's thrown back, his jaw's clenched tight, and his fingers hold on to my hips possessively.

And then ... then he begins to move.

Rossi sets a punishing pace—like a man on a mission to make sure I get what I need from him all while taking what he does too.

He's high praise and dirty words.

"Fuck me, Sofia. Fuck me like you're desperate for my fucking cock."

I'm powerless against the sensations coursing through me. It's him and his actions controlling my body's pleasure.

"Take it. Just like that. Take every goddamn inch of me until you can't take any more."

My breath becomes ragged, and I grip the sheets beneath me, my nails digging into the cotton as I try to hold on to some semblance of control. He leans forward, surging to blissful depths as his lips find my ear, his breath hot and heavy against it.

"Does this pretty pussy of yours want more? Tell me. I need to hear you say 'fuck me, Rossi.'"

But he doesn't give me any control. He continues to move. In, a grind against me to push even farther, out, to where he withdraws completely and slaps his cock against my clit. I yelp from surprise but then sink into the sting of it. I welcome the sensation.

"I love the way your tits bounce. The way you tighten around me. The way you're begging for me to stop and keep going at the same time."

He drives us both closer to the edge. The room fills with us. The slap of our skin against one another. The unmistakable smell of sex. The labored pants mixed with murmured mewls.

"Come for me, Bellissima. I'll keep going until you do. Come for me like the fucking good girl you are."

"Yes," I cry out as I tip over that edge, straight into the arms of blinding pleasure that shakes me to my core. I ride the pleasure that surges through my every muscle, my every nerve, and allow it to own me. To sate me. To show me what could be.

I've never felt pleasure like this before.

It's cliché and ridiculous but it's inarguably true and, in the moment, I dare not think what that means for me.

And I can't because gorgeous Rossi is a sight to behold as he braces his hands on either side of me. His olive skin is misted in sweat. His face is pulled tight with concentration. But his eyes ... his eyes hold mine as he works himself to his own oblivion.

I'm his to use now.

His to chase his pleasure in.

And when he hits that peak, when he cries out something in Italian, I can't tear my eyes away.

I don't think I would though ... even if I could.

CHAPTER SIX

Sofia

WE COME BACK TO EARTH SLOWLY.

Hearts decelerating. Breathing evening out. Mist on our skin evaporating.

We lie side by side on my bed as my brain relives every glorious moment of sex with Rossi, and I bask in the bliss before the feeling inevitably dissipates.

Right up until I shift and realize how wet the bed is.

Oh my God. My cheeks heat. *Just after* sex when you've been with someone new is awkward enough, and now I have to navigate the fact that I—

"I'm sorry. I didn't mean to—"

"For?" His voice is sex-drugged and is a whole seduction in itself.

I shift in the bed, pluck at the wet sheet, and die a little inside of embarrassment. "This," I say quietly.

"What was that?" Rossi asks as he turns on his side and props his head on his hand. I can feel the weight of his stare and see him smirk in my periphery, but I don't dare look his way. "Simply Sofia, what did you just apologize for?"

I want to die a thousand deaths. "This. How wet everything is." I pluck at the sheet again without fully processing how I climaxed like that when that has never happened to me before.

And of course, it happens with Rossi.

He leans forward and presses a kiss to my lips. "And I've never slept with a teammate's sister before so we're both embarking on new territory here. Either that or I'm just *that* good."

"Oh Jesus." I roll my eyes and press against his bare chest but more than grateful for his playfulness that immediately eases the awkwardness.

"I mean"—he cuffs my wrist with his hand and then shifts to straddle my hips in seconds—"I *am* that good." There's no way to avoid Oliver Rossi or staring at him regardless of how uncharted this territory is. He's buck naked and his cock may be resting on my stomach, but his eyes are on me, and his hands are holding mine so I can't hide. "And that was fucking hot. Hands down. Don't apologize for a goddamn second."

I close my eyes and force myself to own the feeling and the moment. I have *never* been so well . . . fucked. *Clearly, Sofia*. But how? How did he make that happen? *Because it felt incredible. And I want it again, if I'm honest.*

His lips find mine in the darkness. They linger and tease and my body is so oversensitive from sex that every touch feels like it's amplified.

"I do believe you just made me more obsessed with you because of it."

"Obsessed with me?"

"Mmm," he says against my lips before rolling off me again and sprawling beside me. "Definitely obsessed."

I sigh and let my eyes close. *Obsessed*. In a sense, isn't that almost what I've been when it comes to Rossi? I looked before but I never touched because he was in the periphery of my world. A different team. A different garage. Sure there was an added mystery to him because of it. Add that to my brother's warning and it created more curiosity than anything.

I haven't had a chance to see what it means this year with him being my brother's new teammate. And this—us sleeping together—definitely wasn't on my bingo card.

"Why'd you agree to Gravitas?"

He belts out a laugh. "Your pillow talk needs some work, Navarro."

"Even footing," I mutter.

"There's that term again. Is this something you do when you get nervous? Get back to the status quo to calm yourself?" He hooks his calf over my shin. "And why are you nervous in the first place? We're two consenting adults. We find each other attractive. We wanted each other. We acted on it."

"You wouldn't understand."

"What I understand is that the warning your brother gave you about me must mean more to you than your own opinion does."

"No. It's not that."

"Then what is it?"

I blow out a breath and stare at the ceiling. Duties. Expectations. Parameters.

"It's hard to explain."

"So I'm only good for rebelling against your norm and mind-blowing sex then, but nothing else?" he teases. He has a point.

Not that I ever thought of Oliver Rossi as a big talker to begin with.

"Yes. Only good for sex and rebelling against warnings."

"I'll wear that badge with pride any day." He gives a definitive nod but continues to stare at me. "*Even footing*. I want to understand."

"Just like I want to understand why you said yes to Gravitas when there are rumors you said you'd never drive for them."

Something glances through his expression. It's fleeting but raw and as soon as it's there, it's gone.

"How about we forget the deep dive, huh? Aren't we Simply Sofia and Just Rossi right now?" he asks. *Okay. It seems I hit a nerve.*

"Hmm. *Just Ollie*," I murmur but am too lost in a silly smile to notice his sudden tensing as anything more than a shift.

"What did you say?" His voice is gruff.

"Simply Sofia and Just Ollie." I shrug. "Rossi sounds so formal and . . . *foreboding*." I chuckle. "Ollie sounds cute and cuddly and . . ." I glance over to him, and he has the most peculiar look on his face—one I don't dare to decipher. It's strange enough that when he paints a smile on his face, his change in demeanor is noticeable. "What?"

"I think we should stop talking."

"We should?"

"Mm-hmm." He runs his hand down my bare abdomen. "Way too much talking."

"Are you trying to distract me, Ollie?"

"Distract? Perhaps. Or maybe this is just my way to get 'even footing.'"

"Funny." But the last syllable stutters as his fingers part me and begin a slow seduction that his mouth follows shortly after against my own.

I moan at the simplistic bliss of the moment. Of his actions. Of him seducing me into submission, because pleasure is more important than the answers to any questions right now.

I came to this festival to have a reawakening of sorts, a carefree moment without anyone knowing who I am, and to forget all familial obligations.

What better way to end it.

With Rossi. Like this.

But as we tangle ourselves in the sheets, there's one very important question we leave unanswered: *what happens next?*

And maybe I get my answer when I wake up hours later to an empty bed beside me. The sheets are cold and my ego's hurt.

Lust is like a drug.

It rules your body.

It mitigates all sense.

It makes you forget the reasons *why* once the high ends.

And it leaves you with a wicked hangover and a hankering for more.

But for me, as I curl on my side, my body deliciously sore from the pleasure Oliver Rossi gave me, I'm reminded of lust's truth.

That it's an unforgiving narcotic that offers pleasure before it burns bright with pain.

But isn't that what I wanted? The bright light? Its blinding euphoria? The chance to be someone else for a weekend?

The walk on the wild side?

Yes. Yes. And yes.

What does that mean though when I'm forced back to reality? How will I feel when I see him regularly? When I'm no longer Simply Sofia from Spain and I want more?

CHAPTER SEVEN

Sofia

"I DON'T UNDERSTAND."

I sigh and cross my arms over my chest. The villa is laid out before me. It's acres upon acres of fertile land that has been in the Navarro family for years. Vines of varying grapes hang from trellises, waiting to be pressed and fermented when the time is right. It's merely a hobby for our private stock and not how the Navarros made their money.

There's history here. Our ancestors being tied to the Spanish monarchy in some shape or form is where the money and land originally came from. That money had been invested wisely but it was my grandfather, el patriarca, who made Navarro a revered name in motorsports. The first Spaniard to win a Formula 1 championship and one who's made a lasting impact on the sport.

I glance over to him now. He's in his wheelchair on the patio. His face is lifted to the sun, but his eyes are closed as if he's absorbing its warmth and finding whatever it is he seeks there.

My heart swells at the sight of a man who's given me so much—unconditional love, temerity, and reprimand when needed. He's the reason I try so hard to hold this family together. Why my last name means so much to me. It's not his fame or fortune I admire, but his quiet, unyielding presence in my life.

When you live in a house of chaos growing up, you cling to the things that ground you. You fight for them. And those two things are people—my grandfather and my brother.

"Did you fall off a cliff?" Cruz asks in my ear and startles me back to our conversation.

"Nope, still waiting subserviently for you to tell me exactly why you don't understand my need to not stand quietly beside you like a trophy. Isn't that Maddix's job?" I say with sickeningly sweet sarcasm, referencing his fiancée.

"First, Madds would kick your butt for even suggesting that she's going to be a trophy and second, what crawled up your ass? All I asked is why you're not coming to the first race of the season. You always do."

Why am I not going? How about because Rossi will be there—*obviously*—and I'm not one hundred percent sure what that means for me yet. Have I wanted more of him? Most definitely. But now that I'm back in my everyday life, Navarro is tacked onto Simply Sofia. And as is with all facets when it comes to my surname, numerous things are unacceptable.

Like a certain Italian who doesn't live up to the family standards.

But oh wait, I can't say that because you told me he was off limits.

"Um . . . because I can't." *Brilliant answer. One for the ages, Sofia.*

"Because you can't." He chuckles and it has that big brother snark to it that tells me he's not buying shit and is already trying to figure out the why behind it.

"Exactly what I said. *Because I can't.*"

"I see," he says and falls quiet as I move a few feet away from el patriarca as to not disturb him. "Who is it that you're avoiding?"

Shit. Am I that transparent?

"No one." I roll my eyes even though he can't see it.

"It's not my crew, it's not my team, and it sure as shit isn't Rossi." He emits a low hum of disapproval in reference to his new teammate while I quietly prevent myself from audibly choking on a breath of air. "So who is it?"

"Oh my God, you're maddening," I say. "You think the only reason I'm not coming is because I slept with someone on the circuit? Wow. Chauvinist much?" The minute the words are out, I cringe. El patriarca just heard that. Awesome. I don't care how old you are, your grandfather hearing you talk about sleeping with someone is *always* embarrassing.

"The girl goes to a music festival and comes back with even more sarcasm and sass than when we sent her." He chuckles playfully.

"You didn't send me anywhere. In fact, you didn't even want me to go."

"Is there a reason you haven't said a single thing about said festival?"

He's always had a good nose for smelling bullshit.

"There's nothing to tell," I lie. *Traitor.*

"Bullshit," he coughs out.

"Fine. A lot happened. A ton. I drank. I streaked naked through the crowd. I went to a wild—" I wince and glance my grandfather's way.

"El patriarca is right there, isn't he?" Cruz chuckles and the knowing sound grates on my nerves.

My lack of a response is his response. "Maybe I want to keep the experience for myself. Did you ever think about that?"

"Secretive and hostile."

"Now, how about it was a transformative experience, one you wouldn't understand even if I could put words to it."

"Translation being you definitely have regrets over whatever it is you did there."

"I'm going to hang up on you. You're being ridiculous." I huff. "I'm going. See—"

"What if something happens to me?" he asks just before I click end on my phone.

Here comes the guilt.

"It won't. You'll be fine."

"What if it does?"

"Then Maddix will be there," I say. The pang of guilt will hit in seconds.

Yep, there it is. Right on time.

"Sofia. I want you here. Besides, you're the only one who can run interference with Mamá or Papá or whoever decides to show up."

"Ahh, that's why you want me there."

"No. I want you there because you've never not been to an opening weekend," he says quietly. "Is it so wrong of me to ask you to come?"

Fuck. I pinch the bridge of my nose. All was fine with lust and sex when I was at the festival. It was simpler. Easier to figure out. To understand.

I've never once considered what happened a mistake—no way in hell do mistakes feel that good—but I wouldn't say it was one of my better decisions either.

You have a one-night stand with someone you'll never see again. With a person you leave behind and then out of the blue, wonder—*or not*—how they're doing.

You don't do it with the man you've been warned about. A man you know you're going to see often.

A man you can't stop fucking thinking about.

"You're going, Sofia," el patriarca says in his shaky but authoritative voice from across the patio. "Navarros support Navarros. You will be there."

"But I have stuff to do." *I'm trying to rid his touch from my mind. His taste from my lips.* "I'm trying to get everything—"

"Yes, well, this family comes first. No?" he asks without looking my way.

Cruz chuckles in my ear—clearly hearing him through the connection—and then gloats. "Perfect. See you there, Sof."

"Grr," I say softly into the phone. But when el patriarca speaks, we all listen.

Cruz hangs up and I'm left lost in my thoughts.

I feel like a traitor.

Isn't that just like being a woman to feel guilty for taking pleasure in something?

"My Sofia," el patriarca says.

"Yes?" I move toward him, thinking he needs me to get something for him. His nurse is usually at his side but I told her to let us have some time alone. It's been two weeks since I've seen him, and I want this time.

"Sit." He pats the arm of his wheelchair to reinforce his words.

"What is it?" I turn to face him. "What do you need?"

"No more talk of the festival, *si*? You went, you had fun, but it's not preferred to have you speak of your . . . *exploits*. We are Navarros. We have a standard to uphold. We have a reputation to maintain. There are expectations we must exceed."

And yet Cruz could fuck around and all was fine.

I bite my tongue and nod.

"I was talking with Emilio the other week while you were off in America."

"With all due respect, el patriarca, I have no interest in dating his grandson regardless of how good his pedigree is." The only way I get away with rolling my eyes is because they're hidden behind sunglasses. "I love you. I'd do almost anything to make you happy and proud of me, but that is not one of them."

His sigh settles in the quiet between us until he speaks again. "This *stuff* you were talking about. Does that have to do with this hobby of yours . . ."

"It's not a hobby. It's what I want to do. Open a gallery. Showcase artists." I pause, needing to make sure my voice doesn't sound like I'm pleading for him to understand. His blessing to proceed and not piss off the delicate family balance is all I'm asking for. And it's one step closer than I've ever come to actually doing this. "It's a passion that I've always had. Just like your racing was a form of art, this is mine in a sense."

He nods. "But you're not making it."

"No. I'm showcasing it so others can see it. Can fall in love with it. If I made it, I assure you no one would show up to look at anything."

He chuckles. "True. Do you remember that time you—"

"No." I laugh and reach out and pat his hand. "We don't need to rehash all the ways Sofia tried to be an artist only to fail miserably. At least I have one thing in common with all the Navarro men."

"What's that?"

"I know how to stay in my lane."

His laugh is deep, one of the things I love best. "That's my girl." He pats my hand back. "That's my girl."

But he never gives me his blessing on it. He never tells me it's a good idea. He never says *do what you love, Sofia*. He just nods quietly and then looks back toward the fields that generations of Navarros have stared at.

We sit beside each other on the patio watching the butterflies flit around the flowers in the garden and the rabbits nibble on the clover.

It's quaint and peaceful but pressure builds in my chest. Over who I am. Who I want to be. And a longing to reclaim that carefree feeling from my time in America.

It's been three weeks since those nights.

Three weeks where I've jumped head first into looking at rental spaces and contacting artists to see if I can showcase their pieces in my soon-to-be gallery.

Three weeks of being brought back to the reality of what's expected of me as Sofia Navarro of Spain's elite Navarros.

Days of being in nonstop motion and thought, but when I lie down in my bed at night, I wonder if Rossi thinks of me like I do him.

For a man who followed me around like a stalker, it's amazing how that stopped when he got up from the bed that morning. The minute he got what he wanted.

But isn't that what I'm struggling with? It's what we both wanted. Both agreed to. And yet I haven't heard a word from him.

I guess, knowing his reputation, I should have tempered my expectations. The player. The fuckboy. The man who's only serious about himself. I knew that when he pursued me. I knew that when I pushed open my front door that night.

And yet I still agreed to it. I still wanted it and now I have to walk around in my real life with his touch seared in my brain as distinctly as the tattoos on his body.

Knowing it and accepting it are two different things.

At this point, neither feel great.

CHAPTER EIGHT

Rossi

There's nothing like race week, but when it's the first race of the season, everything—the excitement, the anticipation, the possibilities—is tenfold.

And this time around, my emotions are charged with uncertainty.

I told myself I'd never race for this team. For Gravitas or the family who owns it. Never. Not after those words were uttered years ago. The ones I held tight to as a driving force behind why I'm here. The ones that fueled the animosity for most of my career.

But when that career was on the line and the possibility of not having a ride was front and center, you swallow your pride—and your animosity—and sign on the dotted fucking line.

Then you're left with a whole offseason to question yourself, your integrity, and how it's going to feel trying to win for a team and a family you despise.

Buono fortuna. My nonna's voice fills my head. Her call to wish me good luck before every race was a staple.

This will be the first time in my life I won't hear it.

It's a welcome dose of humility every time I step into this uniform, into these team colors they've overhauled for the season when they added me to the team. Cruz gets to keep the team's trademark orange. I get a white fire suit with a touch of orange—almost as if they're afraid I'll taint his precious fucking image by having the same uniform as him.

I glance around. *Christ.* Life can change at the flip of a switch, and sometimes you have to swallow your pride to move forward.

I'm not a fan of fucking either—change or having to swallow my pride.

But here I go, putting one foot in front of the other.

Does Stavros even remember those words from years ago? The crushing of my young hopes? And if he doesn't, do I really want to win for a man who tries to ruin a man's career and doesn't recall doing it?

Such complex and conflicting emotions.

So far, I've worked only with his son, Philo, who's taken over most of the day-to-day operations. Yet I know the time will come when I'm face to face with Stavros. What will I say? Will the man I've become be able to temper the hurt of the teen I once was?

Maybe I should thank him. Maybe I should turn my back without a word.

All those unsettled feelings return with a vengeance as I walk through the paddock and see Philo talking to Cruz. His profile matches the one in my memory of his father.

Déjà vu hits with a bang. I'm transported back to that track, to those harsh words, and to the crushing feeling of letting my family down.

I shake my head. I've dealt with this already. *Own this season. Win as many podiums as possible. Create the opportunities I didn't have last year.* Then wash my hands and walk away from this team after they realize how much they need me.

That's the plan anyway.

Whatever lies let me sleep at night, right?

"Rossi. Looking great in that new color," Philo says when he sees me. His grin is wide as he puffs out his barrel chest and reaches one of his meaty fists for me to bump like we're best buds. *We're not.* "We ready for a good week and your first race on Team Gravitas?"

I bump his fist. I have nothing against Philo other than his last name, and that his father's an asshole, but we can't all be rock stars like me, can we?

"Always ready for a strong showing," I say.

"Alec said the car is at peak performance," Philo says, referring to my race engineer.

"Seems to be. We'll know more with testing. See if we can get it dialed in a bit better once we see the track conditions and figure out how best to adjust to them."

"I'm hearing medium tires are what everyone's doing."

I purse my lips and nod. "And I'm thinking hard might be the way to go."

Philo tilts his head to the side and studies me. *Yes, I will speak my mind. No problem there.* "I guess we'll see what we end up with."

"I guess we will," I murmur just as someone motions Philo over to them. He apologizes as he excuses himself.

Cruz and I are both left to stare after him. "Medium is the way to go," Cruz says.

Ah, his royal highness speaks. No doubt he has the best wisdom in all the kingdom.

"I differ in opinion." I turn to face him now. To meet the eyes of the man I've wanted to knock off his pedestal my entire career. Is he better than I am? Who knows? In this field of twenty drivers, it's a matter of mere inches or the slightest of circumstances that catapults one of us to the podium over the other. We're all talented, all practiced, all disciplined . . . it just depends on the day that our slight difference in skill or machinery helps or hurts us.

And despite or because of that, we're both standing here. Both deserving. It's just that one of us wasn't born with a silver spoon in our mouths and is given things because of how bright that Navarro serving spoon shines.

"You would differ, wouldn't you, just to be difficult," Cruz finally says.

"You don't have to like that I'm on your team, Navarro. Just as I don't have to like that I'm on yours. But it is what it is and we can both be professional. Or at least I can. You'd think with that last name and all, you'd be able to do the same."

His chin stiffens as he struggles with my backhanded insult. "I've seen how you treat teammates, Rossi. A little clip from behind. A sudden loss of radio comms so you *can't hear* the directive to defend for your number one. You think I don't know you play dirty? It's not a big secret. Everybody knows."

I chuckle and it holds zero amusement. So this is what he's been waiting to say to me? Why he's been hanging around to get me alone so he can get this total bullshit off his chest.

Fuck him.

"Then I guess you can take that as fair warning, right?" I say with a lift of my eyebrows and a glance around.

"I don't think you have a fucking clue who you're messing with," Cruz says.

"Is that a threat or a promise because I mean ... that's no way to take a new teammate under your wing." My smile is a complete *fuck you.* "I'm sure Philo would be shocked to hear you speak like that to me."

"Like you'd tell him."

I shrug. "I'm a wildcard. Nothing's off the table. Isn't that what you expect of me?"

"You're an arrogant prick."

"And you'll learn to love me. Everybody does. *Eventually.* Don't believe what they tell you about me though. I'm even better." I wink, step in closer, and lower my voice. "Do you want to know what the upside to being your teammate is, Navarro?"

"No, but I'm sure you'll tell me."

I can't resist. He wants to fuck with my head, I'll fuck with his. "Seeing as we're supposed to be family and all now, I finally get to meet your sister," I say, and by his quick uptick of breath, I'd say it works.

"Over my dead body," he grits out.

I slap him on the back and laugh loudly. "You drive better angry. You can thank me later when you fly around the track with the fastest lap time."

But as I walk away, Spanish cussing is muttered at my back.

Serves the fucker right. He wants to issue me a warning? I'll fire right the fuck back.

Last season was rough at Apex, but regret is a useless emotion. I can't change what happened—between my teammate Lachlan and me, between my ex, Blair, and me—or the shitty way I treated them both. I can only move forward and hope I'm a better man because of it.

I chuckle. Moving forward doesn't mean I'm not still a prick though. That part has been ingrained in me for years. When push comes to shove and all that.

"Thank you," I say to my PR handler, Carina, when she hands me my cell phone as I walk into our team garage. I'm about to say something more but the words die on my lips when I look up and lock eyes with Sofia across the space.

I'm fucking sucker-punched.

It's not like I forgot a single thing about her—the taste of her kiss, the scent of her skin, the sound of her sigh, the way she felt tightening around me—and yet until this moment, I might have put those thoughts to the back of my mind.

But they're front and fucking center now.

I agreed to one night. I fought not to chase after her here on our home turf. To not show up at her front door, seek out her number, ask her goddamn brother for it—but I agreed to her request in the moment. I respect her enough to not go back on my word.

But *fuck*.

Standing here? Seeing her again? Having every quickened breath and stuttered moan replay in my head? It's taking everything I have to not close the distance, drag her against me, and take another hit of her.

Christ.

I've relived every second of that night and it still isn't enough.

I cross the space without breaking the hold of her stare. Carina gets whatever hint it is that I'm giving off and walks away.

Sofia's smile flickers but is hesitant. "Mr. Rossi," she says as I approach.

"Mr. Rossi?" I ask, my head spinning as she takes a step back. *Mr. fucking Rossi?* "Really? That's how you're going to greet me?"

"Yes. Hi. Look." Her words are stunted, quick, as if she's going to be in trouble for speaking to me.

My brother has warned me about you.

"You look gorgeous." The words are out before I can stop them.

"Don't do that," she says, her head shaking back and forth.

"Do what?"

She glances around us before lowering her voice. "Don't pretend like we're something."

"Or that I know you at all, huh?"

"You knew this was a one-time thing. You were okay with it. An in the moment thing. A—"

"I got the hint," I respond. *But* I can also see that she's affected by me.

Her nipples have hardened against her shirt, and her pulse flutters against her throat.

"Just give me one night."

"That's all there can be."

You agreed to those terms, Rossi, hard and fast and without hesitating, so now you need to live with them. Respect them. And especially when your body didn't get the damn memo.

I glance at her tits, because . . . well, I'm a man and she's stunning. And because I remember their weight in my hands and their smooth skin in my mouth.

She crosses her arms over her chest. "I mean it."

I grin. "Okay, okay. We had our fun. You used me for your pleasure and it was—"

"It was a mistake," she says quietly.

Of all the words she could have said, those sting. We both know it wasn't anything near that. The chemistry was there. The lust was on point. The connection was indisputable.

"A mistake?" I repeat.

"Yes," she whispers.

"What's wrong? You reclaim that last name of yours and now you're too good for me?"

"It's not like that."

But I see it. *It is.* The way she glances continuously over her shoulder to no doubt where her brother or God knows who is. The way she shifts her feet and keeps fidgeting.

She's embarrassed that she slept with me.

Holy fuck. Like . . . I shake my head and try to process that reality but it's just not computing.

"It's not?" I finally ask. "Because from where I'm standing it sure as shit looks like that's the case."

She blinks rapidly and then averts her eyes. "Isn't this who you are? So I'm not quite sure what you're not understanding."

"Who I am?" I cross my arms over my chest. "And what exactly is that?"

"Not one to stick around after you get what you want . . ."

"Wow. Okay." I purse my lips and nod. "So I'm one-night stand material. Rebellion against your family material." I lean in closer and lower my voice. "Definitely orgasm material. But that's all I'm good for?"

She clears her throat as a response.

"Don't look now, Bellissima, but there's so much material here, you might just be able to make a dress of shame that you slept with me and wear it."

"That's not"—she sighs—"I told you, Simply Sofia." As if that explains everything.

"Yep. Got it. I was good enough for the peasant but not for the princess." I take a few steps back, smile insincerely, ego fucking bruised.

When someone shows themself to you, then you best believe them.

Too bad I thought the real Sofia was the one from the festival.

Reality check given.

Even footing found.

I'll be what she expects of me. Nothing less. Nothing more.

Lesson goddamn good and learned.

CHAPTER NINE

Rossi

"THE CAR'S RUNNING GOOD? FEELING GOOD? YOU'RE READY TO prove to that prick he made a mistake?"

"*Babbo*." Dad. "If you came to a race, you'd know."

There's the same pregnant pause on the other end of the connection that I get every time I say this. "I can't leave work."

I grit my teeth and pull down on the back of my neck. I know it's coming but it still fucking irritates me every time he says it. "I've paid off your house. I've sent you enough money to live out the rest of your life. I did what you asked of me—succeed . . . and yet you're still working."

"I am. Yes. It's busy here. There's never enough time in the day. You know."

Fucking frustrating. *No. I don't know.*

"You're good though? Your head's in the right place?"

"Why wouldn't it be?"

"It's the first race since Nonna . . ."

I nod and stare out the window of my hotel room at the city coming to life beyond. "Yeah." I clear my throat. "I'm fine."

"Oliver?"

"Nonna's gone. Isn't that how this world works? You live. You die. Others move on?"

My words are coated in bitterness.

He should be here. Him. My mamma. They should both be here.

Yet work calls.

It always fucking calls.

"You're going to have a good race. I can feel it."

"That's the plan."

"Oliver . . . we'll try to make it to the next one. You know we're so very proud of you."

"Hmm. Yeah." My mind disconnects as per usual. "I've got a meeting. I have to go."

"Okay. Call after the race when you can."

"Got it."

But when I end the call, I have nowhere to be. Just the confines of my empty hotel room. Just the silence that comes with it.

I'm Oliver fucking Rossi.

Good enough to race in F1. Great enough to beat all the other bastards out there who want to be in my shoes.

But not good enough to look up and have his dad in the stands with the pride he says he has brimming in his eyes.

Yep. I'm that fucking awesome.

I sigh.

The loud pumping music of the local clubs calls to me. The lights. The women. The attention from fans.

My usual reprieve.

And yet, my feet stay rooted in place.

It doesn't feel the same anymore. It doesn't make up for what I lack.

And I'm beginning to realize it hasn't for some time.

CHAPTER TEN

Sofia

"Please tell me you didn't invite Mamá."

It's enough of a nightmare keeping him on a leash from exerting his nonstop pressure on Cruz. the last thing I need is to deal with my drunk of a mother.

"No. I know better than that," my papá says evenly.

"Cruz did well today."

He clears his throat and clenches his jaw. No doubt the sharp criticism he's used to delivering burns like acid on his tongue. But he's heeding my warning. He's holding back and not saying shit. Well, well, well, maybe you can teach an old dog new tricks. Either that or Cruz's threat to ban him from the garage is the culprit.

It wouldn't be the first time. Sadly, despite recent progress, I don't think it will be the last.

But for now, the threat keeps his comments to a mumble and his criticism silenced. *And my headache over worrying about all of the above, a dull throb.*

"Good. Great. Cruz is done for the day if you want to go do whatever it is you want to do," I suggest. I appreciate my brother allowing our father to be back in the pits but that comes at a cost to me. It makes it my job to corral and redirect him. Sure, this is a family thing, but that makes the family part of it fall on my shoulders if I want Cruz to keep his mind focused on the task at hand—being safe—I don't have any other choice.

"Yes. Okay. I was going to meet up in the trophy room," he says, referring to a private lounge where past drivers meet up and hang out at this particular track.

"How nice for you to get to reconnect with old friends."

"Nice would be being here and getting to be with my son, but that's not happening now, is it?" he mutters.

"No, but it's how it has to be." Kid gloves. All day. Every day. "Go meet your friends, Papá."

Do something, anything that will make you feel as important as you actually think you are here at the track.

He grunts in response.

"It'll be fun."

"If that's what you want to call it," he mutters, grabbing his cup with force before stalking out of the viewing deck above the garage that overlooks pit row. It kills him to hold his commentary in.

And it makes my life way fucking easier.

I watch him leave and then let my shoulders sag when I realize I'm all alone. Finally.

It's been two days of trying to avoid Oliver Rossi . . . *and* his cold shoulder. That's what I wanted, isn't it? To push him away so Cruz doesn't see anything there? To step back into the shoes of Sofia Navarro, the woman who keeps this damn family together when all it wants to do is tear apart at the seams. To fulfill my role as the prized daughter and esteemed granddaughter, who's told that she needs to shine in her own right despite always being swept into the shadows of the Navarro men.

I step toward the edge of the booth and look at the F1 cars parked in various places in the pits. It's like Noah's Ark—two by two of each team—but when I look down to the cars of Team Gravitas, my stare stutters. Rossi is standing there with his hands on his hips as he nods in response to something one of his crew says. They point at the nose cone and then the rear wing. More discussion ensues that I don't even deem to assume what it's about . . . and it wouldn't matter anyway because I'm too busy admiring and wanting what I can't have.

I'm too busy wishing I were Simply Sofia, back at a festival, and flirting with Just Ollie.

"Can we talk?" Cruz asks at my back.

I hesitate, when I never hesitate. Cruz is not only my brother, but I truly consider him my friend. My other half when it comes to navigating the Navarro waters and our screwed-up parents. And yet I've found myself avoiding him over the past few days. It's part irritation that I'm forced to be here, part necessity so he doesn't see right through me.

And maybe so I don't look too closely at myself, if I'm honest.

"What's up?" I give one more look at where Rossi was moments before and then turn to face Cruz.

"What are you thinking?" he asks curtly.

"Um, a million things. None of which would be of interest to you."

He chortles. "Funny."

"I wasn't exactly trying to be." He had a good day of testing. Qualifying is tomorrow. Why does he seem so pissed off? "What's going on?"

"I told you Rossi is a hard no," he spits out and has me doing a double take.

"I don't understand. What—"

"I've stood by for two days and watched you follow him around with big puppy dog eyes. You wait till everyone's focus is elsewhere, and then you turn yours on him."

"I've never hidden from you that I find the man attractive." At least I'm not lying.

"And I've never hidden from you that he's not good enough for you."

"No one's good enough for me in your eyes so that falls on deaf ears."

"I'm serious, Sofia."

"So let me get this straight, you're so concerned who I may or may not find attractive that you're watching me?" *What the fuck?*

"No, I'm concerned that you're going to act on that attraction and embarrass our family name."

Wow. That was a zinger if ever I've been given one.

"You're serious, aren't you?"

"Do I sound serious?"

"No, you sound like an asshole, but I guess I can forgive you for that . . . eventually."

He sighs, lifts his hat, and runs his hand through his hair. "That came out wrong. I didn't mean that."

I twist my lips and stare at him. "In case you forgot, I'm a grown woman, capable of making decisions for myself."

"Exactly," he murmurs, irritation etched in the lines of his expression.

"Excuse me?"

"Exactly what I said. You're a grown woman. Your mistakes aren't looked at or as easily forgiven as they would be, say if you were a teenager."

"My mistakes?" I laugh out.

"You are in the public eye."

I stare at my brother like he's just grown two heads. This asshole thinks he has a foot to stand on when it comes to looking pristine in the public's eye?

"Wait a second." I hold a hand up. "I'm old enough to keep our family together. To be the one you call to manage Papá or Mamá or give advice on how to best win back Maddix, but I'm not old enough to make choices for myself?"

His sigh is heavy and the only answer I need to know. Yep, I nailed that on the head.

"What is it exactly that Rossi did to you that you feel the need to continuously warn me away from him?"

His Adam's apple bobs. His voice is even with a hint of reticence. "We expect better for our family."

I bark out a laugh. "Oh, so you can fuck around all you want, party it up and have photos posted online in every damn tabloid, be the playboy you once were—go *slumming* so to speak—*but I can't?*" Is he really serious, right now?

"We're Navarros. We have a reputation to uphold. A certain—"

"Jesus Christ, Cruz. I thought we were on the same team with this. That we're who we are and that we're going to live our lives accordingly. When did you turn into Papá or el patriarca with this bullshit?"

I know my words hurt him, but he hurt me too.

"I'm not Papá."

"No? Because it sounds like you are. You can screw up all you want yet I'm supposed to be perfect?"

"Not perfect. Just not *with him*."

"But why?"

"He's selfish," Cruz spits out.

"That's rich considering I'm staring at a man who used to be the epitome of selfish. That's not a valid reason."

"You'd simply be a game to him," Cruz says quietly. "Something to distract him for the time being, to toy with, and then to fuck over simply to get to me."

I hear his warning, but it doesn't ring true with the man who protected me, who followed me, who looked at me with confusion in this very garage two days ago.

"Why does this always come back to you?"

He levels me with a glare. His patience with the conversation about as done as mine is. "It's not about me. It's about him. I know the man."

And so do I. The same man I know I hurt days ago.

"Controlling. Condescending. Beyond the pale? Like you're being right now?"

He crosses the space and stands in front of me. Eyes the same cognac color as mine look back at me.

"I'm going to win a championship this year, Sofia. I can feel it in my bones. Everything is in place. Our family dynamic has . . . *improved*. I have Maddix and she's . . . everything. And I feel like the team is top notch."

"Including having a man you hate as your teammate."

"I don't hate him. I don't particularly like him. Regardless he's a damn good driver."

"What does any of this have to do with me or who I might find attractive?"

"It has everything to do with it, Sofia. Everything."

And when Cruz is called away seconds later, I can't help but stare after him and shake my head.

This is my family.

Who I was born into.

But truth? I don't like them very much right now.

CHAPTER ELEVEN

Rossi

"Decent quali, mate. Great job."

"It's not the front row, but it'll do," I say to one of my crew as I tuck a duffel bag under my arm.

"Having both of our cars in the second row gives us a good shot tomorrow. All of us are perfectly okay with that."

"Agreed. See you tomorrow." I push the door open to the Gravitas hospitality suite and welcome the fresh air and the lack of any expectation to have to talk to anyone.

Today was good. Quali was good. And to say I'm not a little drunk on the high of a good starting position with a new team after a pretty shitty week otherwise would be a lie.

People still mill about in the paddock despite qualifying finishing hours ago, but there's a calm to the bustle now rather than the chaos from earlier. This temporary city feels like it never sleeps during race week.

I turn the corner past our designated area, head down, hat pulled low, and fuck me, come face to face with Sofia.

Of course, I do.

Every emotion wars within me—need, want, confusion, disbelief. *Aversion.*

"Have a good one, Navarro," I mutter and move past her.

"Ollie," she says and sighs. I soften at that stupid nickname.

I've only ever allowed my nonna to call me that and yet, I can't bring myself to tell Sofia not to.

I don't ever soften. *What's wrong with me?*

I turn back to face her. "What? I'm abiding by your parameters. I thought that's what got me into this mess in the first place?"

"Mess?" she asks.

And truth be fucking told, I don't exactly know how to navigate these waters. To want a woman but to not pursue her? That just isn't me. But then again, I heard the words come out of her mouth when she was arguing with Cruz last night. I happened to be in the right place at the wrong time and those words hit me hard. They fucked with my head. *Slumming.* Isn't that the word she used? The one that's eaten at me, has provided fuel for me to drive the fuck out of the car, all goddamn day?

"Yeah. Mess. But then again—" I just shrug.

"Can we just talk? This feels all wrong."

"Mistakes usually do, don't they?" I ask, not giving her a fucking inch. "But no. No need to talk. I can do my own postmortem of everything. No need to involve you in that. Later, Sofia."

I lift a hand to wave goodbye, torn between why I'm walking away when I don't want to and doing the one thing it seems no one in her family does for her—respect her and her decisions. But the hand I wave with is quickly grabbed by her to prevent me from leaving.

"What, Sofia? *What?* You can't tell me you don't want me, tell me to regard you as just some random woman I fucked, but then get mad when I do just that. You can't have it both goddamn ways."

"My brother is your teammate. My family is . . . they're complicated."

"Both things you knew weeks ago when we slept together, no?"

"Yes, but . . ." She scrunches her nose up as bits of the conversation I overheard ghost through my mind.

"But what? Help me then because I don't understand how your family being complicated has any bearing on this conversation."

"I'm a game to you. Nothing more, nothing less."

"Seems someone is listening to outside voices and letting them influence her opinion rather than make her own decisions and stand by them."

"I know you. I know guys like you. You like the chase. The game . . . and then once you get what you came for, you're gone."

"Right. Glad you think you have me all figured out."

"I don't have to look far. The internet shows the history of women you've been through."

A history that may or may not be full of shit considering I was with the same woman on and off again for ten years.

"Make sure you believe everything you read on the internet. It's the gospel. On the bright side, that means you have been looking me up, so at least you're thinking about me."

"No, more like solidifying what I know about you."

"And what is that? That I'm good enough to screw around with but—"

"But nothing. The only reason you're standing before me is because I said no, and you're not used to hearing that word."

I meet her eyes. See the lie in them. See her trying to believe said lies. And know there is so much more happening here that her pride won't let her admit to.

She has no control over certain aspects of her own life. That much was true in what I overheard. I know something about that feeling of helplessness. Know how it drives you to do things you're not proud of.

"I'm more than familiar with rejection, but think what you will. You can justify your actions a hundred different ways, but there's only one truth. You believe what people are saying rather than trust your own experience. Trusting what you know to be true of that short time we spent together."

"Why is this so hard for you to understand? Why were you willing to accept the parameters that night but not now?" She throws her hands up and tears well in her eyes.

"I did accept them. I do accept them. But it's you standing here arguing a point I already thought was moot that's making me think you're lying." I glance around to make sure we're still alone. "The question you're not asking yourself is what about you, Sofia? What are you willing to allow yourself to do or be or have? What are you willing to believe you deserve? Because it's a hell of a lot more than what you're allotting yourself." I clear my throat. "Or rather, what your family is allowing you to allot yourself."

She squares her shoulders and lifts her chin. On the defense. I'd probably be and do the same. "Says the man who'd be gone in a heartbeat."

"Says the man standing before you. You know, the man you decided to go *slumming* with when you asked him into your bed."

She gasps as her eyes widen and expression falls. She shakes her head, rejecting the words she now knows I heard.

Something I had no intention of telling her. Guess that cat's out of the bag.

"Rossi." I stare at her stone-faced. "*Ollie*. I didn't—"

"You won't be the first to think it. You won't be the last. No skin off my back," I lie and shrug to sell it. Because she's not the only one being hurt by words here. "You're the one selling yourself short."

"I have to go."

"The carriage turns into a pumpkin at midnight?" I ask, so very perplexed over how I'm feeling.

I want her. Plain. Simple. Have I had multiple women since Blair broke off our relationship last year? Yes, and I'm not ashamed of it. But no one has tempted me for a repeat. With Blair, it was just . . . easy. Comfortable. We grew up together, then we grew apart. I took advantage of that history for some time. I'm not proud of it, but it is what it is, and we've both moved on.

But Sofia is right in a sense. I didn't have it in me to stick to Blair. *I'd be gone in a heartbeat.* Not like I'm going to fucking tell her that, but there is something about Sofia Navarro that has taken hold and that I can't seem to shake loose no matter how hard I try.

Call it lust. Call it infatuation. Call it magnetism.

Maybe it's that I can relate to the need to be someone else for a while. The want to hide behind something else instead of face some harsh truths.

And maybe it's because a part of me needs her to understand just how free she'll feel when she finally does something for herself. Hell, if she thought a weekend at a music festival was enlightening then a lifetime of it would be liberating.

She's struggling with whatever she's wrestling against. I can assume, but that's not my place. I've been conflicted like she is. I had to learn that my duty and time had been served and that I was only truly happy when I lived for myself.

"No," she finally says, referring to my carriage question. But I can see the confusion in her eyes. The conflict in her posture.

"Then why are you running if there's nothing here worth running away from?" I ask as she purses her lips and shifts on her feet. "But you're not leaving, are you? There's all this space around us and yet you're standing right here in front of me." My tone is gentle, understanding.

"I can't..."

Slumming? She's full of shit. She doesn't believe it either. The waver in her voice and the sincerity in her eyes tell me. Besides, if she did believe it—the word I'm more certain than ever she used to shut her brother's bullshit down—she'd be long gone by now.

I can't... but her presence here? It's a testament to how she sure as hell wants to.

Maybe I can help her along with that. Call me a selfish bastard since I'll most definitely benefit from it. I'll wear the label as proudly as I'll wear her kiss on my skin.

"What you need to figure out, Sofia, is whether you're going to live for you or live for them. It's a fucking hard, terrifying leap, but one you need to take or you'll never truly be happy."

"You're telling me you're happy? That you're thrilled with being at Gravitas with a teammate you don't particularly seem to like?"

Even footing.

That's what she's doing. Barking back to find the shaky ground beneath her feet. But this time, I'm going to rock it a bit more.

"I'm me, Bellissima. The good. The bad. The arrogant. The no fucks to give. And I think that scares you when it comes to me. That I don't care what people think or what they say. That includes your family, your brother, the press... anyone. I make my own bed. I lie in it. And I sleep just fucking fine."

God. She's gorgeous. Even with her eyebrows narrowed and her eyes willing for me to walk away. To be who she needs me to be. To not be who she wants. She's exquisite, and that pulls on parts of me I wasn't aware could be pulled on.

But I did try to walk away. I did try to respect her. She's the one who pulled me back. She's the one who pursued when she said she wasn't pursuing.

I step forward, fill the space between us so she's forced to look at me, to meet my eyes. "When's the last time you felt alive, Sofia? Be honest with yourself." She opens her mouth and then closes it, struggling to speak the truth. "You didn't answer the question."

"I don't have to." The words are whispered, and I know the answer she's refusing to acknowledge.

I chuckle and watch the goosebumps chase over her skin despite the warm night air. "You're right. You don't have to, but we both know the answer. We both know it was with me." I reach out and tuck a strand of hair behind her ear and then rest my hand on the curve of her shoulder. Her pulse beats erratically beneath the pad of my thumb as I lean in and put my lips near her ear. "You can discount me, Bellissima. You can believe whatever it is, whoever it is that's telling you things about me. You can hold tight to those family rules you think you need to hold tight to in order to be loved by them. You can write me off and ignore the sense I'm making all you want. But you know when you lie in your bed at night, when you cup those gorgeous tits of yours, and when you slide your fingers down and part that pretty little cunt of yours, that you're thinking of me. Of how I felt buried in you. Of how I tasted. Of how fucking alive I made you feel." I take a step back, teeth sunk into my bottom lip, and just hold her eyes. "You deserve to feel that way all the time. The question is, Simply Sofia, how long are you going to deprive yourself from feeling it again?"

Her breath is shaky and the darkening of her pupils turns me on. "You're full of shit."

"Maybe I am." *I'm not.* I take another step back and adjust the bag under my arm. "Maybe I'm not." And another. "But I'll wait. And I'll bide my time. And I'll remind you every chance I get at how goddamn good the sex was." I drag my eyes up and down the length of her and hope I'm making the right decision here. "Good night, Sofia."

Then I turn and walk away.

I head back to my empty hotel room.

I fall back on the bed.

"But I'll wait. And I'll bide my time. And I'll remind you every chance I get at how goddamn good the sex was."

What. The. Actual. Fuck.

I don't chase. *Ever.*

And yet . . . it seems I'm chasing Sofia Navarro.

Because she's worth it, Ollie.

She could be the one for you.

I repeat. What. The. Actual. Fuck.

CHAPTER TWELVE

Sofia

"I WAS SO SURPRISED WHEN YOU CALLED ME LAST NIGHT AND ASKED me to meet you here today," Marla says as she moves around in the space behind me. Her heels click on the stone floors as I stare out the windows to the turquoise water of the Mediterranean and try to quiet the adrenaline coursing through me.

You really did just do this, Sof. The keys in your hand are real.

I squeeze my hands around the cold, hard metal of them. Yep. Definitely real.

Holy. Shit.

"Me too. It was a—" A knee-jerk reaction? A way to avoid being at the race and caving to every person with an opinion about who I am or what I should be doing? What I should have done a long time ago? *My first step in rebellion?* "I've been vacillating on doing this for weeks and it was time to finally act on it."

I laugh nervously and turn to face the real estate agent. Her smile is wide, her hair's perfect, and her power suit is immaculately tailored. "It was. I told you that this spot was going to go fast once I listed it. Plus the fact that it's already set up for what you need is kismet. Great lighting. Open floor plan. Great display space. In the heart of town so you attract attention from tourists and collectors alike. And this view." She shakes her head and opens her arms up to it as she takes it in. "It's simply stunning."

"It is. I fell in love with it instantly." It doesn't hurt that money isn't an issue for me either since this storefront comes with such a hefty price tag.

"Well, congratulations. Selfishly, I think it was the perfect choice." She laughs and adjusts the bottle of champagne in the bucket of ice she brought. You know you're in Monaco when the real estate agents carry around buckets with ice and champagne to possible showings. "I can't wait to see what you do here. You have an excellent eye, Sofia. I saw that last year during the artmonte-carlo," she says of the annual art show here in Monaco. "Every painting you pointed out to me was sold by the end of it."

"Thank you. Clearly art is subjective, but I know what I like when I see it."

"And clearly others like it too. Do you plan on having the gallery open for this year's event?"

I lift my eyebrows. "That's a tall order to fill, but . . . I'd like to try and make it happen if it's possible." I start calculating what that would mean time wise and hate that it's not much time at all. Leave it to me to jump feet first off a cliff and overcommit simultaneously. And yet, I want to make it work. Have to. "At the end of the day, it mostly depends on how many artists I can approach about showcasing their art here."

"I'm sure they'd all jump at the chance to have a Navarro champion their work." *The Navarro name.* The name that opens doors and greases palms.

"One can hope." But that's a lie, isn't it? I want my name, Sofia, to be the draw. My name, my attention to detail, and my knowledge on what to curate to encourage potential artists over my family's name.

Something of my own.

"Do you have a name for the gallery yet?"

"Not yet, but I'm sure it'll come to me at some point."

"I'm sure it will."

I smile and spend the next few minutes trying to get Marla out the door. While I welcome her profusive positivity, which I take with a grain of salt as she did just make a hefty commission off me, I need a few minutes to myself. Plus, with her gone, I'll be assured there won't be any witnesses when that momentary freak-out over what I just did makes its impending appearance.

"Well, congratulations. *Again.*"

"Thank you."

It takes a few minutes after she leaves for the silence and the magnanimity of what I just did to hit.

For the doubt to meld with my excitement. For the uncertainty to pair with my optimism. For the holy shit to recognize my defiance.

That whole bottle of champagne is looking good about now.

I jump when my cell rings and answer on the second ring.

"You text me, *I'm doing it*, with no other context and then don't answer your phone the numerous times I call over the past hour so that I'm left to freak-out and wonder if *doing it* means that hot Italian hunk from the music festival again?" Lilith all but screams as a means of greeting.

I laugh. It's all I can do and exactly what I needed in this very moment. God bless Lilith and her perfect timing. "No. This has nothing to do with Rossi." *But at the same time everything to do with him and the truths he said to me last night.*

She's quiet for a beat and then, when I don't add to my explanation, says, "Well, you're a fount of information now, aren't you?"

"Always." I chuckle.

"But you're not at the race—which by the way, right now both men on Team Gravitas are holding their own in," she says, making that pang of regret and dose of reality hit me even harder. I'm so wrapped up in this, in me, that I may have subconsciously pushed the race to the back of my mind. More like ignored it so I could forgo the guilt. "So that means you defied your grandfather about needing to be there, apparently said fuck you to Cruz by leaving last night at some point—"

"More like I sent him a text this morning saying I had to leave. That there was an emergency with one of the charities and I needed to be there."

"And I'm sure *that* didn't raise any red flags," she says sarcastically.

Well, it was either that or cave to the number one, walking red flag my brother keeps warning me about like I found myself wanting to.

Who knew I was attracted to red, huh?

"I've received a bunch of texts from Maddix on his behalf trying to make sure all is well. I've assured her it is. That all was taken care of but then I freaked out that I messed with his head and he had to race and . . . oh my God, Lil, it sounds so ridiculous now, doesn't it? An emergency at a charity?"

"You've yet to tell me what it is that you did, so I can't exactly say if it sounds ridiculous or not . . . but I'm going with a yes at this point," she teases.

"I rented the space."

"Whoa. I think I need a moment to process this." She takes a dramatic pause. "You mean you actually did it?"

My grin widens, as the approval and pride in her voice means everything to me. "I did."

"Just like that? After all this time saying you were going to . . . you actually did it?"

I nod even though she can't see it, as if the action will push the burgeoning panic away. "Yep. Just like that."

"And which place did you decide on?"

"Monaco. On the main drag. The one with—"

"The incredible view?"

"That one. Yes. It was too perfect to pass up. It was already set up as a gallery space so not too many tenant improvements are needed."

"Okay, so that comes back to my question from the get-go. Why the sudden urgency to act when this has been something you've talked about for a year but never pulled the trigger on? I mean, let's be honest, you have all the money in the world so starting the gallery isn't about making it. You have charity work coming out of your ass so that keeps you busy, not to mention keeping your family together and functioning is a whole other job we're not going to even get into . . . so tell me the one thing you didn't answer me before, *why now?*"

"Maybe it was because I couldn't before."

"And you can now?"

I slide down the wall at my back, suddenly feeling so insignificant in this space, and acknowledge the truth. A truth that was possibly instigated by Rossi's words but instigated, nonetheless.

"I felt like if I stayed at the race for one more second, I was going to suffocate," I whisper.

"Now we're getting somewhere," she murmurs and then falls quiet so I can process and think.

I nod, bottom lip worried between my teeth. "I have no sense of purpose. Everything I do is for somebody else. Maybe I wanted to do something for myself. Something that fills up my cup. Something that makes me more than just Cruz's sister or el patriarca's granddaughter."

"Understandably. But what happened to make you feel that way? Did your crazy mom show up? Did your dad and Cruz have a fight? Like . . . what happened?"

Rossi happened.

He's my first and only thought. His words. His hard truths. His veiled snippets of experience that said he might know what I'm feeling. Almost as if he was encouraging my rebellion by reminding me how incredible my rebellion with him felt.

"I'm twenty-five years old. Isn't it time I figure out my own path? Will my family really implode without me holding the reins or boxing gloves? I don't know, but it shouldn't be on my shoulders, and I'm so exhausted from being responsible for keeping everyone on their sides of the ring all the time."

"You're not going to find me arguing with you on this. You know I feel the same. I'm just glad you've come to the realization on your own." She falls silent for a beat, and I close my eyes to collect myself. "Saying it and acting on it are two vastly separate things."

"Believe me, I'm well aware." But it feels good to say it, to be free for a few minutes from the weight of it, even if I know the minute we hang up, that burden will remain.

"I'm proud of you for acting on it, Sof. On your own terms. On your own timeframe."

Her words mean more to me than she could ever imagine. While my family has always been supportive of everything I've ever done, always proud of whatever it is one of us chooses to do, there's always an underlying tension if it's outside the normal parameters of what they deem as appropriate for a Navarro. And I've yet to determine whether this is one of those times.

The fact that el patriarca has brought it up a few times means he might be warming up to the idea but it's a far cry from his "making money off other people's art isn't a respectable position. It's poaching," comment when I first broached the subject.

"Thanks."

"Come on. Give me more enthusiasm than that." She laughs.

"There was freedom at the festival," I explain. "I was just me, the real me I can be without anyone knowing who that was, and no matter what I did, no one looked twice or cared. My actions weren't going to affect or change anyone's world, and then I step foot back here and the pressure returned and felt . . . more stifling, more fatalistic."

"Not to mention when you're at the track, you probably look up to see Rossi everywhere you turn as a reminder of just how incredible that feeling was."

Literally and figuratively.

But I don't say it. I don't want to acknowledge the discussion with Rossi from last night, the delicious threat of reminding me how much I do want to be with him again, and the staggering words he left me to think about so much that I called our pilot and asked for a return trip here to Monaco.

And while I made this leap, this step, and bolted out of town and away from the race . . . maybe it was because this was the least of two rebellions. This was something my family will bitch about but eventually find acceptable.

But Rossi . . . being with him, wanting him, anything with him, would cause a major upheaval.

Maybe this is enough for me. Maybe this will satisfy my need to have something that's mine. Something tangible.

And maybe I'll stop thinking about Rossi at some point too.

"It doesn't hurt," I finally say, answering the question.

"How does it feel?"

"Terrifying, freeing, confusing, exciting."

"All are warranted." She pauses briefly. "I don't pretend to understand anyone's family dynamics, let alone yours, but do you really think your family is going to disapprove of you doing something that you love?"

"It's outside the family business," I murmur.

"Well, they're not exactly letting women behind the wheel of an F1 car yet so . . . they can't expect you to carry on a tradition that's not yours to uphold."

"I think it's more along the lines of me not having time to do the things I'm supposed to do as a Navarro or . . . I don't know . . ."

"So you're going to try and be She-Ra and handle all things Navarro as the constant peacemaker, the referee, and the publicist, all while trying to set up a gallery to open . . . when again?"

"By artmonte-carlo."

She barks out a good-natured laugh. "So you're shooting for the stars after jumping off a cliff. Sounds about perfectly Sofia Navarro to me."

"Doesn't it?" I chuckle and love that I have a friend who knows me well enough to know I needed to do this.

"It does." She sighs. "And I'm going to wish you amazingly well from my perch across the Atlantic and expect many texts about updates and an invitation to its opening."

"Sounds like a plan."

"What are you going to name the gallery?"

I twist my lips. "You'd think that's something I'd already have figured out with as long as I've been thinking about this . . . but I don't."

"That's okay. You have time." She chuckles. "Well, not too much time, but you know what I mean."

"Funny."

"Hey, Sof? I'm proud of you and I know your family is going to love what you'll end up doing with it almost as much as you will."

A lump forms in my throat. "Thanks, Lil."

"Anytime. You know I've got your back."

The call disconnects and I'm left in the silence of this vast space. Its floors are a gorgeous tumbled stone. Its walls are a soft ivory with lights mounted just off the wall to shine on whatever I'll be hanging there. The glass wall of windows at its front is vast and allows all the light in the world to come in along with the breeze off the ocean.

It's perfect, but I've known that since I first walked past it over a year ago. How was I to know the spot would become available? How was I to know that the timing would work with my courage?

"You have one night, Sof," I mutter to myself. Of panic. To be wishy-washy. To wonder what the fuck you've done. And then after that? Tomorrow? *You need to get your shit together, lean into the fact that yes, you're a motherfucking Navarro, and get this done with the confidence you're letting the uncertainty smother.*

It's normal to freak-out.

But if you're going to rebel, then you need to fucking do it to perfection.

I rise from my seat and move to the table. I have the cork popped and the champagne poured in a flute in a matter of seconds.

"Cheers, Sof. To something that's finally yours." Tears well as I take my first sip but they're because I'm excited. Because I'm proud. Because I'm terrified.

And then I do what I've always done my whole life. The only thing my family has ever known, I turn on the broadcast of the race on my phone to check in.

I watch the two Gravitas cars dueling for position. I look at the ever-changing leaderboard and see my last name. See Rossi's. And feel conflicted.

Over what I know is expected of me.

And what I know I think should be expected of me.

What about what you're willing to allow yourself? What about what you deserve?

Call this the first step in my rebellion.

Call this reclaiming a little piece of me.

As I lift the glass of champagne to my lips and watch the cars zoom around the track, I can't help but like how this feels.

CHAPTER THIRTEEN

Rossi

I STAND AT THE SIDE OF THE PITS AND WATCH THE DOG AND PONY show on the podium. Not a fan of the show per se but am never mad when I've placed high enough that I get to be up there performing for it.

"Tough one out there," Alec says as he steps up beside me, "but we fared well. No one is going to complain about a sixth-place finish."

But I am. But I will.

I nod. "I can do better," I say.

My timing was off when it's never off. The car needed more push. It has some understeer that I fought all day. The fucking heat ran the car ragged... but my choice on the tires was the right one.

When I move through the crowd and back toward the hospitality tent, I glance in Cruz's garage. I see him, his fiancée, his father, but don't see the one person I'm looking for.

She's not here.

And I don't know if that pisses me off or makes me proud of her.

A part of me wants to ask Cruz where she is, stir that pot, but think better of it. Last thing I need to do is cause more conflict for her with her family when it's clear she's conflicted enough.

But it makes me surly. When's the last time I looked for anyone after a race? *Blair.* When Blair was mine. I used to look for her before and after every race, but now I can see how truly selfish I was. Demanding. Expecting.

Not caring about her needs. *Fuck . . . the things I said to her? The ways I made her feel less than?* Not my proudest moments.

But she's found the man who does. The right man for her. *So at least there's that.*

I head toward my driver's room, wanting a quick shower before heading to face the media, and come face to face with Stavros.

Vitriol pools on my tongue but I bite it back. "Sir," I say and go to walk past him. Better to not say anything than to fuck things up and say what I really think.

"Why the hostility?" Stavros asks, causing me to stop.

"Hostility?" I meet his dark brown eyes and bushy gray eyebrows.

He nods. "I'd think you'd be a little more gracious, don't you? You're lucky you have a ride after the stunt you pulled with Evans last season," he says about an on-track incident I had with my then teammate. Tires touched. Blame was put my way. I took the punishment from the FIA. But I don't respond, I just lift my eyebrows in response. "In fact, you should be kissing my ass you have a ride."

"Good to know you still hate me then," I say with a tight smile.

"I still think you're reckless and a danger to everyone on that track, but hate is a strong word for a man I'm paying to win for me."

I nod and glance over my shoulder. Guess my decorum lasted a whole five minutes. "Let's get one thing crystal fucking clear. I win for me and no one else. Sure, if I win, you make money, Stavros, and that must kill you to know that. But at the same time, we both know there's no better driver on this track that you could have gotten than me. So love me, hate me, it doesn't fucking matter which one you decide on because both fuel me. Just know that everything I do on that track is for me and me alone. Anything you get in return is simply dividends."

He stares at me, eyes blinking and lips pursed. "Exactly. You just proved my point. You're not a team player."

"And I wonder who made me that way? *Huh?* Now if you'll excuse me, I have to speak with the media and then do our team debrief after. All things you are also paying me for." I start to walk away and then turn back to face him. "One more thing. By season end, I'll have earned more points for this team than my counterpart. I promise you that."

I push into my private room and shut the door at my back.

Cruz isn't the only one who can race on this team.

I'll fucking prove that.

CHAPTER FOURTEEN

Sofia

"Yes. That would be perfect. I'm happy to take whatever piece you're willing to part with and display it in the gallery." I do a mock fist pump. It was definitely worth stopping my run to take this call.

"I think *Lying in Wait* is the perfect piece, especially with the demographic of your clientele there," Arturo Caminiti says about my favorite painting of his.

"Great. That's . . . amazing." I grin and gesticulate wildly, grateful he can't see me silently freaking out.

"Once you have the space ready, let me know and I'll get it packaged and shipped your way."

"Or I can arrange that for you. Whatever you're most comfortable with."

"We'll work that out as the time draws near."

"Thank you, Mr. Caminiti. Like I said, I'll have my lawyer reach out to you and yours with the contract and terms. Get that all squared away on their end and then we'll talk soon."

"Adíos."

I end the call and do a little hip shimmy in excitement. That's five pieces so far. Five handpicked paintings from artists I love who have agreed to let me showcase their art in my gallery.

A part of me feels like a hypocrite. These artists are agreeing, despite my lack of experience, simply because of my last name. I'm definitely aware of that.

Caminiti's call has given me a renewed excitement and encouragement to complete my run so I can finish and get back to work making calls. But just as I turn to start, I'm met with a pair of amber eyes and an undeniable presence.

"Sofia?" Rossi says, equal parts surprise and confusion. "You're here. In Monaco."

I nod to try and buy time for my body to recover from the sight of him. He's simply devastating. There's no other way to describe Oliver Rossi. The olive skin. The intense eyes framed by thick lashes. The . . . very naked chest and sculpted abs with a dark sweat stain down the front of his shorts from his workout.

"Hi. Yes. I'm . . ." Jesus. Every part of me wants him. "*Here.*"

It's the first time I've seen him since the race. Since his subtle dress down. Since his dark promise to not let me forget how good we were. The funny thing? He doesn't have to say a word because the sight of him is enough of a reminder for me.

"Since when?" His eyes roam up and down the length of me, stuttering over my leggings and sports bra. Seeing his pure male appreciation for me in his dark gaze is thrilling.

"We've always had a place here, but . . . work. I'm here for work for the time being."

"We? You and your . . . *boyfriend?*" He narrows his eyes and takes a step closer.

"No. My family. We have a place here . . ."

"Mmm. And you're here for work. What is it that you do?"

"A little bit of this. A little bit of that."

"Is that so?" He furrows his brows as he steps forward so that someone can pass around us on the sidewalk.

And I don't think I'm ready to share the answer with him just yet. Especially not with this man who unnerves me on so many levels—good and bad.

"Yep. You seem to have opinions about everything I do so, maybe, I'm choosing not to tell you so I don't have to care what you think."

His chuckle is a low rumble and that smirk of his lopsided. "So you do care, huh?"

Our eyes meet and hold. Amusement dances in his.

"No. I don't." But even I'm not convinced from those three words.

He leans in. "I think about you, Sofia. All day. Every day. I think about you. What you looked like coming for me. What you felt like wrapped around me. The way your nails dug into my back. What a good fucking girl you were for me, taking me until you couldn't take any more. Mm," he quietly groans. My skin feels like it's being lit on fire. "Do you think of me? Do you miss the way I felt buried in you? Are you willing to admit you want me?"

I take a step back, breath shaky and body on high alert. Listening to his words, knowing he's thought of me . . . *of me coming.*

Fuck. That's hot.

"I don't want you," I whisper as I swallow forcibly and fist my hands.

He laughs softly. "We both know that's not true." He reaches out and traces a line with his finger from my temple to my jaw. I fight the urge to lean into his touch. "But keep lying to yourself. Your body will win this fight." His eyes flicker down to my lips and then back. "I have no doubts there." He takes another step back. Smirks. Nods. "Off to finish the rest of my run."

"Rossi?" I call out as he runs a few steps.

He turns to face me, jogging backward as he does. "I'll see you around, Navarro. I'm sure of it."

I stare after his back as he runs effortlessly down the boardwalk and hate that I want to run after him.

That his pull on me is that strong.

But it doesn't stop me from wondering.

Or wanting.

Or rationalizing.

Would going after him cause an irreparable problem in my family?

CHAPTER FIFTEEN

Sofia

"Show me, Sof," Cruz says as he takes a left-hand turn.

"No. Not yet," I say from the back seat. "I want it to be perfect before you see it."

"Well, what if I want to see it now?" he asks like a typical big brother.

"Cruz, you're—"

"You're not respecting your sister's wishes," Maddix says in the front passenger seat to my brother. "You're a perfectionist too. Let her do her thing and then show it to you."

"Thank you, Madds," I say with a definitive nod to which Cruz just glares at me from the rearview mirror.

I smile sweetly. He hates when his fiancée and I take the same side. I love when we do. Any way to make him irritated is fine by me. Especially since we haven't exactly talked besides more than just insignificant bullshit since our fight.

"No prob," Maddix says.

"I've been outnumbered. *Again*," Cruz teases as he makes another turn so that the city is laid out before us with its lights twinkling through the dark night.

"I appreciate the backup there," I say just to poke Cruz one more time. Maddix turns and smirks back at me.

"Has el patriarca called you yet?" Cruz asks.

Not Papá. Not Mamá. Just el patriarca. Because while we love our parents in their own interesting way, el patriarca has always been our measure. Our North Star. The opinion or judgment we care about. *Respect.*

"No," I say and meet his eyes once again in the rearview mirror. "Not yet. Have you heard anything?"

"He mentioned the gallery to the Correas," he says, referring to our close family friends.

"And?"

"And nothing. It was mentioned. That's a good enough sign for now, right?"

"I don't get why it's such a big deal. I'm not asking for his blessing on it. More for his understanding."

Our eyes meet briefly again. "He'll give it. I have no doubt on that. It'll take him some time to adjust to the change, and if he doesn't, I'll go to bat for you like I always have," he says. Maddix reaches out and links her fingers with his in a silent show of support.

"Thank you. I think it's ridiculous that you even have to. I'm a grown woman who can make her own decisions for herself and her career."

"And we both know as a Navarro that those words are so much easier said than done." He falls quiet for a beat as he continues to navigate the streets of Monaco. "And I'm sorry for that. I'm sorry that it's tougher on you being a woman."

I nod, not trusting my own voice, because hasn't life always been tougher for him in all other aspects? The expectations of being a Navarro. The prodigal son expected to bring racing fame back to our family.

So the fact that he even voiced anything close to this when I've stood sideline to the hell and back he's been through means the world to me.

"Thanks." I blink back the tears that threaten. "So, enough about me," I say through a laugh. "We're going out to celebrate Maddix tonight." I lift my hands and do a little dance in my seat. "So let's stop the serious talk and get this party started."

"Sounds like a plan to me," Maddix says and then squeals as Cruz presses down the throttle.

The club is packed. People mill about everywhere and anywhere but Cruz rented out the entire top floor that peers down on the rest of the club. Our floor is flowing with friends, industry people, and racers alike, all welcoming being back at home and with a weekend off.

Balloons and décor placed throughout the space are an added flair for Maddix's birthday.

The music is good, the drinks are nonstop, and I feel the stress over the gallery dissipating bit by bit. Song by song. Laugh by laugh.

And something I never expected is that the sight of my brother completely enamored with his fiancée makes me happier than anything. I know he loves her but watching a man, who used to be so egotistical, dote on someone else, want the world for someone else, makes me forget his asshole-ish behavior from the last race and believe that love really can make someone change for the better.

"A toast," Cruz says, raising his glass as the music in our section lowers. "A big thank you to all of our friends for being here tonight to help me celebrate the birthday of the best thing that's ever happened to me—Maddix." A cheer goes up along with the glasses in a toast as Maddix leans over and presses a kiss to my brother's lips. "Isn't she the fucking best? And a quick congrats to my little sister on her new gallery." He points to me, and I stare at him with doe eyes. I wasn't exactly telling people about this yet. "It's a big leap and I hope you all go there when it opens and buy the shit out of her stuff."

Another cheer goes up and I'm patted on the back. The well wishes barely register through the shock, but I guess if anyone should know what I'm doing it's these people here—the who's who of Monaco.

"You promised me a dance, Navarro," Lucas Chamalet says as he drapes his arm over my shoulders. A notorious playboy among those in our circle, he's more puppy dog than pit bull and completely harmless. To the rare few who know him like I do, his fluid sexuality makes him a fun man to hang and flirt with without the fear of leading him on.

"A dance? With you?" I tease, pressing a kiss to his cheek and snuggling up against his side. "Why would I ruin my good reputation for something like that?"

"Girl," he says, twirling me out and then back against him so he can grind up against me. "I'll make your reputation."

We both laugh as I spin around and he pulls me back against him, so that my back is to his front. His hands hold my hips as I lift my arms over my head and sway to the music.

I open my eyes and am pinned motionless by a pair of amber ones from across the room. *Rossi.* He lifts his eyebrows and holds his own glass up, but the glare he's giving me is anything but amused.

More like predatory.

And it's a total turn-on.

What's he doing here?

My heart beats an erratic staccato and adrenaline begins to race through my veins. I feel like I'm in trouble when I've done nothing wrong, and the look he levels me with is enough to replay in my mind every slow, sensual moment of our one night together.

It's another man's hands on my body right now, but it's Rossi's I'm thinking of. It's Rossi's I still want.

And now with those eyes bearing down on me and some liquid courage, I don't break our stare this time. I don't pretend I don't see him. Rather, I pin him motionless with his lips on a bottle of beer and his face in the shadows.

We're in a room full of our peers, full of eyes, but it's only each other we see.

"Who are we dancing for?" Lucas asks in my ear, clearly sensing something is suddenly different.

"No one."

"You are so full of shit, Sofia, but so long as I'm not going to get my ass knocked out, I'll keep playing."

"Sounds like a plan," I say as we keep dancing.

And Rossi keeps watching. Much like he did at the music festival but this time around we're not Simply Sofia and Just Ollie.

This time the world is watching.

And hell if it doesn't make the pull to him—the forbidden—that much stronger and more intense.

CHAPTER SIXTEEN

Sofia

I FOLLOW AFTER HIM WHEN HE LEAVES THE VIP LOUNGE. OUT THE doors to the darkened balcony that overlooks the whole of Monaco with its sparkling lights and obscene real estate.

He's a shadow in the night on the far end, and I swear he's the flame because, like a moth, I'm drawn to him.

I move in silence toward him, his eyes on me the entire way. It's only when I stop a few feet from him does he make a show of lifting his beer to his lips and taking a long draw on the bottle. The action may be slow, deliberate, but I don't overlook the insatiable gleam in his eyes.

"Congrats," he says evenly. "Apparently they're in order."

I nod, uncertain why I'm suddenly nervous.

"A gallery?"

Another nod. A glance over my shoulder. A shaky inhale.

"He didn't follow you out here," Rossi says.

"Who?"

"Chamalet."

"I didn't . . . want him to."

"Why not?" He purses his lips and shrugs ever so slightly. "He sure fits the proper pedigree befitting someone like you."

"Someone like me?"

"*A Navarro.*"

There is a delicate dance going on here. One I know I'm a participant in but that I don't know the choreography to.

And for some reason I feel like playing with fire.

"Jealous?" I taunt.

"What? Of him?" He scoffs and lifts his chin in the direction over my shoulder. "Old money? Void of character? Spoiled rotten? Lacking in class?" His chuckle is low and unforgiving. "No. I've had you, Bellissima. By the way he was puppy dogging you, he hasn't." He angles his head to the side and studies me. I've never been more aware of how someone's gaze can feel like it's touching my skin than I am now. "In fact, I'm pretty sure no one's touched you since I have."

"That's none of your business and not a fair assessment." The words are meant to be said with more vitriol than breathlessness.

"No?" He steps in closer to me, and I fight the urge to reach out and touch him despite hating him in this moment.

"No," I say more resolutely.

"I'm sensing some sexual frustration, perhaps?" He lifts his eyebrows and I want to kiss that smirk off his lips.

"What?" *Yes.* "No. I'm perfectly fine." My voice cracks.

"Seems like it."

"I am. I'm fine." My nod is a little forced, as if I'm trying to sell myself on my own words. Our attraction is irrefutable. His eyes on me on the dance floor and my body's heady reaction to it says as much.

But we're in public and egging this on is playing with a fire I don't think I'll be able to control.

"Ollie?" I ask.

His eyes soften. His lips purse. "Hmm? Please don't tell me you're going to ask for even footing here because I rather like talking to you."

His words are unexpected. "Exactly. On the liking talking part. Not the even footing part. I mean, I just—"

"Why do I make you nervous, Sofia?" he asks and reaches out and tucks a strand of hair behind my ear.

I step back. His touch. It's . . . like a drug. "A truce. That's it. That's what I'm—"

"A truce?" He angles his head to the side and studies me.

I swallow. "Yes. I've been having such a good time tonight, and it seems every time we start down this path—"

"You mean acknowledging our attraction?"

"I mean sparring over it like it's a game to be won . . . when games always have consequences."

"Go on."

"It seems one of us gets our feelings hurt or walks away angry. So let's . . . I don't know . . . do something different."

"Like a truce?" he asks and I nod. "And what does that entail?"

"Us talking."

"About?"

"How about the last race? You did a great job in your first one with the team."

"It was mediocre."

"You all say that unless it's a win, but everyone's talking about how well you managed a difficult car."

"I could've done better."

"And I have no doubt that you will."

"Why?"

"Why do I have no doubt?"

"Yeah," he answers with a smirk. Man, I wish he didn't smirk like that. *He's . . . irresistible.*

"The fact that you were brought into Team Gravitas speaks for itself, right?"

"I guess." But the look that flickers over his features seems agitated. *Does he really hate the team that much?* "I'm going to head inside, Sofia." He shakes his head, looking resolved. *Angry?*

"Rossi—"

"Look, Sofia. You know how I feel about you. You know I want you. But small talk with you is making me want you more, and even though you want me, you won't act on it." *Well, that's the end of that short-lived truce. The problem is who could walk out any moment. We're in a place where everyone would talk. But how do I verbalize that?* "I think I prefer even footing to truces. Even footing means you at least act on what you want."

"That's not fair."

"Isn't it?" He smirks again. "Great talking to you then. Go back to

Chamalet. Dance as provocatively as you want. I'll watch. I'll want. And I'll remember every damn second we were together."

He goes to walk past me. "Rossi." Those two syllables have never sounded more desperate.

He spins.

I hesitate.

"What is it that you want this time, Sofia?"

"Don't be angry with me. You have every right to be. I want you and that means you're unknowingly caught in this fucked-up tug of war I have going internally, but—"

"But nothing." He shrugs and his indifference makes my stomach twist. I'm a riot of conflicting emotions that I can't seem to control. "I understand. Good sex can't override . . . all of that."

But there's more than just sex here. The words come out of nowhere and fuck with my head even more. Luckily, I'm astute enough to not speak them aloud.

If only my family wasn't so overbearing. If only I was brave enough to take what I really want—him. If only I wasn't . . . so chickenshit.

"You don't deserve to be caught up in my issues," I say.

"But I can be tangled in your sheets. Yep. Got it." His smile pulls tight, the muscle pulses in his jaw, and hurt—*is it hurt?*—flashes through those stormy eyes of his.

My chest aches as my mouth goes dry.

"I deserve that," I whisper. *It is hurt.* What does that mean?

"Nah. You deserve a whole helluva lot better than that." He leans in closer, his lips a whisper from mine. I can feel the warmth of his breath. Can smell the scent of his cologne. Can almost taste his kiss.

I dart my tongue out to wet my lips. I don't dare talk because anything I say right now would be a lie, and doesn't he at least deserve better than that? If I'm going to be the chickenshit, the one who can't cut the ties with her family, then it shouldn't be at the expense of hurting him.

But it was. *It is.* And I don't know how to right that wrong. Or maybe I do but I don't have the courage yet.

Unable to resist, I reach out and run a hand down his cheek. It's my apology. It's my punishment.

He steps back, but his voice is a low growl. "Fuck your pedigree, Sofia.

If you want me like your eyes say you do and like your lies pretend you don't? Next time you call my name? *Don't. Fucking. Hesitate.*"

Without a second look, he waltzes away and back toward the party. The door opens, and I'm met with a rush of sound that stops just as soon as it begins when it closes behind him.

I stand there staring, wanting to chase after him but not sure exactly why. While his words hurt, they're true. They're raw and honest and—

Another rush of music as the door pushes open again. I turn immediately toward the skyline to act like I wasn't just out here looking after Rossi.

"Sof?" Maddix calls out, followed by footsteps. "You good?"

I straighten and turn with a smile plastered on my lips. "Yeah." *Fake it till you make it, right?* "I'm fine. Why, what's up? What did I miss?" I ask, trying not to oversell with fakeness.

But my heart is racing, and that ache is there with a vengeance.

Before Maddix can make it the short distance to me, the door opens again and we both turn to see Cruz standing there, looking from her to me and then back. "You guys good? Party's inside." He hooks a thumb over his shoulder.

"Yes. God. I'm fine. What is it with you?" I snap at him.

"I saw Rossi storm in. I wanted to make sure you were okay," he says. "Just stay away from him."

I think Maddix and I tsk at the same damn time. No doubt we might have the same expressions on our faces if I'm reading the one on his correctly.

"You're the one who invited him," I say.

"He's my teammate."

"Well then, don't get mad if I talk to the guy." I lift my eyebrows in challenge.

"There are plenty of other people you can talk to here that aren't him."

"What is your fucking problem?" I shout at my brother, fed up with men inferring that I don't have any choices. Maddix's eyes grow big and she winces, but she doesn't interfere and for that, I'm grateful. "I'm so over people telling me what I can and can't do."

I go to push past him and he steps in my path. "Sofia."

"No." I throw my hands up to get him away from me. "Just no. I'll talk with who I want to talk with. I'll dance with who I want to dance with. I'll—"

"What's gotten into you?" he asks.

"You. That's who," I shout back but know it's so much more than that as I yank open the door and head back to the party.

And back to the alcohol that will numb me from all the things I want to ignore.

CHAPTER SEVENTEEN

Rossi

"Is it true, Ollie?" Sofia's slurred words call out to me and give me pause.

I've watched her all night. Drink after drink. Dance after dance. Almost as if each one is another step, another way, to try and forget the words I said to her on the terrace. Almost as if she believes she can.

We both know the truth. She can't.

What's worse? I can't either.

She's struggling with shit I can't even imagine. I'm struggling with shit I won't talk about.

I should walk away. Cut my losses. Chalk it up to great sex—right person, wrong time. And yet when she walks toward me, when those lashes flutter and she looks up at me, I know I'm not going anywhere.

This damn woman owns me in ways I don't understand.

"C'mon, *Just Ollie. Truce Boy.* Is it true, yes or no?" She punctuates each of the last three words like a kid in a sing-song voice.

I turn to face her. Her hair is mussed, her clothes askew. She looks properly drunk and indisputably adorable as she concentrates so very hard to walk in her heels.

The anger and desire that have owned me all night soften slightly as she reaches me. Her smile widens and she reaches out to grab my arm to steady herself.

"We have to stop meeting like this," she says breathlessly. "Especially because I'm mad at you. At least I want to be but you make it really hard to be."

"Agreed," I say cautiously as I try to gauge how intoxicated she is. I glance around. There are several people out front of the club in much the same state that she's in. A little drunk, a lot relaxed.

"So is it true?"

"I need to know the question so I can answer it for you, Simply Sofia."

She twists her lips and giggles. My balls draw up. Why can't it be as simple as this—nothing more, nothing less?

"I like when you call me that. Do you like when I call you Ollie?" Her eyebrows narrow.

"I've only ever let one other person call me that before."

"So is that a good thing or a bad thing? You like it? You don't?"

"I like it," I murmur, realizing just how much I do.

"Mm. Me too." She smiles. "I stopped you for a reason though. I'm trying to remember what it was." She pouts for a beat and then her eyes widen as she remembers. "Oh. Yes! The girls! We were all talking inside."

"You were, huh?"

"Yep." She gives a definitive nod that has her hair bobbing with it. "Do you like Peach Rings or Gummy Lifesavers better?"

She blushes and fuck if those eyes, those lips, and the flush of pink doesn't already have me getting hard. I chuckle. "Are we talking about eating them or . . ."

"Sucking on them," she states matter-of-factly. And the blood drains to my lap. Making a man watch what he wants for weeks on end is one thing. Hearing her talk about it, make the sucking sound with those painted lips of hers, that's a whole other level of torture. "And the question came up over whether guys like them to be used when getting sucked off." *Oh, I'm well aware.* A siren's smile crawls across her lips. "And I figured you'd be the perfect person to answer that question for me."

The visual. The thought. *Christ.*

"Yes. Or. No," she whispers.

Fucking little tease.

The worst part? She's not trying to be. She's playful because she's drunk. She's carefree because the alcohol has taken away the burdens she wears like a suit of armor. Doesn't that make her being like this even sexier?

"I think you should be careful asking questions like that of guys like me."

"And who are guys like you? Tough guys who're all talk?" she asks.

Guys worth slumming with. I wince. No matter how much I know she didn't mean it . . . I still can't shake hearing her say it.

"Guys who might take advantage of the situation."

She wobbles before stepping into me, poking me in the chest, and whispering, "You forget, Rossi. I already had you too."

"That's not something I'll ever forget," I murmur and resist the urge to reach out and cup the side of her face. I'm not one who touches, who needs to touch, and yet when it comes to Sofia, that's all I want to do. It's maddening. "You should probably go home."

She pouts and studies me. "The hard to get thing gets old, Ollie. Two steps forward, one step back."

I bark out a laugh. "Yes. Of course. How dare I play hard to get with you?"

As if I couldn't like her any more than I already do.

"Make no mistake, Sofia. I'm not playing hard to get with you. I'm letting you make every decision. Every step of the way."

"Is that why you haven't called?"

Her words and the brutal honesty in them startle me. "Called?"

"For a stalker, you sure didn't try very hard."

I step forward and lower my voice. "It's a fine line between respecting your wishes like you deserve and telling you you're mine and only mine like I want."

"Respecting my wishes? Ha." She blows raspberries at that.

"Yes. Respecting your wishes, Sofia. Do you think it would go over well if I go around the paddock asking for your number? If I ask Cruz for it?" I narrow my eyebrows and chuckle. "For a woman who wanted one night, nothing more, nothing less, that doesn't sound like I'd be respecting your wishes."

"But you . . . you said you want more. Again. Another time."

"I did. I do. But fucking you over to get that isn't respecting you either and, from what I gather, that seems to be what many men in your life do to you—disrespect and disregard you—for one reason or another. I won't be one of them."

"But you said you wanted me," she repeats.

"And you said you weren't sure what you wanted. Last I checked, Bellissima, that's on you, not on me. I'm a fucking guy. You can't say one thing to me and mean another and expect me to interpret it. I . . ." I take a step back and run a hand through my hair. I'm frustrated and about two seconds from hauling her against me and kissing her senseless to stop the questions and doe eyes. She's way too innocent for the thoughts about what I want to do to her that keep running through my head.

"Sofia," a voice shouts down the sidewalk, followed by a waning click of heels. I look up and meet the eyes of Cruz's girlfriend, fiancée, whatever the fuck they are. She eyes me warily but then gives me the slightest of nods and a ghost of a smile. "Everything good?"

Sofia makes a dramatic show of giving a thumbs up.

"Everything's fine," I say to her.

"Are you . . ." Maddix eyes Sofia and then me, clearly assessing the situation.

"She'll get home safely. Yes. I'll make sure of it," I say.

She contemplates that for a few seconds before she nods and takes a step back. "I'll tell your brother you got a ride home with a friend."

"Perfect," Sofia says before turning to face me—a little too fast by the way she catches herself from stumbling—then raises her eyebrows. "Where were we? Lectureville?"

"We shouldn't be having this conversation right now." She's drunk and I'm trying to reason with her when there's no such possibility. She won't remember shit. "Forget it." I wave a hand her way.

"Fine." A nod.

"Great."

"And if you think I'm going home with you, you're out of your mind. I'm a goddamn prize." She does a shimmy that has the lights reflecting off her dress. "And if you don't want me, someone else will."

"Careful, Sofia." *You're striking a match you might not want to light.*

"I'll find someone else who'll answer my question, then." She makes a sucking noise with her lips. "*Ciao.*" She gives a mock salute before walking toward a party attendee heading our way on the sidewalk.

"Hey. Hi. He's cute," she says to me about the man she's approaching.

"Sir." She waves a hand to him. "Hi. Yes, you. One quick and *very important* question. What do you prefer? Peach Rings or—"

"Nope. Not going to happen," I say. Sofia yelps as I pick her up and throw her over my shoulder.

"Rossi." She beats on my ass. "Put me down." A hard spank on mine to which I reciprocate in kind on hers. The difference is that one gives me way more pleasure than it should.

"Nope. Not on your fucking life and not when you're asking questions like those to random men. You're drunk. You need to sleep it off."

"I do not. The party is just getting started. You're the fuckboy. The king of the party." She laughs in protest. "Put. Me. Down."

"Don't mind us," I say to a few people who've stopped and stared. It's not like I can get away with not being recognized in Monaco, but at least they can't see her face right now. At least no one can pin us as being together.

She gripes all the way home. When I finally set her down and push her into the car. When I all but carry her up the stairs into my penthouse. When I force her to sit and drink a full glass of water and take two ibuprofen.

"You're a party pooper," she says and sticks her tongue out at me seconds before she sags on the stool.

"I know," I murmur as I walk over to her.

"Wait. This isn't my house. Why didn't you take me to my house, Ollie?" she slurs.

"Too many eyes on us here, Sofia. I know for certain that my place is private."

"Oh. Yeah. Good point." She closes her eyes and is laughing softly until her head droops. "I think I'm a little drunk over here," she whispers.

"Well aware," I say as I take a sip of the beer I've opened. Something tells me it's going to be a long night.

"The best part about being drunk?" She chuckles sleepily. "I don't have to care about what anyone thinks of me."

I nod, understanding and not understanding at the same time. I lean over, press a kiss to the top of her head, and murmur against its crown. "You never have to worry about that with me. I don't judge you. I understand you more than you might think."

"No one's ever said that to me before," she whispers and then for the slightest moment, as I breathe in the scent of her shampoo and the even cadence of her breathing, I think she's fallen asleep. "I'm so tired, Ollie."

"I know you are." It takes no effort to gather her in my arms and carry her into my bedroom. But it's the way she rests her head on my shoulder, how her lips find the underside of my neck, and my name in the softest of sighs that makes putting her down on the edge of my bed almost impossible.

Her lips find mine. Our kiss as reflexive as my next breath. It's what I've craved. What I've been desperate for.

But not like this.

And as much as it pains me to end it ... to pull her hands off my neck and set them in her own lap—to adjust my hard-on so that it doesn't hurt as much as it already does—I do them all and then take the hardest step back I've ever had to take in my life.

My breath is pained, ragged, as I stare at her. At what I want. And deny myself once more out of respect for her.

"Rossi," she murmurs, eyes trying to flutter open to meet mine.

"Sit here for a sec." I offer a strained smile as the taste of her kiss continues to consume and wreck me.

"No." She reaches out and grabs my arm. "Don't leave me. Everyone always leaves me alone."

I stand there in my room, our fingers linked, those eyes of hers drowsy but more sincere than I've ever seen them before, and with words I can completely understand.

"I'm not leaving. I'm just getting you a shirt to sleep in."

She nods. "Mm-kay." Then she closes her eyes.

I spend the next few minutes taking off her boots.

Pulling her dress over her head and telling myself not to peek, not to want, before slipping one of my T-shirts over her head.

But hell if I do either. I peek. And I still fucking want.

"Lie back," I tell her and pull the covers up and over her. "Get some sleep."

She makes a noncommittal noise as I brush her hair off her face.

Now this is a side to Sofia Navarro I have never seen before. Sexy and seductive. Professional and cold. But this? Serene and unguarded isn't something I was ready for. If I wasn't mildly obsessed with her before, I might just be now.

I go to take a step back.

"It's okay you know," she murmurs.

"What is?" I ask, not expecting her to answer.

"Us using each other for whatever it is we both need."

"I know," I murmur, thinking that what I thought I needed from her that first night in America and what I need now are two completely separate things. "I know."

It's only seconds before a soft snore begins.

I back up a few feet, thoughts on all of the things I'd rather be doing right now with Sofia than watching her sleep. But I drag a chair from the sitting area near the bed.

Don't leave me.

I sit.

I watch her sleep.

I left her asleep the last time I was with her. I got up as the early morning sky turned gray, stared at her, and walked away to respect her wishes.

This time I'm not leaving. This time is different.

And I wonder if that's enough for me.

CHAPTER EIGHTEEN

THE ROOM IS AS LIGHT AND AIRY AS MY HEAD IS GROGGY. THE BED is luxurious—a soft mattress, what feels like miles and miles of a weighted comforter, the cool cotton of the gray sheets against my bare skin—and the shirt I have on smells like Rossi.

And I'm not mad about it.

Before I can question how I ended up here, flashes of last night make their appearance. The club. The balcony. *Fuck your pedigree*. Peach Rings or Gummy Lifesavers. I wince at that one.

Don't leave me.

Oh boy. That's . . . an unexpected one. *Thanks for that, Mamá.*

What else might I have said that I don't remember?

What else did I do that I might regret?

I shift in bed and sit up, one thought heavier on my mind than others.

Did we have sex last night?

It's a question I've never had to ask myself and one that I'm embarrassed to ask myself now but . . . there's no forgetting that kiss last night. The one we shared when I was sitting in the same position I am right now—legs dangling over the edge of the bed.

I'd like to think I wasn't too drunk to remember the incredible hands and skill of Oliver Rossi, but if I was drunk enough to pass out and not sleep with him, then something is seriously wrong with me, right?

To be in his room, in his shirt, in his bed, and to not have acted on it? I mean . . . that's a sexual travesty, is it not?

I smile at my ridiculous thoughts—my *even footing*—because being drunk was easy. Letting my guard down was fun. Being free to say whatever I wanted and having an excuse as to why I said it was great.

But *now* is the hard part.

Facing Rossi. Living up to whatever ridiculous thing I said. And then extricating myself from the situation if need be, despite feeling like we're in a better place than we were.

With a reluctant sigh, I slip out of bed and head to the bathroom. The first thing I notice is the new bottle of water there, the two ibuprofen, and the new toothbrush in its package beside them atop a fresh towel.

I stare at them for a beat. I don't know whether I should feel cared for that he has these out for me or weirded out that he does this so much that he has a routine.

Regardless, I use them all and head out to find him. My footsteps are soft as I walk down the tiled hallway toward what sounds like music playing softly elsewhere in the house.

The ambition to keep walking leaves me when I step into the edge of the kitchen and find Rossi. His back's to me. He's only wearing a pair of sweatpants and nothing else. He's tanned and toned and I watch the chain reaction of muscles bunch and move as he moves about his kitchen.

The counter is covered in an array of pastries and breakfast sandwiches. The scent of coffee lingers in the air. And when I see beyond him into the great room the kitchen overlooks, there's a blanket and bed pillow askew on the couch. It's clear that's where he slept.

Respect.

Words float back into my mind. Things Rossi said last night about me, about respect, that I know I need to hold tighter to but that I can't one hundred percent remember.

And I stand in his kitchen, in his T-shirt, and I know that right or wrong, there is something here between us. And by him sleeping on the couch, he respected whatever that is.

What happens when you're the mouse in the cat and mouse game and you suddenly want to be caught?

"I wasn't sure what you like so I got a bunch of different things," he says over his shoulder like me being in his place is the most normal thing in the world. Again, I question if this is his normal MO.

"How did you know I was standing here?" I take a step into the kitchen and stop when he turns to look at me. His eyes say so many things—none of which I'm able to decipher. They're guarded in a way I haven't seen them before, and I'm not sure if that unnerves me or makes me more at ease.

"When you've lived alone since you were sixteen, you know when someone's in your space."

"I'm sorry. I didn't mean—"

"That wasn't inferring anything, Sofia. Simply a statement of fact." He holds up a coffee mug. "Black? Cream or sugar?"

I stand in his kitchen and stare at him. "Cream, please."

"One sec." He moves with an unexpected efficiency as he doctors my coffee. "Grab some food. Unless that head of yours is hurting. If that's the case, then—"

"No. It's fine, it's . . ." This is all just so normal. So domestic. "It's fine." I busy myself grabbing a croissant and some fruit. "Thank you for the toothbrush and ibuprofen."

"It's always weird waking up somewhere different. I figured you could use them," he says like it's no big deal when it is. I don't think anyone has ever done that for me before.

"Thank you," I repeat as I follow him to where he sits down at a breakfast nook to eat. And when I say nook, I mean a carved alcove off the side of his kitchen with floor-to-ceiling windows that have a breathtaking view of the sea. It's a clear day and beyond the harbor, yachts move lazily in the distance while smaller boats zip around.

I take a seat opposite him, one foot on the chair so my knee is to my chest, as I bring the cup of coffee to my lips and take my first hit. "Hmm. That's good. Thank you."

"Of course." He nods and looks at me over the rim of his own coffee. Our eyes hold before I focus on the croissant in front of me and begin tearing little pieces off it. I have no interest in eating at the moment, and it has nothing to do with the amount of alcohol I drank last night or an upset stomach because of it. It most likely has everything to do with the man sitting across from me.

"What do you mean you've lived alone since you were sixteen years old?" I ask.

"Technically I've been on my own since I was sixteen. It wasn't until I was eighteen that I actually had a place of my own," he says like it's no big deal. "So I misspoke."

"But still. Why were you on your own at sixteen?"

"Racing was an expensive sport. It was either putting money into the car and growing myself and my brand or using what I earned to go back and forth between wherever I was and home." He takes a sip and hisses at the heat. He gives the slightest of shrugs. "We didn't have much, so I decided to ease the burden on my family and not go back. I sent the money I made or won back to help out. I kept a little for myself and I couch surfed from one place to the next in between races."

"With whom?"

"Crew members. Friends I'd made along the way. Other drivers' families."

I stare at him but don't equate the man before me with someone who was essentially homeless for years on end. He was one of the best of his class and yet . . .

"It's not a sob story, Sofia. It was a choice. I lied to my parents so they thought I was taken care of. And I was fine. I had a dream and wanted to live it, and they wanted that dream for me but couldn't afford it. We all make sacrifices to get what we want."

He is so matter of fact but I knew him back then. I saw him at races when he competed against Cruz and I had no idea. Absolutely no clue that he was living how he was living.

"I know, it's just . . ." I shake my head and take a small bite of the croissant. "You could have slept in your bed last night."

He chuckles. "I didn't divulge that to make you feel guilty for sleeping in it. And it was testing my restraint enough to have you in my house and not be able to touch you. Don't kick a man while he's down. Besides, the last thing you needed was to wake up in a strange place feeling uncomfortable that I was there."

"Rossi. We've slept together—"

"You can stop reminding me of that. It would do me a lot of good if you did." He mock groans as he adjusts himself where he sits in his seat but his ghost of a smile is there. As is the look in his eyes when he angles his head to the side and studies me.

It's the weirdest feeling but I've never felt more seen in my life.

"Tell me about it," he says quietly.

He just sits there quietly and looks at me. I get the sense that he's hurt or upset over something I don't quite understand, and I don't know what it is. "Tell you about . . . what?"

"The gallery."

"Oh." Why does the mere mention of it make me feel vulnerable in front of him?

"Why are you hiding it? Why wouldn't you tell me that was the work that brought you here? Why did you seem embarrassed about it when your brother brought attention to it last night?"

"It's complicated."

He smiles. "Try me."

"Jumping off a cliff into the unknown is scary, is it not?"

"Yes, but if you're opening a gallery, I'd assume that's because you are either educated on, acquainted with, or thoroughly enjoy art. Or all of the above. And if that's the case, then it's not really the unknown, now, is it?"

I go to open my mouth, to refute him, but know he's right. "I think it's more the stepping into new territory. Setting myself up for failure. Doing something a Navarro doesn't do."

"And what's that?"

"Something outside of racing." My smile is bittersweet but a small part of me feels relief that I actually just admitted that. Out loud. To someone other than myself.

A huge lump balls in my throat, and it's hard to swallow over the emotion lodged there.

He nods, his eyes full of understanding. "I'd think they'd be thrilled you are wanting to make your own way. Carve your own path."

"There is a precedence for what's expected. Going rogue is not that."

"And why not?"

I purse my lips and fight off my family's unspoken answer. *Because that is what my mamá did. Took off. Carved her own path.* Cheated on our papá. Fell more in love with the drink than her children. Is determined to fuck over every member of the family in one way or another.

Taught me that those you love the most, leave.

I blow out an unsteady breath and muster a smile.

"It's okay. You don't have to answer," Rossi whispers, somehow reading my *non* answer as a sufficient answer.

"Thank you." I blink away the tears that threaten and the sudden rush of sadness edged in anger.

"Don't thank me. You're allowed to feel whatever way you need to feel . . . but you don't need to be embarrassed by it. You should be thrilled. Ecstatic. Shouting about it from the rooftops. Keeping the gallery quiet isn't doing you any favors. Not in this city. Not with these citizens who love their glitz and talking about discovering the next great thing." He takes a sip of coffee. "Use your name even if you don't want to. Use it to create the buzz. Then capitalize on it with your expertise."

"I know, but . . ."

"But nothing. Use your name to your advantage."

But why do I feel like he'd look differently, negatively, on me if I did? And why do I care so much if it did?

"I know. I am. I guess I just don't want to be too optimistic in case it doesn't pan out the way I'd like it to."

"You need to stop owning the person that people expect you to be and own the person you are, Sofia." He angles his head to the side and simply holds my gaze, and the conflict no doubt evident in my eyes. "Making someone see someone/something else's beauty is admirable."

How can he say something like that and not expect me to respond? To be able to speak when those words just spoke to my soul more than he ever could have imagined.

I rise from my chair and move about his great room, taking it all in as a means of distraction from this unexpectedly poignant conversation. It was dark last night, I was drunk, and I didn't get a chance to see this side of Rossi. The racing magazines piled on top of art books. The framed pictures on tan walls. A leather couch that looks well used and very comfortable. The few pictures on the shelves that depict friends but not too many.

"Do you like art, Rossi?" I ask as I lean over and open one of the books on the coffee table and thumb through it. Pictures of paintings enrich each page and draw me in to look and study. The pieces shown are from artists unknown to me and are fascinating.

But when there's no response to my question, I look up to find him on the edge of his own family room. He looks as if he wants to say something but doesn't. Instead, he gives a tight smile with a quick shake of his head—almost as if he thinks better than to say whatever he was going to say. "Not really."

"Why all the books then?"

"Interior designers love that shit."

I close the book and look at the spines of the rest of them spaced around. "Whoever it was has good taste. A good eye."

"I'll let her know if I ever see her again," he says.

"This one has . . ." I pause when I flip through the next book to find notes next to images. Dates and locations in chicken scratch beside photographs of famous paintings and sculptures.

"Some are my nonna's books too. She was the art lover," he murmurs but there's peculiarity about his expression that I can't read.

"Then I like her already."

"Mm," he says and rests his ass against the back of the chair as he crosses his arms over his chest and watches me move about his space.

I'm keenly aware of his eyes on me. On my bare legs beneath his T-shirt. On my braless breasts beneath the fabric.

There's something real, something honest, about this conversation that I don't want it to stop.

It's that Rossi's a real person. Someone beyond that nonchalant, ruthless persona he wears like a shield at the track. There are stories behind his hesitant responses, truths I have a feeling he keeps close to the vest, and I'm utterly curious about every single one of them.

The question is, will he let me see them? Or will the real Oliver Rossi step back into the shadows?

CHAPTER NINETEEN

Rossi

SHE'S IN MY SHIRT.

In my house.

Her hair is a mess. Her face naked with a little of last night's mascara smudged beneath her eyes. Her tan legs look a mile long.

But it's the expression in her eyes when she looks over her shoulder where she's standing with the picture window and the ocean behind her that has me struggling to breathe.

She's fucking gorgeous.

And yeah, Blair was beautiful. *Still is*. And while she was mine on and off for so long, I never looked across a room at her and felt like my heart was going to explode. I never wondered how I could stop time, how I could preserve the moment, because I feared it would be ruined the minute she realized I wasn't good enough for her.

That I was exactly what they all say about me. My fellow racers. The media. The fans. Stavros. Fucking Navarro.

Great sex is one thing.

This . . . this weird feeling in my chest and sudden flush of heat is entirely different.

Why do you think everyone leaves you, Sofia?

"What?" she asks me as she trails a finger over a cabinet on the far end of the room. She offers a half-smile before turning back to unabashedly look at my things.

There's a part of me that wants her out of here. Out of the inner sanctum of who I am. The real me.

But I brought her here, didn't I? I brought her here when I knew I wouldn't be taking advantage of the situation. I forced myself to show her this part of me. Hints of the truths I hide from the public.

This one's on me.

"Nothing." I smile and reach for my coffee. I then glance at my kitchen counter and realize how utterly ridiculous it looks right now. How much I overdid the breakfast shit because I didn't know what she liked and wanted to make sure whatever it was, was here.

And I wanted a reason for her to stay longer.

"You were at the party last night," she says over her shoulder.

"Apparently."

She chuckles with a quick glance my way as she thumbs through yet another art book. I fight the urge to tell her I got that on a private tour of a gallery in Florence. She'd understand, right? She'd appreciate that?

"Why?" she asks.

"Why, what? Why was I there?"

"This book is incredible by the way." She nods and sets it down like it's an artifact, which makes me smile. "But yeah, why were you there? I thought you hated my brother."

My smile flickers. "I was invited."

She laughs, her nipples jogging against the fabric with the motion. "But no response to the *you hate my brother* part."

I drag my eyes up to meet hers, trying to ignore the fact that I want her with every part of my being but talk of her brother isn't exactly arousing.

She smirks.

She knows where I was looking.

"I don't dislike your brother." I set my coffee mug down, feeling like I might need my hands free.

"But you don't like him either." She turns and mimics my posture, ass against the windowsill, legs stretched and crossed out in front of her, arms now crossed over her chest.

"History is sometimes a hard thing to overcome." If I dislike her brother because of everything he stands for—affluence, legacy, presumption, reputation—then don't all the same things apply to her? Shouldn't I have the same animosity toward Sofia?

"But history is made to be learned from." She points to the art books as if to say case in point. And only if she knew how true that was. How many hours my nonna spent teaching me the history of each of those pieces.

"True." I nod.

"So you *do* like Cruz then?" she presses.

"He's a competitor. We compete. Against each other. For each other. No doubt at times we'll like each other and at others we'll not. It's a flawed system to have men want to beat each other but at the same time protect each other."

She nods slowly and I can see she's processing what I've said. "So you're refusing to answer."

I chuckle and push off the chair and move toward her. "My answer is irrelevant and definitely has no bearing on this, right here."

"It doesn't?" She moves a few steps toward me.

"No." I close the gap, reach out, and tuck a piece of hair behind her ear. "It doesn't."

We stand in this space, so close yet so far apart.

"Thank you for making sure I got home safely." She reaches out and rests a hand on my chest. Her hand is cold but it feels incredible because, all of a sudden, I'm pretty fucking warm.

"Always," I murmur, moving my hand to cup the side of her face and run my thumb over her bottom lip.

There's a ragged inhale of breath, and I'm not sure if it's hers or mine because I can't hear properly over the thundering pulse in my ears.

Our lips meet. It's a slow burn of a kiss. One with our hands in each other's hair. With our bodies aching for more but some fucking thing holding us back. Making us take our time.

Anticipation. Desperation. Both are a dangerous drug to mix but not as dangerous as she is. As this woman before me with the wild eyes and the sleep-mussed hair.

"You usually do this before you spend the night," she murmurs as she kisses her way to the underside of my jaw.

"I'm coming to find out that whatever this is between us, Sofia, it's anything but typical."

I lean forward to kiss her again and she hesitates. She's thinking way too much. About why. About how. About whether this is a good idea or not.

And I'm so sick of all these thoughts. The only thing I know for sure is that I've never wanted anything more. I've had her. I know how good the reward is. How incredible she feels. But I've never had to wait for anything. Never had to want anything. It's always just been there.

And then there's Sofia.

Fucking Sofia.

"Stop thinking," I murmur as our lips meet.

"Then make me."

No sexier words have ever been spoken.

And as much as I want to rush to the next part—to our skin on each other's, to me being buried in her—I savor her kiss. The slow steadiness of it. The quiet command of it. The enjoying each other to simply enjoy each other.

The room's bright.

There's no dark to hide behind.

There's no alcohol to dim the haze of desire or veil the desperation in our need.

There's no rush to finish before the weekend is over.

It's just her pink lips parting for me.

Her tongue darting out to dance with mine.

My shirt coming off over her head so that her breasts are free.

God. This woman. This moment. It's going to be my fucking undoing, and I'm goddamn good and gone.

"I want you, Ollie," she murmurs against my lips as her fingernails skim down my naked torso. It feels like fire scorching its way under my skin. "I've always wanted you."

I hiss out a breath as her hands slip beneath the waistband of my sweats and encircle my cock.

"I'm sick of fighting against myself over it. Of denying myself just how fucking good you are. How good you make me feel."

My hands shove down my sweats allowing her the freedom to stroke me. And when she does, when she tightens her fist over my cock and takes it from root to tip, I lose all sense.

I've been stroked by dozens of women. Not a boast, just a fact. But fuck if her touch isn't the most intense feeling—like ice and heat and every damn sensation in between.

"Sofia," I groan and welcome her lips on mine as I run my hands up her bare back. As I soak in the warmth of her skin and the taste of her kiss. As I jump into this chaotic pleasure that's welcome right now but that she might run away from tomorrow.

"Thank you for respecting me last night, Ollie," she murmurs as her lips find my ear and her teeth tug on the lobe. "But for the love of God, disrespect me right now."

Jesus.

I lean back and look at her as I wrap her messy ponytail around my fist. I love the little gasp that escapes her mouth as I tug it back. I love how her lips part just enough that I know she's as affected by me as I am by her.

My chuckle pairs with her labored breathing until she tightens her hand on my cock and strokes again. Then I'm back to hissing. To wanting. To dragging my mouth against hers as we move to the couch.

"Jesus," I murmur as I step out of my pants and push her to sit on the couch. "Spread those thighs, Bellissima. Show me that pretty pussy of yours."

With her eyes on mine, she scoots her ass to the edge of the couch and does as I ask. There's no hesitation. No shyness. Just pure unadulterated lust in her eyes as she opens up for me to see.

And what a sight it is.

A trimmed strip of curls. The light pink skin glistening in her arousal. The smooth, toned thighs on either side.

I groan and run my palms up and down the length of her thighs, grazing my thumbs over her center so her breath hitches and her hips buck.

I do it several more times. My eyes flicker back and forth from the darkening of her eyes to the clenching of her pussy with each and every turn.

"What do you want?" I murmur. "My fingers? My tongue? My cock?"

"You," she pants out breathlessly. "I want you."

Every part of me reacts to those words. To that admission. To her blatant desire.

And so after another circuit of my hands on her thighs and with a cock so fucking hard it hurts, I hold her knees apart and dip my head between her thighs. My tongue finds her clit and circles lazily around it before parting her slit and dipping down into her well.

Heaven.

My first and only thought—because no other thoughts are possible as I inhale her scent and savor her taste on my tongue. Sweet perfection. I bury my tongue in her, using short, quick strokes to give her what she needs and take exactly what I want. Her. All of her. Every fucking scent and flavor and reaction until she realizes that no other man will ever pleasure her like I am.

"Rossi." Her hips buck up when I move my tongue to her clit and add my fingers to the mix. "Ollie." Her fingers grip my hair as I pick up my pace. "Please. Yes." She tightens around me as I continue the sensual assault with my tongue and my fingers. "Oh God."

And when she comes, when her thighs tense on my shoulders and her muscles pulse around my fingers, I let her have the moment. Every blissful and aching moment of it. I try to be patient, I try to give her time, but like a man desperate for water, I withdraw my fingers and bury my tongue in her to taste my reward.

I lick and suck on the sensitive flesh as she squirms beneath me, her pants becoming murmured *Ollies*.

Her fingers loosen their grip in my hair.

Her thighs slowly relax and fall back open.

And when I can't wait any longer, I quickly protect us, and then I push into her. My vision goes white as I fill her as full as possible. Our joint moans are like an aphrodisiac. Pleasure. Longing. Need. Greed. All four mixed up in that one sound.

"Feels. So. Good," she murmurs as her eyes drift shut.

She doesn't know the half of it. How she makes me feel. How strong the goddamn ache is to draw this out *and* to fuck her into oblivion. To savor and destroy simultaneously.

I lean forward and slant my lips over hers. Our tongues meet as she brings her hands up to my neck, holding me there. Needing me close.

And it's then I begin to move.

In. Out. Over and over.

With her hands on me. Her lips against mine. And every fucking thing about her seared into my mind like a painful brand I welcome.

Because this is pain in its most beautiful form. To want something you're not good enough for. To need someone you know will leave. To become infatuated with someone you know you can't have.

And yet I'm still here.

Still driving myself to the brink of release from what she makes me feel.

"Sofia," I grit out as my body takes over and my control snaps. Her laced fingers behind my neck ease up as she meets my eyes.

"Let me watch you," she says, and those are the last words I hear as I succumb to the moment. To the lust her body brings me. To the desire just being with her creates.

I hold her stare as long as I can until I can't anymore. With my eyes closed, I shout as I come. Hard and fast and overwhelmingly.

It was a forgone conclusion.

One that shouldn't rock boats or move mountains.

But I am rocked.

And I am moved.

And when I stop jerking my hips, when I collapse onto her sweat-misted chest, when her fingernails skim up and down the length of my spine, I'm at a loss for so many things.

The biggest one is ... where do we go from here?

CHAPTER TWENTY

Sofia

IT FEELS LIKE LAST TIME—THE PLEASURE, THE SATISFACTION, THE want for more—but so very different.

He's still here beside me.

He's more than just a mystery now.

He brought me home last night and didn't try anything with me.

We lie on our backs in the bed where we've migrated to, in that awkward, *we just had sex, what do we do now* moment, and I struggle with what to do or say.

"So, what do you like to do in your time off?" I ask.

He barks out a laugh. "Are we back on this whole even footing thing?" He shifts, turning on his side to face me and resting his head in his hand. "It's okay to have sex and it not be awkward. It's okay to have sex, decide you're both going to take a shower, and then . . . have more coffee. And it's okay to lie in this bed that still smells like sex and relive every incredible moment of it."

I turn, mirroring his posture, and smile. Jesus. He's . . . so damn attractive. Bedhead. Scruff on his chin. I just had him and I already want him again. "It was incredible, wasn't it?"

My grin never stops. How can it? Neither does the ache that that simmering look he gives me continues to stoke.

"It was." He reaches out and cups my breast, letting his thumb run absently back and forth over my nipple. I think the man is slowly trying to kill me by sensual torture.

"You're not anything like they say you are, you know," I murmur.

He purses his lips and gives the slightest of nods. "You forget. I don't care what anyone says about me."

"Everybody cares, Ollie." *There are times that I wish I didn't.*

"What do they say about me?" He leans forward and takes my breast between his lips. "That I'm difficult?" A kiss to my sternum. "Selfish?" A warm suction on my other nipple. "Reckless?" A slide of his tongue up the line of my neck. "Out of control?" An open-mouthed kiss on that spot just beneath my ear. "They're all true. Every single one." He brushes his lips against mine. "I hope that answer doesn't disappoint you."

I thread my fingers through the hair at the back of his neck and pull his lips back for another kiss as an answer.

It's long and languorous. A slide of tongues. A whisper of sighs. A slip of the two of us into something so much more than just lust.

And when the kiss ends, when between my thighs is slick with arousal and my body burns so bright I fear it could detonate, Rossi tucks me in beside him, with my head on his chest.

We lie there in the quiet. In a silent acknowledgment that whatever's between us hasn't been sated with sex. It has been stoked.

When my phone vibrates on the nightstand for the fifth time, Rossi sighs. "I think you're wanted in reality, Bellissima."

I sit up, grab my phone off the nightstand, and cringe.

"Hello?"

"You alive?" my brother asks.

"I'm talking to you, aren't I?"

"Why haven't you answered?"

"My phone was dead. I was busy. I didn't want to. All of those answers should suffice." I melt into the feeling of Rossi reaching out and running his fingers up and down my bare back. There's something so casual about it, so intimate, which sounds ridiculous considering the sex we just had, but it's true. It's an unexpected touch, unneeded, but given, nonetheless. As if he can't resist having his hands somewhere on me at all times.

"Someone's hungover." He chuckles. "Open up. I'm outside. I have stuff for you."

"Um." I glance back toward Rossi and smile. "I can't. I'm not there."

"Why the hell . . . ohhhh." It took him long enough. *"Where are you?"*

You'd kill me if you knew. "None of your business. I hope Maddix had a good time last night."

"Sofia."

"Cruz," I repeat back in the same warning, disapproving tone. "I'm fine. I'm busy. I'll talk to you later."

And with that I end the call, put my phone on do not disturb, and toss it on the far end of the bed.

"I just love when the big brother calls to check up," he says sarcastically.

"You should," I say, turning and crawling to straddle his lap. "It's to your benefit."

"How's that exactly?" he asks as his hands find the sides of my waist and I feel his cock harden beneath me.

"It makes me want to do everything he thinks that I shouldn't." *Can his hands never leave me?* "He makes me want to rebel against all his rules."

"Like?"

I grind over him with only the sheet between us. My body is so deliciously sore but it's ready for more. I lift up and free him from the fabric, then I line him up at my entrance. I'm already so damn wet for him. So ready to be pleasured into submission again.

His fingers tighten.

He hisses out a breath.

I lower myself ever so slowly onto him. Each blissful inch feels like the best kind of torture.

And when I bottom out, when he's bucking his hips, his fingers bruising and his restraint held by a thread, I rock my hips forward and whisper, "Like you."

CHAPTER TWENTY-ONE

Sofia

"At some point, I probably need to take you home," Rossi says as he wraps the towel around his waist and walks out of the bathroom toward me.

"Probably. Unless you want to do something else."

"I have stamina, Bellissima, but even a man in his prime has to have a recovery period now and again."

I laugh and roll my eyes. "No. I mean . . . never mind."

"No. Tell me." He gently fists my hair and forces me to look up at him.

"It was a stupid thought. It's imposing. It's—"

"Keep the wishy-washy for your family, Sofia. When you're with me, you ask for what you want. That's the only way to get it."

Why does shit like that turn me on?

I meet his eyes. "I like this Rossi. My Ollie. The one I've gotten to know today, and want to get to know him better. That's all."

"What if I had plans today?"

"Then I could do them with you."

"Really? Just like that? You go from telling me *not in a million years* to *hey, let's hang out?*"

I shrug. It does sound stupid. "I was always going to cave."

"I know."

I scoff. "Whatever."

"You were. I was. There's something here between us that's . . . *undeniable.*"

And that feels out of control. "I know. I just . . . maybe I didn't want it to go away just yet." I blush with the admission but after everything we've done to each other over the past few hours, that should be the least of things I blush about.

"So . . . what? If I had things to do out on the town, you were going to go with me? Let it be known we were hanging out together?" he asks as he turns to his closet to grab a shirt, but there's something in his voice that I can't quite pinpoint. An emotion that's being held back.

"I—uh . . ." I didn't think about that. "We could watch a movie. Order takeaway. Let me cook for you. Sit in the jacuzzi on your deck and . . . never mind."

"What did I say to you? I don't do *never minds.*" He meets my eyes. "What is it?"

"I've had a great time with you. I don't want it to end. But at the same time, I can't exactly have you drop me off at my place and kiss me goodbye out front."

"Who said I was going to kiss you goodbye?" Rossi asks, giving me a glimpse of the man I see in the paddock. The cold heart. The guarded man.

I open my mouth and close it then make a ridiculous sound in response. I struggle with how to say anything when I feel like I was blindsided.

But isn't that just how I made him feel? Like I can fuck him in private but I can't acknowledge him in public?

"Touché," I finally say.

"That wasn't my intent, Sofia. I don't say things to hurt you. I told you all along I'd respect your wishes, and I'm trying really fucking hard to, but it's difficult when I don't know what game it is you're playing."

"I'm not playing any games."

He moves to hang his towel up. "So then what are you saying?"

"I like whatever this is. I want to do whatever this is *again.* Spending time with you. Having sex with you. Getting to know you. But it's probably not the best decision right now to be public with it."

He nods. "And why's that?"

"You're on a new team. With my brother. The last thing we need is to cause turmoil at Gravitas."

"So it's for my sake, then?"

"Last year was a shitshow for you with Lachlan and Blair," I say referring to his teammate and his ex who started dating each other. There were a few public scenes that occurred that painted him in a less favorable light. They only served to encourage the negative things people think and say about him. "You were accused of hitting your teammate out of revenge, Rossi."

"I'm well aware. I paid the price for it. Your point?"

"Don't you think it would look bad for you to be back in a garage on a new team and be at odds with your new teammate too? Because that's exactly what would happen. Cruz wouldn't let this go without a fight. I don't know what's between you two, but I know that for a fact. Then what? Then you'd look like you're the problem and nobody would see it differently."

His jaw sets and his teeth clench. I know he can see what I'm saying, and luckily for me, it plays perfectly into what's truly necessary.

The last thing *I* need right now is for this to get out. For the fact that we're . . . whatever we are, to be known. Does that make me a chickenshit? Yes.

He steps toward me and cups my face. His eyes are serious. "You told me last night it was okay to use each other for whatever it is we need to use each other for."

"I did?" *Shit.*

"You did. And last night—*and* this morning—happened with me knowing that's how you saw me. You're using me. I own that. I accepted that before you even woke up."

"There's nothing wrong with you. I promise. It's me. It's . . ."

"What are you using me for, Bellissima? To get back at your brother? To rebel against your grandfather? To get that carefree feeling back you had from the festival?"

"It's none of those," I whisper.

He nods and I swear to God he can see through the lie that I can't acknowledge yet. "You just keep thinking that, and I'll just keep pretending the real reason you're here is because you want to be. Because you think I'm good enough."

"It is. I am. You are." *Get it together, Sof.* It's wrong that my family and my insecurities are making him feel less about himself. And I have no idea how to fix that. "How can you think differently? If I didn't want to be with you, I would have asked to go home. This morning never would have happened. *After* this morning never would have happened." I lean forward and press my lips to his, hating this conversation. "I'm just getting used to the idea of this. There's a lot of outside noise. For me. For you. And maybe it's best if we figure out what song we prefer before we let any more in."

He purses his lips. "Tell me something real about you, Sofia. Tell me something to prove you're invested in this as more than a *fuck you* to your family."

My gaze flits around the room almost as if I'm desperate and know what he's going to ask but don't want to address. "Sure. Yes. Only if you do the same."

"I don't believe I ever gave you anything to question when it comes to my investment in you, but sure, I'll play." He crosses his arms over his chest. "Who left you?"

Shit. My pulse pounds and my chest aches. I opened this door. I know it, but that doesn't mean I hate him for walking through it. "My mamá," I whisper. "She left us. And then came back and made me believe I was a good enough reason for her to stay before leaving again."

"I'm sorry." His expression is as pained as my voice sounds. "I shouldn't have asked."

But you did.

"And when she left physically, it feels like my papá left mentally too. So yeah, it sucks. I'm over it. It's not a big deal."

And yet when you get drunk, Sofia, you tell the man you like you're afraid he's going to leave.

Rossi just nods quietly. "It has every right to be a big deal though." He closes his eyes for a beat before opening them and offering me a reticent smile. "You can use me for your pleasure. You can use me to prove not everybody leaves. You can even use me until you get the strength to tell people we're whatever this is. But don't you dare use me to lie to yourself. You're better than that."

But don't you dare use me to lie to yourself. You're better than that.

Rossi's words are a constant refrain in my head that wades through the guilt that feels as thick as sludge.

But he said them. He put them out in the ether and then he let them go like he never even thought them. What I'd give to be able to do the same.

But I can't.

Not when I'm cuddled up beside him with his arm wrapped around my shoulders. We're watching some oddly interesting documentary. Yet another unexpected surprise about Oliver Rossi—that he likes documentaries.

The conversation has been incredible. We've covered an array of topics from surface level things to the theoretical.

He continues to impress me with his knowledge. With the way he sees the world. With his command of what he wants. But there are a few things he switches topics on.

Any mention of his family is met with a sarcastic comment. "My parents are . . . my parents. Stuck in their ways. Married to jobs they don't need. I know this because I've sent them plenty of money to make sure of that. They say they're proud but who knows . . ."

Blair. His ex who was on again, off again during a ten-year span. "She was what I needed at the time, but we grew apart. I was a complete asshole. No excuses there, I was. I see that now. And someone loved her better. She deserves that because I didn't."

The perception of him. It's our last topic as he drives me home late that night. "They can call me whatever they want, but they'll sure as fuck be on their toes when I'm in their rearview mirror or racing beside them."

"So you race dirty on purpose?"

"I race the way I race, Sofia. It's gotten me this far, hasn't it? And even if I don't race dirty, people perceive that I do so anytime there is a wreck, it's my fault. People love a villain."

"But you lean into it. Don't you want people to know the real you?" I ask.

"No. It's easier this way."

"But why?"

He turns and looks at me. "Because you get sick of trying to show people the real you but not be believed. It's easier to be what they think you are. You know all about that, don't you?"

His words serve their purpose—to stop my line of questioning—and to maybe put me in my place.

I clearly hit a nerve.

"I still think you should let them see the real you," I whisper but say nothing more as he makes the final few turns to the Navarro family home I've been staying at since I committed to the gallery space.

It was built in a crowd of luxurious homes at the base of the hills of Monaco. The drive may be windy and private, but that doesn't stop the neighbors or their security from looking closely at the cars that drive down it.

And in a town full of extravagant cars, everyone knows the drivers and theirs.

I turn to look at Rossi through the darkness. I take in his profile—eyes, lips, expression—and I wonder what he sees when he looks at me. The Navarro privilege in a town full of it? A spoiled rich kid? A woman with First World problems he never thought in his upbringing he'd be a witness to?

"Who else calls you Ollie?" I ask and get the faltered and puzzled response I was looking for. It's the same look he gave me the first time I called him that.

"Why would you assume that?" He glances over to me.

"It's just a hunch," I shrug. "But something about the name softens you."

"I am *not* soft." He tsks but a smile curves one corner of his lips and tells me I've guessed right. "And if you ever tell anyone that I am, I'll deny ever knowing you," he teases and squeezes my thigh.

But I let the question die as we drive in silence.

"My nonna called me Ollie," he says quietly with a reverence that's almost tangible. "I hated the nickname with everything I had but somehow she took it, turned it into something good so that . . . when *she* called me Ollie, it felt like she loved me more than the whole world."

"Oh." My tongue feels thick in my mouth. "Why did you hate it?"

He gives a subtle shake of his head and doesn't answer my question when he speaks. "It's why I went to the music festival. She was my biggest cheerleader in all things—on and off the track. She'd passed away and I needed time to clear my head, to get lost in everything I wasn't, before the season started."

I rest my hand on top of his that's on my thigh and squeeze. "I'm sorry."

"Don't be. It's the cycle of life." He shrugs it off but I know there's a lot more than just the death of his beloved nonna.

"I—I won't call you that anymore. I'm sorry—"

"No. I like it. It makes me smile." He sighs as he takes a left. "And you're right, it softens me. You soften me."

Oh. My.

There's a weight to his admission that I'm not certain either of us are ready to address and so I leave it be. I let the silence eat at its edges so that we can be more comfortable with it. Or not be.

"This one here," I say, the impending turn forcing me to find my voice.

"I know where the Navarro house is," he murmurs as he turns into the driveway. "Everyone in this town does."

I nod, knowing that statement has its benefits and its disadvantages. But I don't put words to what he already knows. To what I feel like he partially resents me for but that I don't truly understand.

"You sure you don't want to stay with me?" he asks as if we're not already sitting in my driveway.

"I do. You know I do." I smile, suddenly having a mini-freak-out over what happens next. Is this something you talk about on a first date? But is this really considered a first date? *No. It's not.* "But . . . if I stay, I'll never get to the gallery tomorrow."

"Why's that? Do you think something might distract you?" he asks as he runs a hand up my thigh. I squirm away from him, knowing if he finds purchase where I want him to, there will be no getting out of this car.

"Very distracting." I shift and link my fingers with his to stop him. "And if I don't go to the gallery, then I won't be ready in time for artmonte-carlo."

"The art show? Is that the plan?"

"An ambitious one, but one nonetheless."

"Ambition is never a bad thing. Are you still looking for more pieces?"

"A few, yes. My feature piece for sure."

"You haven't found it yet?"

"I have a few in mind but so far no one's buying what I'm selling."

"And what are you selling?"

"Space in a well-trafficked area. A smaller than usual commission structure for the gallery. I figure I need to take a smaller cut initially to entice artists while I grow my name and brand."

"Are you telling them who you are though? Your name? Your family?"

"No. Yes. I don't know. Whichever one I tell you, you're going to tell me I'm wrong. If I do use it, then I'm not being true to myself, and if I don't use it then I'm not leaning on what I was born into. It's a no-win situation from where I stand and where you judge."

He falls silent almost as if it's an acknowledgment of the truth I just levied him with. His hands are on the steering wheel and his thumb's thrumming a beat. He stares out at the darkness in front of us. "If you could have one piece, what would it be? Your dream piece to showcase?"

My smile is automatic because the answer is that simple. "You wouldn't know it."

"Humor me. That way I can pretend to know it when you eventually acquire the rights to show it."

"*Midnight Madness* by Mikah Mastroni."

He raises his eyebrows, starts to say something, and then stops himself. "*Midnight Madness*. Is this a well-known artist or piece?"

"In the art world, yes. Rumor is that he doesn't loan pieces out. Hell, he rarely even allows people to see his work. The piece I love—*Midnight Madness*—is only known because someone snuck a picture of it from a private gallery and posted it—which tells me he will in fact loan a piece out for the right person, price, reason ... hell if I know."

"And the painting is good?"

"It's incredible. It's moving. It's ... *everything*."

He nods but doesn't say anything more as I study him. This man, who has owned my mind for a month.

And now he's beside me. He's talking to me. He's validating my dreams and aspirations. *It's an incredible feeling to have someone like him listen.* I know I won't be able to think about anyone else.

"I might know a little something about that feeling," he says quietly.

My mind stutters over how to respond, but fears anything I might say would ruin the moment, the softness to a man who's rarely soft.

"Good night, Ollie," I whisper.

He leans over and brushes his lips to mine. "Good night, Bellissima."

CHAPTER TWENTY-TWO

Rossi

I DRIVE THE COAST.

It's late and the moon is out, but there will be no going back to my place where pieces of Sofia are everywhere and she's not.

I don't know what the fuck this is, but it's like nothing I've ever felt or experienced before. And that's not a slight to Blair.

But maybe . . . just maybe, I can comprehend the pull Blair felt toward Lachlan last year. That draw. That certainty between them. That all-consuming something that would drive you to lie, to hide, to do whatever it takes so that feeling doesn't fucking stop. That Lachlan would risk his new contract—the one I have now that I took out from under him without him even putting up a fight—simply so he could be with her.

It made no sense to me then. Racing and keeping your ride were what you did at all costs. But now? Now there's more sense to that madness. More reason to why you'd do something so counterintuitive to all you've worked for.

And it's the weirdest fucking feeling.

What I've known of love has been skewed.

My parents loved me enough to push me. To not want me to live their life. To feel obligated to support them because they drove me to want more. But once they didn't have to live the life they didn't want for me, once I paid off all their debts and set them up comfortably, I don't see them any more or any less. It's not like they've chosen to come to races.

Blair loved me as best as I let her. That's no fault of hers.

Then there's racing. That relationship is a contemptuous bitch where I love what I do and sometimes it loves me back. But it seems that it too, wants something in return. It wants the show, the façade, the risk-taker people expect.

And now Sofia. What the fuck is this? The feeling. The borderline obsession. The need.

I scrub a hand over my jaw and exhale.

I've lived a life disregarding the things I've loved.

A life with one goal.

It's jarring when the entire fabric you've built your world around seems to no longer hold its weight. Nor do you think you want it to.

So I drive.

The hills of Monaco.

Over to Nice.

To the twisty roads beyond.

And I try to undo these feelings. I try to rationalize, to justify, to eradicate them—play them off as just good fucking sex . . . but it's so much more than that.

Sofia's so much more than that.

She's lived a life in Cruz's shadow.

But I see her there.

I can't see anything else.

The question is . . . do I really want to?

CHAPTER TWENTY-THREE

Rossi

"I KNEW I'D FIND YOU HERE," BLAIR SAYS FROM BEHIND ME.

Fuck. Of course she'd know.

"Maybe I came here to be alone." I take a sip of my coffee and look out at the empty track before me. The morning sky still has hints of that dawn gray that the rising sun is chasing back into hiding. The garages to the far right of me have crew members milling about but nothing chaotic like there will be in the coming hours.

"And maybe you came here because you're brooding about something and don't know how to deal with it."

"That's a stretch," I mutter. This is why I don't let people get close. Close people can read into things when you don't want them to.

Blair snorts. "Hardly. And no, I'm not asking if I can take a seat because I've earned that damn right when it comes to you."

"God help Lach," I tease.

"So. Oliver. What's going on?" She tucks her knees up to her chest and wraps her arms around them. I study her for a second, the familiarity of how many times we've talked like this during the years, and feel a little more at ease.

"Nothing much. Just taking it all in and getting a little perspective before hitting the track today like I sometimes do."

"Hmm," she says and takes a sip of her coffee. "You forget that I know you. I know you pull away when you don't know how to deal. That you stomp around the garage when you don't want to talk. I'm the closest thing you have to a best friend—like me or not." She hits her shoulder against mine. "I'm here if you want to talk to someone about whatever's going on with you. Your car was sensational in testing yesterday so it's not the car."

"It's not the car," I say.

"I think it's whoever you're googly-eyed about."

Fuck. Leave it to Blair to notice.

I blow out a breath as the last few days play through my mind. The confusion. The want. The need. *The silence.* "She hasn't said two words to me."

"She?" Blair prompts.

"Mm."

"Has she said two words to you like this whole week? This month? Like is this a normal thing or is this a *because of the race* type of thing?"

I purse my lips and steer my gaze over to the Moretti garages where one of their cars is being pulled onto pit row. "She's texted only."

"Were those texts nice or flirty or strictly business or whatever it is between you?"

"They were... friendly. Sexy. Flirty." I pause and realize what they really were. "Cautious."

Is that what they were? I was so busy tripping over myself from the onslaught of emotions I was feeling while Sofia was wherever she was being... cautious when it came to us. Is that what's bugging me?

"Can you blame her for being cautious when it comes to you?" Blair asks. I level her with a glare. She shrugs. "I mean, can you?"

"What's that supposed to mean?"

"You're far from perfect, Oliver."

"No shit."

"And you don't exactly have a track record for being anything more than a player."

"Yep. Got it. Don't you need to go plant flowers with Lachlan or something about now?"

She laughs. I knew she would. Thank God.

"I don't know, Blair. It's..."

"It's what?"

"It feels different with her."

"Oh." The sound she makes is mirrored by the sudden tensing of her body. "That's ... well, that's unexpected," she says gently and knowingly and neither make me feel like the ass I expected to feel like.

"You're telling me." I match her tone, my eyes fixed on the Gravitas garage and Cruz's car in the stall next to mine.

We sit in silence for a bit, both digesting this most unexpected revelation. "Then what's stopping you from ... whatever it is you're stopping doing?"

"It's complicated."

"No shit." She chuckles. "Who is it?"

"Don't ask."

I can see her expression in my periphery—the purse of her lips, the narrowing of her eyes, the subtle nod of her head—and I know the minute she thinks she has it narrowed down.

"It might piss a lot of drivers off if you were to say, date their sister, but I have a feeling there's one in particular that might cause you the most problems."

"Perhaps." It's all I'm going to give her. I trust Blair. That's not the issue. But I've never been one to blab about my affairs, and I sure as shit aren't going to start now.

"Fight harder."

I snort. "Yeah. Sure. Okay." I roll my eyes but keep looking at Cruz's car.

"I'm serious. She likes you for whatever reason she likes you—"

"The good sex," I tease, needing to add levity to the conversation.

"You can't be too lovesick if you're still saying shit like that. Good to know you haven't changed much." She knocks her shoulder against mine. "But I'm serious. If this really is different like you say it is ... then you need to let it grow like it is. You've planted the seed—no pun intended—and now you need to sit back and do something I know is impossible for you."

"What's that?"

"Be patient." She waits until I meet her eyes. "Sprinkle some water on it, let it get used to that so it can bloom. If you flood it with water, it's going to drown."

"You're talking in gardening terms about my sex life."

"Love life," she corrects, which has my hands tightening on my mug. I hear her but I don't respond at all.

"My life."

"Noted." She takes another sip. "From what I've learned, that family is a complicated one. Very. I mean this with all due respect, you're not Spanish, you don't come from a well-known family, and you're known for being slightly . . . unethical and brash. None of those traits would seem to be who they'd pick for their prized daughter and granddaughter."

"Way to boost a man's ego."

"For a man who has no problem telling me like it is, you sure don't want to hear it."

"I like her, Blair. Like . . . *I like her* in ways that make me understand you and Lach and how last year happened."

"So then don't screw this up."

"I love how you stroke my ego," I joke.

"We're way past that part of the friendship." She rises from her seat and dusts off her ass before she picks up her mug of coffee. "From what I know of her, she's a good match. I don't know. You're finding your footing on this new team and she's finding her footing in her world. Maybe the timing is right. Maybe it's not. Either way time is what you need. To bide. To sit back and let her take the lead. To just let it breathe."

I draw in a deep breath and sigh. "Thanks."

"Any time . . . it also wouldn't hurt for you to actually try and be on talking terms with your teammate. That could make this whole thing swing one way or another."

"There's—"

"History? Yeah. I know. But that history isn't exactly his fault now, is it? He's bore the brunt of it simply because of his last name much like it seems she has to in other aspects."

I grunt in response. The last thing I want to think about is Cruz in this whole mix when I'd much rather be thinking about Sofia.

"I've got to get back but good luck this weekend."

"Good luck to Lachlan but apologize to him in advance for me."

"For?"

"For kicking his ass."

Her laugh stays with me as I watch her take the long walk back to the pits and to Lachlan.

Sprinkle it with water.

Let it breathe.

This is definitely new territory for me if I'm thinking in terms of shit like this.

I push up from my seat. Chicanes. Grid positions. DRS. Boxing.

Those are much better terms.

Terms that make me feel like me.

Terms I repeat all the way back down to the garage.

CHAPTER TWENTY-FOUR

Rossi

"Have them look at adjusting the wing," I say when I see Cruz staring at the back of his car like he's trying to solve the world.

It's mid-morning. The garages are empty as most of the crew is in a team meeting.

It's my absolute favorite time on the track. I can sit with my thoughts. Can settle the squirrely-ness that seems to hit me on race weeks.

"Yeah. Sure. Like they haven't already thought of that," he says, disregarding me.

"They have, but they're doing it wrong."

"What the fuck, man? You think you can come on this team and tell people what to do and they'll do it?" Cruz straightens up and stares at me.

"No. I think my car outperformed yours yesterday, and if we want to secure a one-two finish or a two-three so that we're both on the podium, our cars should be in sync. Nothing more. Nothing less. But think whatever the fuck you want to think. Not my fucking problem."

I go to walk away the same time Sofia walks into the garage.

And just like every other time I see her, the air is stripped from my lungs.

Our eyes meet. My feet falter. And I suddenly need to do something useless in the garage rather than leave.

She gives me the slightest of smiles—like a goddamn moment of sunshine before the clouds close back up—and then her dad walks behind her.

"Cruz. You need to have your crew get their shit together and figure out why your teammate's car was faster in testing," Dominic Navarro says, choosing to act like I'm not there.

I chance a glance at Sofia again and she mouths that she's sorry.

"Already on it. Probably a wing adjustment," he says, taking me by surprise.

"It's not a wing adjustment. Only a fucking amateur would say something stupid like that and if they did, you should fire them on the spot."

He's such a prick. Why do I forget shit like this all the time?

Cruz clears his throat. "I beg to differ. I'm pretty sure that's the right move."

I do a double take and meet Cruz's eyes briefly. So I'm wrong unless it comes to trying to stick it your dad. Good to know.

At least I'm good for something.

"And then you'll finish in the last half of the grid, out of the points, with your number two driver in front of you. That's a bad look for the team. He's two, you're one—"

"And he's standing right here, backing up your son's opinion," I say. I don't care if he's a prized fucking Navarro or not. I deserve the same respect he gives his son . . . then again, I wouldn't exactly call it respect.

Mr. Navarro snorts as he eyes me with disdain.

"Papá, I think you've worn out your welcome in the garage," Cruz says. "I make one exception and you overstep—"

"You shouldn't accept mediocrity like this—"

"Out!" Cruz says, pointing to the door, his teeth gritted and the tendons in his neck taut.

"C'mon, Papá. Let's go see what's happening at the hospitality suite," Sofia says without looking either of our way. Her head is down, and she ushers Dominic Navarro like an exhausted nanny who's embarrassed by her charge's behavior.

They leave the garage and I'm left staring after them wondering if this is the norm for this family. And if so, "Cruz—"

"Leave it," he says, our eyes meeting briefly.

I don't know what else to say—I'm not good at this shit. But it doesn't matter because before I can say anything at all, Cruz stalks out of the garage without another word.

A dozen excuses run through my head.

At least your dad is here.

At least you're not alone.

At least when you talk to your dad like I did mine earlier, he didn't make excuses why he couldn't be here.

But they're all bullshit.

And I hate that it humanizes Cruz while making me understand Sofia even more.

I sit in my private driver's room in the Gravitas hospitality suite. Most of the drivers are in media interviews, but mine was scheduled earlier. This is my moment to get my head straight before I jump on the track and qualify.

Knock. Knock.

I glare at the door but don't answer. This is my time, my space, and most people on the team respect that without infringing. And if I'm needed, then my PR handler, Carina, will be the one to interrupt me.

Knock. Knock.

This knock is a little bit harder. With a huff, I yank the door open. I'm shoved backward when I'm met with the weight of Sofia against me.

Our lips find each other's in a torrent of need. Of lust. Of greed. Of desperation.

The days feel like years since I last tasted her, and I'm so overwhelmed by it that all I can think, all I can process, is *more*.

"Ollie," she murmurs against my lips as my hands run up and down her back and press her into me.

"What are you doing here?" I ask like an idiot who doesn't want her to stop doing whatever she's doing. *She's here for me.*

"I only have a few seconds. A few—"

Our lips meet again. Her fingers scrape up my neck and her teeth pull on my bottom lip. "You're the only thing that makes me feel good on days when I shouldn't."

"Stop talking then," I say against her lips and slow this kiss down.

Take my time with it. My field of vision narrows, and she becomes the only thing I see. The only thing I feel.

And this time when the kiss ends, the hunger's still there. *It owns me.* But cupping her face with my hands and looking into her eyes? It grounds me.

"You okay?"

"I'm fine. Yes. Of course."

"You sure?"

She leans in to kiss me again. "For a lot of people this is a turn-on. The sneaking around. The stolen kisses. The not knowing when we'll get to see each other next," she whispers.

"And for others, getting to show their woman off to the world and claim her as theirs is the turn-on," I reply.

Her lashes flutter and her lips part as she studies me. "Is that what you want?"

Fuck.

Shit.

"I'm drowning and not sprinkling," I mutter.

"What?" she asks with a half laugh.

"Nothing." I press a kiss to her lips. "Everything." Another kiss as I chuckle at myself. "When can I see you again?"

"I don't know. I'm busy with—"

"Babysitting your papá."

"This is who I am, Rossi." She shrugs but the desire that filled her eyes now gives way to exhaustion.

"I know." I try to let her know I understand. That I'm not judging. "Tonight? Tomorrow? When can I see you?"

"I'm here, but I'm not alone. I can't . . . next week?"

I groan, protesting. "Okay. Yes."

Another kiss.

"Be safe out there," she whispers.

"Always."

She runs her palm down the side of my face—it's something I've noticed she likes to do, and I love having her do—and hesitates as her fingertips linger there. "Bye."

"Ciao."

She opens the door an inch and looks both ways before sneaking out. I'm sure it would go over really well if her brother walked down the hall about now.

But he doesn't and just as quickly as she came, she leaves.

I'm left looking at the closed door with the feel of her lips still on mine.

That's what makes this whole thing so hard to ignore.

To feel the heat.

To feel the passion.

And to have to pretend like it doesn't exist.

CHAPTER TWENTY-FIVE

Sofia

I'm overwhelmed to say the least as I take in the studio. All the windows are taped with paper blocking any view of outside, the floor is covered in drop cloths, and a paint tray with a roller on it is on the far side of the gallery.

One wall is done.

Another is half done.

And I'm in way over my head but determined to do this myself.

I think.

I might be calling in reinforcements because, what looked like a small task now seems insurmountable and then to add to that, the days are ticking down. I have art being delivered soon. This place needs to be ready.

With a groan, I move across the space and wince when I step in a blob of paint that squishes between my toes. My shoes have long since been taken off, and there's absolutely no hope for salvaging this outfit that's now covered in paint splatter.

"Sofia?"

I startle at the sound of Rossi's voice calling in through the back door I've left unlocked.

We've talked nonstop over the past several days but hearing that voice in person has my heart leaping into my throat.

"Hi," I say as the sound of rustling paper bags fills the room.

"That is the most relieved, most desperate greeting I've received in the longest time," he says as he comes into view and holds up the bags I heard. "I brought food."

"You brought food?"

"I did. We got on the jet after the race. Just landed. I made sure your brother went his own merry way and then I came straight here. I hope you don't mind," he says and sets the food down on the folding table I have set up.

"Mind?" My body sags in relief at the sight of him. "Mind?" I step into him and wrap my arms around him, pulling him into me to let him know just how much I don't mind him coming straight to me.

Jesus.

The things this man does to me.

Our lips meet. The kiss is slow and simmering, packing a powerful punch of lust and longing that a simple kiss can't compete with.

I revel in the feel of his hands as they slide up my rib cage, his palms hitting each indentation in slow motion as his tongue dips and dances against mine.

He's the slow dose of a drug I've been waiting to take but now that I have, I fear how quickly the high will be over.

"I've missed this," I murmur between kisses.

"This?" A kiss. "Or me?" A lean back with his teeth tugging on my bottom lip. "Or both?" A deeper, longer kiss. "Don't bruise my ego with your answer, Bellissima," he says, his lips curving up into a smile against mine. "Remember I'm soft, after all."

I meet his eyes, my heart pounding in my chest and butterflies taking flight in my stomach with a giddiness I've never felt before. "Both." A kiss. "You." A longer, deeper kiss. "This." A tease at the nape of his neck with my fingernails. "The thought of you doesn't do the feel of you any justice."

He chuckles. "Lucky for me."

I reach down where he's already growing hard. "And you're definitely not soft."

"No. I'm most definitely not." He groans. "Don't start something you don't want to finish, Bellissima."

"Pretty sure, I'm finishing." I scrape my fingernails against the fabric of his pants.

"The food's going to get cold."

I tug on his bottom lip. "Mm. There are other things to eat."

"The back door is unlocked." He tries to maintain a steady voice, sound unaffected, but it's growing husky with each passing second.

"Then lock the door, Ollie."

"Oh. Might something be happening?"

I chuckle. It's low and deep and taunting. And when I strip my shirt slowly over my head, taking my camisole with it, the weight of my breasts bouncing, his guttural groan echoes in the empty space as his eyebrows raise. "Yes. Something might be happening."

He flashes the sexiest grin as he moves toward the back door, his shirt already discarded and his pants being unbuttoned in the process.

When he returns, we both face each other naked in the muted light of the room. Jesus. It doesn't matter how many times I see his beautiful body, I'm still taken aback by it. His toned, tanned chest. The darkened discs of his nipples. The hint of a happy trail.

"There are people outside," he says and motions to the shadows on the other side of the brown-papered windows.

"There are." I nod and glance around. A lot of shadows, in fact. "What do you think they think we're doing in here?"

"A little bit of this." He takes a step forward, stroking his cock in his hand. "A little bit of that." He groans as his eyes scrape up and down the length of me.

"Oh, and here I thought all we were going to do is paint," I say coyly as I reach out to the paint tray beside me and dip my finger into it.

"Paint?" he says and steps into my space. My body's a ball of need and desire.

I reach out and paint a heart over his heart. He watches as I slowly fill it in and when I finish, his lips find mine in a slow, tantalizing kiss that makes me ache for more.

"My turn," he murmurs. I gasp when he dips both of his palms in the paint and then cups my breasts. When he lets go, there's a perfect set of his handprints holding me there.

"That's some handiwork," I say and kiss him again. "Pun intended."

"Things are about to get messy, Sofia," he says against my lips.

"Perfect. Welcome to my life."

He palms my ass, his hands slick with paint as he presses me against him. His cock is hard against my lower belly and my body's greedy for his. "I've missed you."

It's been less than two weeks. How can I miss him this much? "Show me how much." Our lips meet again. The kiss is tantalizing and hungry. Our hands keep gliding, keep marking each other's skin as we slowly lower ourselves to the floor.

But it's when I lie back, when I spread my thighs for him and earn that growl deep in his chest as he takes in just how ready I am for him, he starts to laugh.

"Um . . ." He purses his lips and holds up his hands coated in paint. It's then that I get what he's saying. He can't hold his cock to guide it into me. There's paint . . . everywhere.

"I'm pretty sure we're skilled enough to handle the challenge."

"Bellissima, I'm a goddamn pro," he says as he grabs my thighs and pulls me toward him. Our lips meet. Our tongues dance. His words incite. "Get on all fours."

Four words. Instant chills.

I keep my eyes on him as I make a show of getting on my knees. Of staring at him over my shoulder as I lower myself to my elbows. As pushing my ass up in the air at the same time his cock presses ever so gently at my entrance.

"Christ," he grits out the same time there's laughter outside the window from unknowing passersby.

I push back and onto him slowly until he's as deep as I can take him. The longing for him while he's been gone along with the desperation of knowing how good he feels combines for an enhanced anticipation that has my nerves buzzing and my pulse racing.

"Sofia. God. Yes. Fuck me."

I smile. It's for myself, but I fucking smile, because there's something about hearing what I do to him in the gravel of his voice that's a seduction all in itself.

And so I do what he asks. I begin to rock my hips back and forth onto his. Teasing and taking and angling so I get as much as I can out of this.

He fists a hand in my hair and pulls my head up so my neck arches. "You're beautiful like this. Your ass. Your pussy stretching around me, taking me as deep as you can. Your arousal coating my balls. Take me, baby. Take all of me."

There's no grace in our actions. No finesse in skill. Just two people desperate for one another. Two bodies needing the release the other one can give. Two lovers covered in paint, laughing when a knee slips in it or my elbow slides some.

But his lips find my shoulders and his cock hits all the right places.

And soon we've forgotten about paint on our bodies and people wandering by outside. The outside noise has gotten lost to the feel of each other. To the delicious pressure and the surge of bliss as I get dragged beneath the first swell and he follows soon thereafter to a tidal wave of sensations.

CHAPTER TWENTY-SIX

Sofia

"You have paint..." He breaks out in a grin. "Everywhere."

"I wonder how that happened?" I reach out and dab a fingertip of white paint on his nose, about the only place on his face that I haven't already marked.

"I don't know but I'd be more than willing to give you a full-body inspection to see if you need more." He holds out a fork with pasta wrapped around it for me to take a bite of. "Eat."

"Mm. That's good."

"I know. That's why I got it." He offers me a shy, lopsided smile. "Good thing you had everything taped off and covered."

"Good thing."

"It gives a new meaning to body painting."

I laugh. It feels so good to. I've been stressed over this place. Stressed that someone would figure out that Rossi and I are involved—because regardless of labels, when you get off an airplane and go straight to the other person, you are in fact involved in one way or another. Over the impending feeling of waiting for el patriarca to acknowledge this gallery. Just... everything.

"Thank you for coming to see me," I whisper as we both lean back against a yet-to-be-painted wall and look at each other across the short distance.

"You talk a good game, Bellissima," he says referring to our numerous sexy text exchanges over the past two weeks since we last saw each other. "I needed to make sure you could back it up."

I blush and roll my eyes, my body already heating beneath his praise. "And?"

"Well, while your painting skills need a bit of work"—his grin widens—"you can definitely back it up."

Our gazes hold a few seconds longer. This is supposed to be fun. Supposed to be sex. It's not supposed to be me feeling all mushy when he shows up here unexpectedly to feed me, to sex me up, and to help.

But that's exactly how I'm feeling every time he looks at me like that.

He blows out a breath and turns his head to survey the space in front of us.

I immediately get nervous, wanting him to like what I've done here and understand why I selected this space. "It doesn't look like much but—"

"I see your vision." He points to the blueprint I have taped to the paper on one of the windows. "And it's going to be incredible."

"You think?"

"I know. Do you have a name for it yet?"

"For what? The gallery?"

He nods. "That is what we're talking about, isn't it?" he asks with a heavy dose of sarcasm.

"Not yet, no. I have dozens of ideas but none of them grab hold of me. I want something meaningful. Something that reminds me how far I've come. Something that's . . . perfect."

"Makes sense." He rests his hand on my knee and squeezes. "When it comes to you, you'll know it right away."

I purse my lips. "I know." I just wish it would come to me sooner rather than later.

He takes a bite and chews as he contemplates the space. "I think your *Midnight Madness* painting will fit perfectly right there in the middle—with a spotlight on it. With the front doors open, customers will have a straight view to the back of the store where it's showcased. They'll need to see more of it so they'll move farther inside and have no choice but to take in the rest of the art. It's a great setup." He stops and tilts his head. "What? Why are you looking at me like that?"

"You remembered the name of the painting."

"Of course, I did." He shrugs. "I even looked it up. It's . . . expressive."

"Expressive?"

"Mm-hmm. Like each person who looks at it will draw something else from it."

"I swear you know more about art than you're letting on."

His expression falters ever so briefly. "Nothing more and nothing less than the average person does."

"Your nonna didn't share her love with you?" I question, thinking about the scrawled notations in the art books at his house. The ones I'd love to look at again but feel like I'm snooping if I do.

"An appreciation, maybe." He nods and changes the subject. "Any luck with procuring the painting?"

I snort at the frustrating week I've had. "No. None at all. I tried—because that's just me—but like I said before, the artist doesn't seem to want any attention. He's not responding, and I've left inquiries everywhere. His agent. Emails. Smoke signals." I chuckle and take a sip of the red wine Rossi brought with him and smile that only Oliver Rossi would bring red Solo cups for a one-hundred-euro bottle of wine and be okay with it. "Showcasing it was a pipe dream. I need to get over it and move on so I can get this place ready."

"It's always good to have a backup plan." He taps his cup against mine. "Like me for instance. If you weren't here, I had a plan to wear a disguise and have a car take me to your place so no one would recognize me."

I laugh. "No, you didn't."

"Want to bet?" He leans over on one hand so that he can press his lips to mine. "I wasn't going another minute without seeing you."

Swoon. And not just everyday swoon but more like I need to *sag against this wall to keep me standing* type of swoon because the way he inserts comments like that into normal conversation should be illegal.

"No complaints here."

"Good. I'm glad."

"You had a great race," I say. For some reason I want him to know I care about his passion too. That his work matters to me as well.

"No complaints on my end. We had a good team showing."

"The adjustments you suggested Cruz have made to his wing have continued to help him."

"As I expected it would." His focus is on the food now, and I don't know if that's on purpose or just because he's hungry.

"Why'd you help him?" I ask. There's a hitch in his movement but it's so very slight. "My papá was rude to you and yet you went back again this race and told Cruz what you thought should be tweaked."

"He told you?" His eyebrows narrow.

I nod. "Your dislike is beginning to look a lot closer to like."

Just like my lust is beginning to look a lot more like . . . whew.

He shrugs. "My loyalty is to my teammate over your father. Like all of us, Cruz needs his head in the right place before he gets in the car. Your dad's comments could jeopardize that. I was just trying to . . . *try*. I don't know. That's not a common thing for me so don't get used to it."

But he did do it. He did intervene in a situation most would have backed down from because it was the revered Dominic Navarro.

"I noticed. Thank you."

"Don't thank me." He looks at me and raises his eyebrows. "Is this . . . never mind."

"No. No *never minds*, remember? Say what you're going to say."

His sigh is heavy, foreboding. "If Cruz is the golden child and your dad treats him like that, how does he treat you?"

His question creates a bitter taste on my tongue. "Cruz is the prodigal son. It's his job to bring glory back to the Navarro name in the sport."

"That's how you treat your prodigal son? Huh."

I can hear the judgment, can feel it. And while he's absolutely right, it still makes me defensive of my family. They are fucked up for sure, but they are my fucked-up family.

"It's . . . yeah," I finally admit.

"And you? The non-prodigal son? How are you treated?"

I twist my lips and stare at my half-painted gallery as I sit beside a man my family would never allow me to be with. What do I say?

"There are different rules for me," I say softly. "El partriarca. My parents. It's . . . complicated."

"And these rules are what prevent you from shouting out about this place from the rooftops? Because if so, that's total bullshit."

"I don't pretend that my family makes sense to anybody else, but it's still my family."

"Oh, I'm aware," he mutters. I don't understand why he sounds so angry. "You're good enough to babysit your father, make sure your brother has what he needs to succeed, and who the hell else knows what, but no one gives a fuck what you need, right? Who's taking care of you, Sofia?"

His words hit me straight in the heart. The way he frames the truth has a way of doing that more often than not, and an even greater way of making me feel like an absolute idiot for being part of it.

"What about you, Rossi?" I ask, definitely on the defensive. It's so much easier to punch back than it is to admit he's right. "You're a world-famous driver, where are your parents at?"

He turns to level me with a look. It's one of nonchalance with a good dose of *fuck you* edging it. "Where they've always been. At home in Italy. Outside of this chaotic world I live in. Proud of me from afar but too goddamn busy to get up close. Is that what you wanted to hear? You happy to know your family isn't the only fucked-up one around?"

"Oliver. I'm . . . sorry." *Jesus*. The hurt in his words own me and make me feel like there's so much more here. Deep down I know even if I asked, he'd do what he always does—divert and deflect. Maybe even be on the defensive.

I might know a little something about doing that myself.

"You asked. I answered. I don't need your pity."

"I wasn't giving it to you."

"Bullshit, but you keep thinking that."

"Why are you being so difficult?" We went from good to bad in a matter of minutes. I shove up off the floor, throw my panties and T-shirt on, and move around the space, pouring more paint in the tray and adjusting the rollers, needing something to do with my hands. Anything other than hearing the dejected, little-boy tone in his voice when talking about his parents.

I glance back his way and he's leaning his head back again, looking at the ceiling. He emits a huff. "Are we having our first fight?" he asks.

"No."

"Yes," he says resolutely.

"Whatever it is, it's stupid. How fucked up our families are or are not, isn't a competition. Especially because . . ."

"Especially because what?" he asks.

Because this can never go anywhere. Because you're you and I'm me and this would never be approved of in a million years.

"Because you just got home and we have more important things to do." I infuse happiness into my voice as he shuffles about behind me.

"Like?" he asks as he steps in behind me, presses his body against mine, and nuzzles my neck.

"We have work to do."

"Work?" His hands slide beneath my shirt, the paint there dry and crackly when he cups my breasts, which are already needy with desire.

I sigh and sag against him, my head dropping back to his shoulder. "Lots and lots of work," I murmur.

"Sofia?" he asks with his lips kissing down the curve of my shoulder.

"Hmm?"

"I don't give a fuck who your family is. What they have. Their history. But how they treat you matters to me. This? Right here? It matters too. You're who matters."

I turn to face him, tears welling in my eyes—unsure of their root cause—and meet his soft smile. "You're what matters too."

He rubs his thumb back and forth over my collarbone. It makes me feel so small and makes him seem so strong. It's silly and not even true, but I still like it. I still lean into it.

"Hey?"

"Yeah?"

"The best part about fighting?" He leans in and brushes his lips against mine. "Is seeing just how good the making up part is."

"Is that what we're doing?" I ask. "Making up?"

"Bellissima, I'll say we're doing whatever it is you want to do so long as you keep touching me."

CHAPTER TWENTY-SEVEN

Sofia

"Talk to me. You've gone radio silent. Either the gallery is so all-consuming you can't see straight or . . ."

"Or?"

"Or you're being sexed so good you're forgetting to call your friend."

I adjust the back of my lounge chair so I'm facing the sun more, fix my bikini bottoms, and take a seat. "What about all of the above?" I grin. It feels good to be able to talk to somebody I trust about this. Somebody I know won't blab to the media for a quick paycheck.

"You know what? I had like five things I could have said but I'm going to say the one that's the most important. Good for you. You deserve someone who makes you feel good about yourself and who you are."

"It's been . . . fun."

She barks out a laugh. "I hope so. If not, he's doing it all wrong."

"Whatever." I wave a hand she can't see. "It's just been fun to enjoy someone else and find out what makes them laugh, what turns them on, what . . . who they are when the world sees them as someone else. And by the same token, it's incredible to be enjoyed by someone else. And to . . . I don't know, have someone in this new city who's not my brother."

"I thought you had plenty of friends there."

"I do, but no one to cuddle up with and watch old movies."

"You're telling me that's what you choose to do with that fine-as-fuck man of yours? Watch movies?" She chuckles.

"No. I assure you we do more than that."

"Just don't be *making* any movies because those somehow always get stolen. That's the last kind of attention your gallery needs," she jokes.

"There will be no sex tape. I assure you." I laugh.

"Good. Now that we have that covered, tell me everything and I'll do the same."

We go on to talk for a bit about her life, about my life, and about things with Rossi as I let the warm sun and the cool breeze relax me.

"This all sounds so normal, Sof. You never do normal when it comes to men." She laughs. "And here I was, certain you were going to go into a rant over how Cruz has put his foot down on this whole fucking his teammate thing."

"Well . . ." I laugh nervously.

Her pause says it all. "I was wondering why you two weren't splashed all over the place yet, but I was reserving judgment until I talked to you. And now I get it. Cruz doesn't know, does he?"

"Well, not exactly."

"And that means what?"

"That means nothing." I scrunch my nose up.

"You are so full of shit. You've just sat and gushed about the man and then you admit no one knows about him but me."

"I didn't say that."

"You didn't have to. So what gives, Navarro?"

"It's my life. I can do as I please," I joke.

"So long as it's in secret." Well, now that she puts it that way. "Have you ever stopped to think how Rossi feels about this?"

"He's fine with it."

"You sure about that?"

And for others, getting to show their woman off to the world and claim her as theirs is the turn-on.

Rossi's words ghost through my mind, but I shake them off. It's just way easier to do that than to hold tight to what they really mean. He wants more than a secret rendezvous with me.

I clear my throat. "Yeah. I'm sure. Us going public—or letting anyone know—would complicate matters for him too."

"Uh-huh. I see," she says with zero sense of enthusiasm.

"Don't do that."

"Don't do what?"

"That judgy thing you do. That sound you've made since you were twelve. The whole *you're saying something but not really saying something* thing you do when you make that sound."

"I haven't said shit," she says but I can hear the amusement in her voice.

"It's just fun. We're just having fun. Isn't that allowed?"

"Yes. Of course it is. But Sof? Normally you don't have to hide *just fun*."

"Lilith," I groan. *I hate when she makes sense.*

"How often do you see him?" she asks. "And don't give me this, *oh, every once in a while* shit because you haven't been calling me back so that means you've been busy with him."

"A lot." That's not exactly quantifiable.

"A lot as in just for booty calls or a lot as in conversation and meals and—"

"As in he's helping me get the gallery together."

"Oh." The sound. *Yep, she gets it.* Maybe it even makes me hear what I'm saying too.

"Yeah. *Oh.* But like I said. It's just fun. It's just a way to feel good. It's—"

"Just you casually denying you're catching feelings for him."

I snort. "I can catch feelings for him all I want. It's what I can't do with him that matters."

"And what's that?" she asks what I've been avoiding myself.

"Taking this beyond what it already is," I whisper.

"And when God forbid, your grandfather has passed on, when you're standing in an empty flat or staring at the ceiling at night, is it really going to matter what he thought about a man you decided to invite into your life who wasn't the right lineage or born into the right family? Are you willing to give up your happiness or what possibly could be for a man who was born in a different century and a majorly different time?"

"Lilith."

"What? I know it's the Navarro women's job to stand by and be the support pillar in the family. To make sure all the charities you've traditionally supported are kept in the public eye. To be at every race as the endearing daughter and sister. To make sure the family is spoken about in the most positive manner—which includes marrying someone of the proper whatever it's called. I'll say what I've always said about that. *Fuck that, Sofia.* Just because your mom failed at it, it doesn't mean it lands on your shoulders to be perfect at all of it. And even if you were, it doesn't make anything right. Not her abandonment. Not your grandfather's antiquated ideals of what you should be. Nothing. The only thing that it would definitely do is make you miserable. And you have been. Right up until you met up with me at the festival."

"That's not true." But even those words are hard to get out.

"You and I both know it is. I love you, Sof. More than anything. So hear me when I say this. There are a few times in your life when you should stand up for what you want. If Rossi's worth it, if the way he makes you feel is worth it, then maybe this is that time."

And long after she hangs up, I sit with my eyes closed and the sun warming my skin. Lilith's words replay in my head.

Over and over.

Guilt chases after them.

Guilt that she's right. *I want more. This could be more. Rossi deserves better.*

No. *Ollie deserves better.*

Guilt that I'm wrong. It's not okay to play with Rossi's emotions. It's not okay to lead him on. It's not okay to essentially be a couple when we can't be one.

But . . .

Are you willing to give up your happiness or what possibly could be for a man who was born in a different century and a majorly different time?

No.

I don't know.

Does he really feel anything for me?

"*Sofia. I don't give a fuck who your family is. What they have. Their history. But how they treat you matters to me. This? Right here? It matters too. You're who matters.*"

And when I don't want to think anymore, I get up from the pool deck and go to the only place other than the gallery that I want to be.

I head to Ollie's.

CHAPTER TWENTY-EIGHT

Rossi

I CLOSE MY EYES AND COMMAND THE WHEEL.

I race from memory. Each ease on the throttle. Each shift of the car. Every chicane to navigate. How close I am to the wall. Even the slightest turn of the wheel.

With my eyes closed, every sense is heightened. My memory. The curves. The bank of the track. My split-second reaction to every scenario the computer throws my way.

And I know the minute Sofia walks into my simulator room. It's the hint of her perfume that announces her presence.

But I finish my lap. Racing against time and my memory. Against the pull of the only woman I've ever let distract me.

And distract me tonight she has when she showed up at my door, her skin still warm from the sun she was lying in and a quiet somberness to her I've never seen. Her only words were, "I didn't want to be alone. Can I just hang here? I won't disturb you."

Doesn't she know though when she's anywhere near me that she disturbs me in the best way possible?

"I know you're there," I say before I open my eyes into the darkened room.

"Sorry. I didn't mean to bug you."

"It's okay. I'm almost done." I can hear her move farther into the room.

"I like watching you work," she says and comes into view.

There's a softness to her tonight. A tentativeness. Something is clearly on her mind, but she'll tell me when the time is right, if she wants to.

I take my headset off and hang it on the hook beside me. "You sure you're okay?" I ask.

Her smile is soft. "I am now."

"You want to talk about it?"

She gives the slightest shake of her head. "Had a conversation with Lilith earlier. I'm tired. Overwhelmed. Just a bunch to think about."

I purse my lips and nod, not sure exactly what that means. "You ever been in one of these?" I ask.

"When I was a kid. I used to sneak into my brother's simulator when he wasn't home. Pretend I was like him and race an imaginary circuit." Her smile is bittersweet.

"The number of times I'd sit in someone else's cart long after their race was over and pretend I was driving the entire course. I probably looked like an idiot to anyone else who wandered past. A ten-year-old, helmet on, eyes closed, making kart sounds as I played out the last lap of a race where I overtook everyone for the win." I smile. It's a memory I rarely think of these days but the fact that I did, and she brought it out of me without all of the other bullshit that usually comes with my childhood memories, says a lot about her and what I think of her.

"That makes me smile," she says.

I hold my hand out to her. "Come drive."

Her head startles as she looks at me with curious eyes. "What do you mean, come drive?" she asks but takes my hand as I tug her toward me.

"Sit." I pull her hips so that she can sit on my lap and then direct her to lean back against my chest. The space is tight and there's no way there will be any accuracy with this drive, but I like her here. I like her like this.

"This won't exactly work."

"Sure it will." I guide her leg over mine and ghost my arms with hers on the steering wheel. "Drive with me, Bellissima."

Her ass is nestled over my cock and her hair tickles my cheek. Her skin smells like sun and her laugh sounds off as, according to the screens in front of us, we sit on the starting grid, waiting for lights out—the start of a race.

"Rossi."

"Shh. Hands here." I put her fingers where they need to be to hit the right buttons and use my feet beneath hers to get ready on the pedals for the start. "Watch the lights," I say in her ear and love seeing the goosebumps blanket her skin. "I'll push the gas, you steer."

"What about shifting?"

I love the sudden panic in her voice, the fear like this is a real car on a real track.

"I'll help you with that until you get the hang of it."

We drive for the next twenty minutes or so. Each lap she becomes more relaxed, more in command, and the little laugh she emits and shimmy she does at the end of each five-lap race we do makes me chuckle.

It's the hardest thing in the world to explain, but that time is the single most sexy and most comforting time I've ever experienced. For her to step into my world, to try it and be hands-on, and to let me guide and help her without telling me she knows what she's doing is . . . incredible.

She trusts me.

I don't know why that strikes a chord in me, but it does. And long after she signs off the simulator leaving me to review the statistics of my drives before she interrupted, that thought sticks with me.

"Sof?" I ask as I walk out to the family room where I expect to hear the television but am met with silence instead.

And then I see her.

She's curled up in a ball on my couch. Some of my art books are open to various pages on the cushion beside her, but she's sound asleep.

There's an inherent need to collect the books, to hide the dates and places beside the pictures I've penciled in as my own private diary documenting the pieces I've seen in person.

But I don't. And for the first time in my life, I don't feel the shame over my love for art. I don't fear she won't like me because of it.

I'm sure this would be a whole other fucking story if she were awake and asking questions about my inscriptions, but she's not. And maybe this gives me time to get used to the idea before admitting to it.

Silly. Stupid. But profound.

Fucking art. It changed the course of my life—for good and for bad.

Simply Sofia. What is she doing to me?

"The girl you love will love the artist within you."

Love?

It's a bit early for that, hey, Nonna?

I stare at her as something in my chest gives way. It's an ache and a swell and a tumble over itself all at the same time. I press the heel of my hand to my sternum and rub, but I don't think this feeling is going to go away any time soon.

In fact, I'm pretty sure I knew that the first night I saw her at the music festival but wasn't quite ready to admit it to myself.

I don't think I am right now either.

Without thinking, I move toward her. Within seconds I have the art books stacked on the table and am gathering her up in my arms.

"Ollie?" she murmurs in her sleep.

God, I love when she fucking calls me that. I've never let anyone else but my nonna call me it, but now? Now it's like when Sofia says it, it makes me feel fucking awesome.

"I'm here," I say.

"What are we doing here, Ollie?" Her lips pull up at the corners and then slowly fall as if she's fallen back asleep.

"I don't know, but whatever it is, I like it," I whisper in the vastness of my place.

"Mm. I do too." She runs her hands over my chest and up to the side of my neck. "Don't leave me."

"I'm not. Don't worry. I'm not leaving you."

She wraps her arms around my neck and nuzzles into it, much like that first night here but it feels so very different this time. So very real and beyond just the sex.

"Mm. Good." She presses a kiss there, her lips lingering. "I'm falling, Ollie. Don't forget to catch me."

And those words. *Fuck, man.* Those words . . .

I nod and grin, pulling her tighter against me as I move down the hall.

She's not the only one.

CHAPTER TWENTY-NINE

Sofia

HIS BODY IS WARM AGAINST MINE AS I BLINK AGAINST THE SUN'S rays lighting up the room.

I snuggle into him. Into his presence. Into the fact that clearly I fell asleep last night and he let me stay here to sleep.

It's a weird feeling but one that is so damn right it's ridiculous.

"You going to tell me why you were so upset last night?" he asks, obviously sensing that I've woken up.

I groan. "I just want to lie here and enjoy this. The quiet. The time without thinking—"

"The avoidance of all the things?"

"That too." I close my eyes and replay the phone call from yesterday after I'd hung up with Lilith.

"El patriarca? Hi. How are you?" If surprise were a sound, it would be my voice.

"My Sofia. How are you?"

"I'm good. Um . . ." *Why are you calling me? You hate phones, would rather talk in person.* "Is everything okay?"

"Yes. Yes. All is good. There's a matter I want to speak with you about."

He knows about Rossi.

It's my first thought. It's my last thought. It's the one that twists my heart.

"What is it?" I infuse cheer into my voice.

"This gallery of yours. The opening will be in six weeks."

"But . . . no. The artmonte-carlo is in five weeks. That's when I'm slated to open it."

"No. You'll move it."

"But . . ."

"I want to throw a party. For Cruz. It is the weekend you want. You will change dates." *Tears well in my eyes, but I don't speak.* "If you want my blessing on this . . . venture . . . you will change the dates. You are needed here at the villa to celebrate your brother."

"Celebrate what though?" I ask.

"Do I need a reason to celebrate one of my grandchildren?" he asks.

"No." *But you could easily use that weekend to celebrate me. Your son's other grandchild.*

"Yes?" he asks.

I stand with one hand on my hip and my vision blurring from the tears of frustration.

To finally get his blessing, but to get it with strings so thick, I'm not sure it's even feasible to cut them.

"My grandfather called yesterday. Said he'd give me his blessing on the studio, but only if I change the opening date," I say and explain the rest of the conversation. Even the words sound stupid to say. I'm a twenty-five-year-old woman who has to wait for her grandfather to approve the things in her life.

But no one understands my family. Understands the tradition we've lived by. Understands the control our family patriarch still holds over us. Nor do they understand why we respect all of that.

It's just how it is.

"And you told him no, right? You told him you've been busting your ass for weeks to get the grand opening *ready* and that you're not changing shit for some party for Cruz."

My silence eats the room. Second after second. I struggle to swallow and my pulse pounds in my ears. "I'll figure it out." And I will. Somehow. Some way.

"No, you won't. You'll give up your dream, your plans, for the good of the family." I open my mouth to refute him but then close it. "I admire that about you but damn it, Sof, I also dislike you for not being more selfish as well."

"Unless you've walked in my shoes, it's hard to understand."

He lets the comment sink into the stifling silence of the room that feels buffered somehow by his quiet understanding and the nonstop tracing of his fingers up and then back down my bicep.

He makes me feel lov—

"Come early to Japan with me," he murmurs, the warmth of his breath heating up my skin and saving me from a thought I can't afford myself to have. "Just you. Just me. Another city. A different bed. Just us."

I don't answer.

I open my mouth.

Then close it.

Then sit there and think how to answer him because I want to, but isn't that why I came here last night? To figure out what this is? Now I'm even more confused.

"I have to go early. Just me. I thought maybe you'd come with me."

"I can't. I have the gallery. Contractor deadlines and . . . *things*."

"Sure. Fine. I understand," he murmurs and presses a kiss to my shoulder.

But I don't.

I don't understand the lie I just told or the distance I suddenly feel the need to create.

It's because you're falling for him, Sofia.

It's because you're falling for him, and you know you can't.

Because if el patriarca won't accept my gallery, he'll never accept the Oliver Rossi I've come to know and . . . *lo*—adore.

CHAPTER THIRTY

Rossi

I RUB MY EYES AND PINCH THE BRIDGE OF MY NOSE. NO ONE SAID pulling a huge surprise off was easy, but now I'm beginning to see why I never put the effort in before this.

It'll be worth it.

I know it will.

But tracking down ghosts and trying to have meetings with them is a ridiculous fucking feat. One that my agent helped with but that I had to handle in person once we knew the contact information was right.

Now, I wait.

And I'm not good at fucking waiting.

I meander throughout the hotel suite, unsettled and yet feeling fucking good about life. About things with Sofia. About the race this week and my chances.

My phone is filled with texts from friends here in town. Ones who have asked that I go out with them tonight. Party with them. Fuck around and see where the night takes us.

Is it pathetic that I don't respond to many and, if I do, I make excuses that I have an early morning with sponsors? I mean, I am having a meeting tomorrow but not early enough to have to worry about.

Nothing used to stop me from a night on the town.

But now... now I want to spend my time with Sofia. The fun times. The quiet times. All of them. And I'm not quite sure what that says about me. All I know is her not wanting to come with me was like a punch in the gut. A bitter pill of rejection. A dose of maybe she's not feeling the same fucking way as I am.

Maybe that's why I'm in a surly mood. Maybe that's why I don't want to go out.

And maybe that's why she hasn't answered any of my texts or calls.

The knock on the door is unwelcome. It's already gotten out that I'm in the hotel. This will be the fourth time tonight a "lost" fan accidentally finds my door.

I'm tempted to not answer it—normally I wouldn't—but for some reason, I decide to.

And thank fucking God I do.

I swing open the door to find Sofia standing there. She's in a trench coat and heels, a designer carry-on in one hand and a brown paper bag in the other, and a grin a mile wide.

"Hi. What are you . . ." I take a step back, my eyes sweeping over the length of her body. Those tanned legs. Her hair slicked back in a no-nonsense bun. Her lips painted a dark red.

"I never meant to say no to you. About this. About being here. I just have trouble learning how to say yes when it comes to things I want. When it comes to things that matter."

"Oh." Christ. The things this woman does to my head and fuck it, yes, my heart.

"This matters." She steps into the room and shuts the door at her back. She sets down the items in her hands efficiently before slowly untying the belt on the coat and letting it slide slowly off her shoulders and to a pile on the floor.

But I don't give a flying fuck about the coat or anything else because Sofia is standing in front of me in a dark red lace bustier with garter belts and no panties underneath.

Lord, have mercy.

"You matter," she murmurs and steps into me, her lips finding mine without hesitation.

"Sofia." *She came.*

"No. Don't talk, Ollie. Just feel. Just let me make you feel good."

She drops to her knees, and I look down at her just as she makes quick work of my pants, freeing my cock at an expeditious pace.

Her grin is wickedly sexy as she reaches out and pulls out a bag of Peach Rings.

"You're fucking serious?" I ask. I'm not huge but I'm above average in girth. Can that fucker stretch wide enough for me?

"What do you think?" she asks as she pulls on the candy with her fingers before placing it over the tip of my cock.

Yes, it can stretch wide enough. Wow.

She licks around the rim and the strip of candy.

I groan at the strange sensation of the pseudo cock ring. It's constricting, adding to the building pressure I have within. Her fingers slowly working it up to the base of my shaft only heightens my sensitivity and anticipation.

"There." She sinks her teeth into her bottom lip as she angles her head to the side and admires her work. "Now let's see if I can get enough of you in my mouth to taste it."

The thought of her being able to take that much of me has my cock jerking and my nipples tightening.

"Sofia," I murmur, my hand beneath her chin.

"This. Matters," she murmurs, seconds before she takes my tip between her red lips. Jesus. My hips jerk involuntarily as I watch it disappear inch by fucking hard inch into her mouth.

I ache. All the fuck over. My balls. My lower abdomen. That beating thing in my chest I swore was dead.

When she looks up at me with her mouth full of my cock, her lips just barely touching the Peach Ring, and those thick lashes fluttering, I'm fucking gone.

And it's not like I had very far to fall.

I begin to move my hips slowly. I begin to fuck her mouth in slow, even strokes. Ones that test every ounce of my control to not make her gag on me.

But I hold the back of her head as her fingernails dig into my ass and hold on.

The Peach Ring edges me out. It's like Sofia's warm mouth and tight suction is enough to make me come, but the goddamn candy brings me to the brink and then backs me off.

It's heaven.

It's hell.

It's a fight between ripping the fucking thing off so I can fuck Sofia into oblivion or letting it stay on and see how intense the orgasm is.

And when Sofia goes down on me one last time, when her lips close over that Peach Ring seconds before she starts gagging on me, I can't hold out anymore.

I come. I come so fucking hard that I see stars. All I feel is the rush, the sweet burn of bliss, and Sofia sucking down on me and taking every goddamn thing I have to give her.

Jesus. Fucking. Christ.

This woman.

I haul her up against me. The Peach Ring's still on, and I'm still fucking hard. It's like I can't get enough of her. I don't think I want to. I pull her onto the couch with me. I hold her hips with one hand as I push up into her.

We both cry out. We both hold on.

Her in that sexy getup and me desperate to show her how she makes me feel.

Crazed. Whole. Incredible.

Enough.

We fuck desperately and hastily. Like it's the first time and the last time. Like if there is a sliver of space between us, it's too damn far.

She's everything I want. Everything I need. And when she cries out my name, when she stares into my eyes as the fucking desire overwhelms her, and when she tightens around me like a vise, there's only one word that crosses my mind.

Mine.

Sofia fucking Navarro is mine.

I pull her down to me, her legs still astride me and my cock slowly softening in her, but I still can't get enough of her.

She's all I see.

She's all I want.

Her lips. Her kiss. Her taste.

Just fucking her.

Our lips meet. Once. Twice. Before I wrap my arms around her and hold her to my chest.

Words fail me. The ones I feel. The ones I want to say. The ones that are definitely here but for some reason, neither of us wants to give voice to yet.

How can we? This was supposed to be . . . whatever this was. One night? A festival fling? Done and over? But hell if I go an hour without thinking about her. Or see something I'd think she'd like. Or try and remember something I want to tell her.

"I meant what I said," she murmurs, lips against my chest.

"What's that?" I run a hand up and down the length of her back.

She hesitates. "This matters."

"I know it does," I say and hold her tighter against me. "It matters to me too."

We leave it at that. At knowing there are stakes here but not defining them.

At knowing there are emotions but leaving them unnamed.

If they're unnamed then no one can leave. And if they're undefined, no one can claim I'm not good enough.

But she's here. On my chest. Against me with the scent of her perfume clinging to my skin. She's here. And I just keep telling myself that's enough for me.

"Well, Bellissima. That sure is one way to kick off a race week."

She laughs and presses her lips to mine. "It sure is. Now, about that Peach Ring . . ."

CHAPTER THIRTY-ONE

Rossi

"LET ME GUESS," I SAY STOICALLY. "YOU'RE NOT COMING. *AGAIN*."

"It's not you. It's . . . work is busy, Oliver."

I swallow forcibly, trying to rid the bitterness his excuses leave in my mouth. And I don't know why I suddenly care, why it's so important to have him at a race, but it is.

Maybe it's to prove to Sofia that I'm normal. Or maybe being with her has made me realize how fucking alone I've been for so long. She has a fucked-up family and yet they're still always together. I don't know. I don't think I want to know, but I answered this phone call looking for a fight. A fight I've held back for so many years and that I'm finally ready to have.

"Of course it is. When have you not picked work over me? Maybe that would be an easier thing to answer for me?"

"I don't pick work over you, Oliver. In fact, it's quite the—"

"Bullshit."

"I pick certainty. I had a life where nothing's guaranteed."

"And I have one hundred million euros in the bank. A portion of that, I've sent you so you don't have to work, and yet you still choose it over me. Every time. Without fail."

"You're wrong," he says in that calm pacifying voice of his that agitates me.

But there's something in its tone. A tremor in the vibrato that makes me give pause.

It's brief though.

"I'm not wrong, Babbo. I'm far from wrong but you never show up. I send you tickets to every single fucking race, and you never show up. So tell me you're working. Tell me you're busy. I don't fucking care anymore. I'm sick of trying and I'm more than sick of feeling like you're still ashamed of me—"

"Oliver!"

"Nah. I'm done."

I end the call and raise my arm to throw my phone, something, anything to allow me to alleviate the hurt rioting through me, when I see her in my periphery.

"I'm sorry," Sofia says. "I heard the last part. I didn't mean to. I . . ." She shakes her head as if she doesn't know what to say. "I knocked. You didn't answer so I came in."

"No skin off my back," I say.

"Don't do that." She walks farther into the room.

"When I gave you a key to my hotel room to sneak in, I guess you weren't thinking that would be the show, huh?"

"Rossi."

"Forget it, Sofia."

"*Ollie.* Talk to me?"

I grit my teeth and pinch the bridge of my nose. The need to walk away, to pull away, calls to me and yet how do I do that when she's been so forthcoming with me about her family, about her struggle? How do I tell her my life is off limits when hers is a fucking tornado we're both stuck in?

I pace. I lace my fingers at the back of my neck and move back and forth across the space of my suite.

"Why won't he come to a race?" she asks softly.

"Because I fucked up as a kid? Because racing wasn't my first love?" I spit out half-truths. "Hell if I know."

"Come on. I'm serious."

"So am I." I shrug. "He's frustrating. Always has been. Seems he always will be. It's always work with him. All the time. And I get it. It's my fault. I made him that way—"

"Whoa. Stop." She shakes her head. "How did you make your dad a particular way? He's the adult."

"Don't... just never mind."

She walks toward me and grabs my hands. "No *never minds*. Remember?" Her eyes meet mine and I swear to fucking God, I feel the first brick in that wall I built around myself tumble off and hit the ground. "What happened?"

"I was in a fancy school. Private. Elite. With all the affluent kids from the area. I had gotten a hardship scholarship there somehow. I'm sure my babbo moved heaven and earth to get it for me." I can picture it perfectly all these years later. The stone walls covered with ivy. The dark blue of the uniforms and squeak of tennis shoes on the hallway floors. The rumbling engines of the fancy cars that dropped them off. The relentless fucking bullying. That's what I remember the most.

"What happened there?"

"I was bullied. *One of these things is not like the others* type of things. They liked counting their piles of cash and I liked . . ." *To spend hours in the art room. To pore over books in the library on it.* "To do other stuff. Stuff my father didn't count as worthy of my time."

"Okay." She doesn't ask questions. She lets me talk and that bolsters me.

"One day I snapped. I was sick of the little shoves from behind. My lunch being stolen for sport. The terror of changing in the locker room. And I fought back."

"Go on."

"It wasn't a fair fight. I should have gotten my ass kicked, but there was so much pent-up rage, so many days of being teased, that once I started, I couldn't be stopped."

"I'm so sorry."

I sniff and roll my shoulders. The memory of coming out of that dark rage and seeing the four boys bloody and gasping and cowering will forever stay with me. "They sued us for everything we didn't have. They pressed charges against me. They got my babbo fired." I swallow. "They tried to ruin our lives."

"Surely they were in the wrong. They provoked it."

"And you know as well as I do that when you have money, your privilege is different than everyone else's." I say the words quietly.

She looks at me. Studies me with those quiet eyes and that soft expression. "And that's part of the reason you've always disliked my brother."

I open my mouth to speak and then close it. Maybe subconsciously it is. Maybe it's not. And maybe that's part of the reason Stavros picked him all those years ago instead of me—because affluence just makes everything easier. "We came into each other's lives when my family was still suffering from the fallout of what I did. I was angry. Resentful. Trying to make it up to my father by doing well at what he was pushing me toward—racing—and feeling like I failed. Especially when Stavros picked him over me."

I can see the light switch go on in those expressive eyes of hers. No doubt she remembers that because Cruz has been with Stavros and Gravitas ever since then.

"We were just different. About as different as I was from the bullies who terrorized me. It wasn't Cruz's fault. It was Stavros's. The cruel words he said. The justifications he used for why he didn't pick me. Right or wrong, when you think you're on top of the world but then have your legs kicked out from underneath you, it sticks with you. And as a sixteen-year-old kid, it crushed me and yes, I still hold a grudge over it to this day."

"As I probably would too."

"Cruz probably knew nothing about what was said, but he acted like it—or in my eyes he did—and for me . . . for me, it just fueled my animosity toward him over the years. I did things I wasn't proud of. Things I was proud of. Things I'm sure I did that I've no doubt forgotten."

Sofia moves to the window of the hotel and looks beyond. She could say a million things to me right now. She could ask me if I think the same of her. She could tell me I'm an asshole because her brother didn't deserve any of my vitriol. She could turn and tell me I'm a petty fucker and ask me why she should stay with me.

But she doesn't do any of them. Instead, she stares out the window at the city beyond, a city we can't be seen in public in because of that same history that's haunted me for most of my life—*that I'm not good enough*—and asks the unexpected.

"What happened? With the bullies? With you in school? With your family?"

I stare at her delicate shoulders, the curve of her hips, and the regal way she holds her head, and I say things only Blair and my parents know.

"Nothing happened to them. My parents had to pay legal fees for them and us. Mandatory counseling for me. Pain and suffering damages. They had to pay back the tuition that was bestowed to me even though I never used it all."

"Rossi." She turns to look at me. Compassion owns everything about her and for the first time in my life, I don't see it as pity. I see it as someone truly caring about me.

"Yeah. It was bad. I went to live with my nonna for a while until the drama died down."

"The *Ollie* Nonna?"

"Yeah."

"The upside is that I was a juvenile, so my record was kept private. My father . . . he shouldered the burden of it all. Worked nonstop to pay as much as he could while pushing me in another direction. Toward the only other thing I'd shown interest and promise in."

She moves to me, her smile soft and her eyes kind. "It's not your fault. You know that, don't you?"

I nod, but the shame sits like a lump in my throat. From loving something so much it ruined my family. For my actions. For so many fucking things. "It changed my family forever though."

But I've made it now. I've changed everything and proven everyone wrong . . . and I still don't have anyone in the stands from my family rooting me on.

So if it's not my actions . . .

Is it me? I am, after all, the common denominator.

"It's not you. It's not your fault," Sofia says as if she can read my mind. She runs her hand down my cheek and pulls me into her. "I'm sure he's proud of you in his own way. Everyone shows things differently. Everyone has battles you're unaware of. Just like you had this battle that I didn't know about."

She leans up on her toes and presses her lips to mine. But it's the way she pulls me into her, the way we shift to the couch so that she's sitting, and my head is in her lap, that allows me to breathe a little easier.

She didn't leave.

I smile and snuggle in more to her hand that's running through my hair. Funny how we both had that fear. She knew hers was there. I didn't.

"Ollie?"

"Hmm?"

"What was it you loved so much that made them pick on you?"

I take a deep breath and feel the shame from all those years ago envelop me. The same shame that led to so much hardship for my family. That has placed a wedge between my dad and me.

"Art," I say softly.

Her fingers tighten ever so slightly. Her breath is a slow exhale.

And for once . . . I truly think we're on even footing.

CHAPTER THIRTY-TWO

Sofia

"Maddix. Hi." I glance over her shoulder expecting to see my father or my brother or someone with the last name Navarro tagging along but there isn't one.

"Hey. Mind if I join you?" She points to one of the chairs in the hotel's cocktail lounge.

"Sure. What's up?"

"You tell me," she says and orders a glass of wine while I eye her.

"What do you mean?"

She purses her lips and shrugs. "You're quiet in the garages. You shy away from hanging with your brother when normally you're in the thick of everything. I don't know. Something's off and I just wanted to make sure you were okay."

I offer a smile. I love my soon-to-be sister-in-law. Adore her actually. And might just wish she weren't so astute. "It's nothing." It's everything. Rossi is everything. "I have a lot on my mind with the gallery and needing it to succeed so I don't let the family down or—"

"It's more than that." She smiles and takes a sip of her wine. "You can say it's not but after knowing you for over a year, it's something more than the gallery and the usual."

I nod and glance around. "Agreed. There's more but it's nothing earth-shattering. It's more that I'm just contemplating a lot of things."

"Like?"

Like how I'm falling for a man who will never be accepted by my family.

Like how I'm so sick of doing what's right and expected of me.

Like how what he loved ruined his family . . . and I fear I might do the same.

"Like I don't think I could ever do what you do," I finally say.

"What's that?" She furrows her brow and studies me.

I hope she doesn't look too closely.

With a shrug, I explain. "Share your fiancé with the rest of the world. Know that wherever you go, you'll always be recognized. Know that no matter what you do, you'll never be considered the *right girl* for Cruz in the eyes of his female fans. Worry every time he gets behind a wheel that you'll lose the father of your children."

"Whoa." She holds her hands up and chuckles. "Well shit, Sofia, way to be a downer."

"Sorry. This is me overthinking."

"Is there something you're not telling me here? You plan on marrying a driver or something?"

"No. Of course not." I smile and then sell the lie. "I saw Erikkson's girlfriend earlier. Her pregnant belly was so adorable. And then there was a situation with a rude female fan saying mean things to her. It just made me question if I could ever do that."

Maddix nods but I'm not one hundred percent sure she's buying what I'm selling. I know I sure as shit wouldn't be.

"Well." She purses her lips and toggles her head from side to side as she contemplates my questions. "I don't share my fiancé with the world. Cross is mine." I love what she calls my brother. "They can have the persona of him all they want. I get the best side of him. You get used to the recognition. I mean, you already get that being his sister so it wouldn't matter if you were dating a driver."

"It's not the same."

"Depends on how you look at it. And the minute you think you're good enough for someone is the day you stop trying to love them with your whole heart. So all that matters to me is that Cruz thinks I'm good enough. That he sees me and our relationship for what it's worth. When I tried to walk away from us, he fought like hell for me. I know where I stand and wouldn't want us any other way. As for the racing part. I can't negate the danger or the worry, but you know that too."

I nod and stare at my own glass of wine, as if it will give me the answers I need. And it won't. I know it won't. Accepting any of these things isn't going to make my family accept Rossi any more than they already do—which is not at all.

He's a man who's already been wronged by people like me . . .

Who the hell am I to put him through that situation again?

"I know. I do, Madds. I know."

She reaches out and squeezes my hand. She saw Rossi and me that night of her birthday party. She's a smart woman. I'm sure she can make some inferences, but she doesn't say any of them out loud.

"Here's the thing, Sofia. No one's going to love every decision in their life. I hated the idea of being your brother's 'girlfriend.' I fought it with everything I had, but fate thought it would be funny to put me in my place and make me fall in love with the guy. Worse things could have happened."

I smile and nod. "True."

"Whatever it is that's stressing you out, will work itself out. You might have to take a stand. You might not. If it's worth it though, you'll do whatever it takes to ensure whatever results you want out of it."

"We're talking about the gallery," I state.

"Sure we are."

"We are. I have a lot of decisions when it comes to it. El patriarca isn't thrilled with me for keeping the gallery opening despite him asking me to move it, but . . . that's my decision, not his."

"It is." She nods definitively. "Just like other decisions should be yours without familial influence."

"Maddix?" I ask.

She holds her hands up. "I love your brother. That doesn't mean I always agree with him. He'll come around. I know he will."

We're no longer talking about the gallery.

"Uh-huh."

And with that, Maddix slides money across the bar for her drink, kisses me on the cheek, and then heads out of the bar.

I stare after her for way longer than I should.

Rossi was supposed to be a fling. A little fun at the festival. But he's become so much more in such a short time.

Our conversation from the other day has consumed me. The burden he's carried for so long. The guilt over his actions, the damage it did to his family—neither were his fault and yet he still wears them like a scarlet letter. He blames himself for something he was pushed to the brink on.

Maybe that conversation with his dad will spur on a change. Maybe it won't. All I know is I feel honored that Ollie trusted me enough to tell me. To let me in.

And then there was the culprit of all of it—*art*. One of my greatest loves and one of his biggest sources of pain.

I sat there with his head in my lap and the silence settling around us, thinking of all the invisible dots that had been there for weeks but that I hadn't been able to connect. The art books with notes scribbled inside. The interest in the gallery. The drawn-out conversations where he'd ask astute questions about pieces I'd said I liked but then played it off like he didn't understand.

All of it.

How miserable to be ashamed of something you love.

How did this happen? How did he become my everything when I was looking for nothing?

He's the person I call when I don't want to be alone or just need a friend.

He's surprisingly handy and doesn't complain when I ask him for help in the gallery.

He's the man I want physically on every damn level.

He's a man who's been shamed by the same passion that has fueled me.

But he's also the man who despises my family for the things I can't change about us.

Our lineage.

My last name.

There are a lot of things that can be overcome in a relationship.

I'm just not sure if that is one of them.

CHAPTER THIRTY-THREE

Sofia

"Marla? Hi. Is everything okay?" I hold my phone out and look at the screen as if to confirm that she's really calling me. It's not like I'm in the market for any more real estate.

"Yes. Of course. I just wanted to call and tell you how freaking brilliant that was."

Um . . . "How brilliant *what* was?" I put my finger to my ear and step out of the garage. To my left, in my periphery, I notice Rossi standing down a ways. We lock eyes and acknowledge each other in the only way we can in a place like this—with a stare that's a little too long. With a curve up of one corner of our mouths. With an ever so slight nod of our heads.

With the invisible string that ties us together.

"The flyer. The contest. The giveaway."

"I'm sorry. What are you talking about?"

"Don't play coy with me. During the yacht races today when the town was freaking packed, you had a helicopter toss flyers out the door and pepper the damn town. It looked like it was raining blue confetti."

"Marla. I didn't—"

"And the contest is brilliant."

What the hell is going on here? "Yes. I mean sure."

"If you want to get local artists involved, get people into the gallery, why not hold a contest to display one of their pieces?" *What?* "Then have the people vote on it during your grand opening during the art show." She laughs. "I mean, so much brilliance in that one action. The whole town has been abuzz. Everyone's talking. People are trying to peep through the torn paper of the gallery. It's like you lit a torch under everyone and got them all jazzed about artmonte-carlo."

"Well, that's great."

"It is. I must go, but I wanted to tell you how exciting it was and how sad I was you missed it all. I knew you were going to do great things with that place of yours. I just knew it."

"Thanks."

Marla hangs up and I stand in the middle of the paddock with my head abuzz, my fingers scrolling through social media to see if what she's saying is true, and a healthy dose of trepidation that it might be. And sure enough, video after video shows the bright blue flyers being dumped from a helicopter over the marina. It shows people scurrying to grab the flyers. Then it shows the flyer.

And it locks in on my gallery opening—its contest and its giveaway—into the date of the art show.

If I didn't already know who did this, I do now.

I look back to my left but Rossi's nowhere in sight. Confused, overwhelmed, and thoroughly shocked, my mind is already thinking of how to spin this. Of how to explain to el patriarca that it was an error, a miscommunication with my assistant, and now I'm forced to open on that date.

Excuses.

Excuses.

Excuses.

I'm so sick of making them. Of living by them. Of needing them.

I stop in the middle of the walkway so that several people bump into me as the epiphany hits.

Isn't that why Rossi did it?

So I don't have to make them anymore? He forced my hand so I couldn't back down, so I couldn't sacrifice myself for my family...so I did something for myself on my terms.

I catch my breath and acknowledge that a fallout will be coming but, you know what? I welcome it. I'll stand my ground.

It's not like I have a choice now.

I turn to head to his garage, to wherever he might be, but then stop when I come face to face with my brother.

"Cruz," I say, startled.

"Someone's on a mission," he says, clasping his hands behind his back and furrowing his eyebrows at me. "Something wrong?"

"No." I swallow and shake my head. "Nothing's nothing."

"*Nothing's nothing?*" He laughs. "So glad Papá paid for that top-of-the-line education. Seems to have been worth it."

"Don't be an ass, Cruz." I look at my phone as a text comes in about the flyers. "I . . . I need to make some phone calls. It's about the gallery."

"Then by all means." He takes a step back. "You're still on for the family dinner after the Miami Grand Prix, right?"

"That's in a few weeks. Why are you acting like I'm not going to see you before then?"

"You're busy. So busy it seems you can't talk to me. Just making sure you'll be there."

"I'll be there, Cruz. When have I not been?" I snap at him.

He holds his hands up in mock surrender. "Just figured I'd ask and get a commitment before you find out that both Mamá and Papá intend to be there."

I groan. Perfect. Just what I need. Both of them in the same place, in public. "Awesome." I start to walk. Then stop. Then look back at him. "Of course, I'll be there. I have to—I have to go."

"Okay. Everything's okay though?"

"Yep. Perfect."

But the farther away from him I walk, the more I realize this isn't the time or place to be having any conversation with Rossi.

And yet . . . I need to.

I don't know how many hours it takes for me to get him alone, but during that time I watch countless clips of the flyer drop. I read the buzz all over social media about the new gallery in town. I see local artists post about how they're thrilled to be included in artmonte-carlo that's typically reserved for the best of the best—and that means most of them come from outside of Monaco's city limits.

The only response I get to the endless texts I've sent Rossi during the day is: **Meet me at your hotel room at six. I'll have thirty minutes between going from one event to the next.**

And you better believe my ass is in my hotel room waiting for that knock on the door. I open it to find Rossi standing there in full Gravitas promo mode—baseball hat, polo shirt, sponsorship luxury watch—and he pushes into my room and shuts the door behind him.

"I don't think anyone saw me. What's up?" he asks seconds before his lips close over mine and he has me pressed up against a wall.

I'm consumed by the kiss, by having him at my fingertips all damn day but never getting to touch him. By wanting him and not being able to have him.

Then sense hits me over the head and my hands are pressing against his chest despite my head leaning forward to savor more of his kiss.

"Stop. No. I'm mad at you."

His grin is cheeky as fuck as he meets my eyes. "Over?"

"The flyers. Monaco. The gallery."

"I don't have the slightest clue what you're talking about."

I hit at his chest and hate that my smile is a mile wide. "Yes, you do." I push harder on his chest. "You papered the town. You thought up a brilliant contest to intrigue people. You locked my grand opening into a date I can't get out of. You . . . you . . ."

"I, what? I believe in you? I want you to do this for you? I think it's your time to fucking shine and that shouldn't be compromised for anyone—even for old family precedents?"

I hold his gaze and shake my head back and forth. A million reasons to be mad flit through my head, but his words mean more to me than anything.

"You can be mad at me all you want but you have to admit, the videos online are awesome. Give me that much. For twenty minutes you stopped that town dead and they haven't stopped talking since."

"The trash," I say, trying to gain my even footing. "I'm going to get in trouble for the trash—"

"It's taken care of. I had permits pulled. Have a staff hired to pick up every scrap that wasn't kept."

"Ollie, this is . . ."

"Insane? Preposterous? *Fucking awesome?* Yeah, it is. Those are all the ways you make me feel, and I thought it was about time you knew how it felt yourself."

There go those jelly knees again. "I'm . . . I should be mad at you," I say with way less accusation than I feel.

"But you aren't." His smile lights up his face.

"But I am."

"Should I be afraid of that whole even footing thing?" he teases.

Even footing? Hell, the man has shaken the ground beneath me. Even footing left the conversation weeks ago. "I just . . . *Ollie*."

He steps into me, cups my face in his hands, and then dips down so we're eye level. "What are you going to do about it, Bellissima? If you tell everyone I did it, then you'll have to explain why I would do such a thing for a woman I barely know. Then people will start digging. Start noticing coincidences that we were at the same place at the same time and maybe they weren't coincidences anymore. And if you say you did it, then God forbid you might actually be taking a stand for yourself, for once."

"You . . . bastard." But the words come out in a laugh and the strangest feeling floats through me.

One that reinforces the many things he's said but that I've never really felt. Words are cheap. Actions are everything. And he just showed his hand by telling the world that someone believes in me. *Which is completely different to el patriarca's actions—to hold a dinner to celebrate one grandchild's dream to ensure another doesn't achieve theirs.*

"Maybe I am a bastard, Sofia. Maybe I'm not. All I know is that you're fucking everything. It's no fault of his own, but no one sees past Cruz into who's standing in his shadow because his light is too bright. I wanted to tell you that I see you. That I want you. That he needs to share the damn spotlight."

Be still my fucking heart.

I stare at Rossi—at the man everyone thinks has a cold heart—and realize how much he has softened for me. How much he has worked for me to see my worth when I should have seen it myself.

I brush my lips against his in the most tender of kisses.

"I didn't mean to upset you," he says between kisses. "I just wanted you to see your own worth."

"Ollie," I murmur.

"I have to go but fuck if you're not making it hard." He chuckles at the pun and then our lips meet once again. "My meeting." Another kiss as he cups my breast. "In five minutes."

We both jump at the knock on the door but keep our lips and hands moving.

"Go the fuck away. We're busy," Rossi groans in reflex.

But the minute the words are out, we both freeze, understanding the gravity of the mistake.

"Sofia?" My brother's voice barrels through the door. His fist pounds harshly seconds thereafter.

"Shit." I hiss the word out. My heart pounds and head swims.

"Fuck it," Rossi mutters and yanks open the door. He and my brother stand face to face, shoulders squared and challenge written in every ounce of their posture.

There is no mistaking Rossi's mussed hair or the flush of arousal on my cheeks.

I wait for a fist to be thrown. For words to be shouted. But it's the expression on my brother's face that I'll never forget. It's the one that has me scrambling after him. *Betrayal.*

"Cruz," I shout.

Rossi looks at me with regret etched in every line of his face. "I'm sorry," he says but I'm already down the hall, chasing after my brother.

"Cruz. Wait."

But before I can get to him, he steps in the elevator, meets my eyes, and utters one, unmistakable command. "Don't."

The doors shut.

The elevator descends.

And I'm left staring at nothing as I try to figure out what to do next.

CHAPTER THIRTY-FOUR

Sofia

THE TENSION IN THE GARAGE IS LIKE A COIL SPRUNG SO TIGHT THAT I'm afraid when it snaps, the reaction will be so violent that everyone will be hit by its shrapnel.

My brother. Rossi. Maddix. The crew. Fellow drivers. The media. Freaking everybody.

My brother walks into the paddock area toward the garage but doesn't look at me. "Cruz?"

Talk to me.

Yell at me.

Fight with me.

But he does nothing. He simply meets my eyes and gives the slightest shake of his head. The disappointment I see there kills me. Because he is my person. Because of everything we've been through together with our parents, he's become the one whose opinion means the most to me. *I care what he thinks.*

I stare after him and where he disappears to. Honestly, I shouldn't have expected anything different. He refused to talk to me last night. Not before he had to go to the sponsorship dinner with Rossi. Not after it when I sat at his hotel room door waiting for him. Not even when he physically picked me up to move me out of the way of the door, telling me to just leave him alone.

I thought it would be my grandfather's disappointment that would tear me up. I was wrong. I haven't even received that yet and Cruz's was painful. Heartbreaking.

And then there was Rossi. Just as busy as my brother on the work spectrum, apologetic that he caused this while at the same time unapologetic over it.

Why does he care so much what my family thinks of him when he couldn't give a fuck about everyone else?

Because you matter, Sof.

Isn't that what this comes down to?

You're falling for a man you shouldn't want, you can't have, and who will make everyone and their brother in the Navarro realm up in arms.

A competitor.

The guy who doesn't give a fuck what anyone thinks.

A non-Spanish commoner in their tunnel-visioned, archaic gazes.

"Excuse me." It's Rossi's voice at my back. I turn to see him there, his PR handler at his side, and his eyes a fleeting glance my way.

For a second, I thought he was trying to speak to me, to . . . I don't know what with me, but I realize he's simply asking to move past the path I'm blocking.

"Sure. Yes. Sorry." The words out of my mouth sound pathetic. This isn't on him. Far from it. But he's trying to take the path of least resistance, pun intended, but continuing to act like there's nothing more, nothing less between us than just a simple contract joining him to my brother.

I step out of the way.

"Good luck today," I say softly.

He turns back to look at me. His eyes are sad. Compassionate. And edged with a small amount of anger.

He nods. "Thanks."

If anyone else saw this non-exchange-exchange, they'd see nothing more than a passing cordiality.

If my brother saw it, he'd know. He'd see my sorrowful, heartbroken expression and comprehend how conflicted I'm feeling.

I'm trying not to hurt anyone, Cruz.

I don't want you to believe you're not important to me, Ollie.

Family. Responsibilities. Pressure. It's all there, boiling inside of me.

But what's the way forward?

Will I have to sacrifice my dreams again so that everything can be right in my world?

Do I have to step back into the shadows where I don't matter?

One man will let me.

The other I know damn sure will not.

CHAPTER THIRTY-FIVE

THE CAR IS ROUGH BUT MANAGEABLE.

That fucking look in her eyes. I put it there. I made her feel that way. I'm at fucking fault.

I push it and test its limits. Hard through the corners. Within millimeters of the goddamn wall coming out of the chicane. I fly down the straight.

I'll place on the podium. I'll make her happy. I'll prove to her brother and her family that I'm fucking worth it.

But Cruz is still ahead of me—within reach—and fuck if I'm not going to finish ahead of him this race. I'm going to. Have to.

The number two driver in the top Gravitas spot.

I'll prove to Stavros that I can be consistently better than Cruz. I'll prove to the fans I'm better than I've ever been. I'll prove to the Navarros that I'm just as good if not better than their prized son. And I'll fucking impress everyone who's ever doubted me before.

Right here.

Right now.

This race.

"You're pushing hard," Alec says in my earpiece. I'm not sure if it's an admonishment or praise.

I don't fucking care.

"How's the read?" I ask of all the gauges and telemetric stats on the car that he has on the massive board in front of him.

"Good. Fine. You're about to hit traffic though. That will slow you down."

"No, it won't," I say as I accelerate around and lap a car. I steer into the slipstream of the next one so I can sling out and around it at the right time.

"Careful, Rossi."

I don't respond. Can't. I'm too busy watching Cruz ease up when he hits the traffic in front of him.

Fuck that.

I'm going for it.

At least that's the plan.

If you don't kill yourself, you're going to kill someone else.

I sit.

You're out of control. A danger to everyone on the track.

And I wait.

A liability I'm not willing to take no matter how much potential you do or don't have.

And I let the slip take the pressure off the car, and at the right time, I whip out and around the car in front of me and use the momentum to gain on Cruz.

"Stay on his wing," Alec says but I don't acknowledge him. "Bustos is coming up hot behind. Defend for Navarro."

I choose not to.

I'm too fucking focused on the cars in front, too dialed in to my own pursuit.

Yes, I'm too fucking selfish. Especially now. Specifically today.

"Rossi." A warning I don't heed.

C'mon, baby. Fucking go.

I repeat those four words over and over and over as I drive the fuck out of my car.

I pass the traffic in front of me.

Then I come wheel to wheel with Cruz.

And I compete.

I don't back down. I don't take this number two driver bullshit. I don't hear the noise in my headset. I refuse to be bullied this time around too.

I play the part people expect of me. The one that earns me fans. That has gotten me this far.

And I fucking compete.

I'd be lying if I said I didn't emit a huge goddamn roar when I edge past Cruz. When I come into the turn like a bat out of hell and pull solidly in front of him.

There's yelling in my headset. A cautious tone from Alec—where he's not sure if he should scold me or cheer me on to chase after the next place—a spot on the podium.

But he knows the world is listening to our exchanges. So do I.

"How fast is Laurent?" I ask of the next car in front of me like I didn't just go against orders.

"You're the fastest on the track right now," he says.

My grin is strained from the Gs but there, nonetheless. Can't blame the faster car for going ahead. *Well, you can, but the public will rip you to shreds.* He knows that. I know that.

So I just keep pushing.

"How far?"

"Zero point six, Rossi."

"Ten-four. I'll reel him in."

And I do. Turn by turn. DRS activation after DRS activation. By tooth and nail, I fight my way to cross the line in third place and take a podium.

And take it I do. I enjoy every goddamn second standing on it, in Gravitas white with a strip of orange, while looking into the crowd.

I meet Sofia's eyes. Pride brims in them and fuck if my chest doesn't constrict.

I hold Stavros's stare. The muscle pulses in his jaw but he smiles. How can he not? I just gave him his first podium of the season.

And I sure as fuck feel the glare from Cruz who placed fifth. Respectable but out of the glory. *And after me*—the guy who's tainting his little sister's perfect image.

When I walk off the stage, covered in champagne and gloating like the motherfucker I am, Stavros holds his hand out to stop me.

I pause. I meet his eyes. I say, "It's amazing how much you like how dangerous I am when I win for you, now, isn't it?"

He grunts, but I don't wait for a reaction. I don't have to. I have media and PR and all the superfluous outside noise that comes with this sport.

It's a love-hate thing when all you want to do is sit on your ass for two minutes, down an ice-cold beer, and relive every glorious second of it.

Oh, and kiss your woman.

Anything to avoid the shitstorm I no doubt stirred up in private. Within the team. With Cruz. With fucking everybody.

But as I enter the garage for the first time, I come face to face with Cruz and the fucking pissed off look on his face.

"That was dirty," he spits out. "But it seems that's all you know, isn't it?"

"What was? Passing you in traffic? Taking the advantage? What was so dirty about it?" But I know he's talking about more than just what happened on the track. *I know.*

"Everything about it. Ignoring Alec on the radio. Pushing when you were told to defend. I've heard the recording of your comms."

"Apparently I didn't." I shrug nonchalantly. "You're only pissed because your ego is bruised. If you'd done it, it would have been the best fucking move ever, no?"

"We're a team. I'm one. You're two. That's how it goes."

I step into him. I welcome the fucking fight. And not just because of right now, but because of everything else he's saying—implying—and fuck him if he thinks I'm going to stand here and take it and not defend myself.

"If it comes down to you and me, Cruz, it's me all the fucking way. Don't you forget that."

"Exactly my point." He glares at me, jaw clenched and hands fisted. His words referring to something way more important than racing.

But only he and I know that. No one else in this garage listening and pretending not to does.

"You'd do the same and you know it," I grit out.

"No. I don't think I would."

I glance over to where Sofia has just stepped into the garage and then falters when she sees us squaring off and the small crowd of crew gathering around us.

"Don't," he warns.

"Don't what?" I taunt. I can't help myself. "You forget, no one tells me what to do. Not you. Not . . ."

"Stavros?" Cruz asks, tilting his head to the side, a slight smirk to his lips as if he just caught me in something I won't cop to while standing in front of all these people.

"Fuck off," I say evenly.

"It still eats you all this time later that he picked me back then over you? That—"

"That you were so awesome your papá paid him to?" The hurt teenager I was lashes out. Even the man I am today can't stop him. Not after years of it building up. "Nah. I earned my stripes. I didn't have anyone paving my way for me. I didn't have—"

"No, but you sure as fuck knew how to screw over other people to get there. Take what you want from them and leave them to deal."

I stare at him. Itching for him to throw that first punch. Needing him to so that I have an excuse to defend myself. To not be who they all want me to be—the aggressor. The villain. The fucker who screws up.

And as much as I want to give that to them, there's a woman standing fifteen feet away who I can't do that to, no matter how fucking bad I want to.

"You got something to say, Navarro? Then say it. Let everyone here know what you really think of me." I open the door for him to see if he'll walk through it.

What's more important, huh? Your sister and respecting her or unleashing your privileged shit on me?

Cruz bites his tongue. The garage is full of people, and I dare him to let the world know I'm sleeping with his little sister. Me, the guy no one thinks is good enough. Me, the one who knows he fucking is.

He just glares at me in the eerie silence of our garage. Sound is everywhere around us—the emcee, the crowd, other garages—but in ours all you can hear is our labored breaths and unspoken anger.

"That's what I thought." I say the words and then turn on my heels and waltz out of there.

I glance quickly at Sofia. She's torn as I expect her to be.

And I wish she wouldn't be because the answer should be so much easier than what she thinks it is.

I love her.

I fucking love her, but I can't tell her because she just showed it. She just fucking hesitated. And that's enough to tell me where I stand.

Acid creeps up my throat. I should be washing it down with champagne, but I don't want a single fucking drop.

I want to own this fury. I want to unleash it. And when I step into the hospitality suite through the private back door and there's a slam behind me, I know he's fucking there.

And I turn on him in an instant with my fist cocked and my hurt overflowing.

"Back the fuck off," I say.

Cruz's chuckle is everything I need to ignite the fuse but for some reason it doesn't click. It doesn't light.

This time the damage would be irreparable.

This time? I'd lose more than just a scholarship to a fancy school and my love of art.

This time, I'd lose Sofia, and I know it.

"Why? You going to punch me, Rossi? You going to ride that *fuck you* bullshit you're known for when you're just a worthless piece of shit trying to be everything you're not? The media may print stories about you, but I know the real you. The real truths."

"Don't throw stones in glass houses, Cruz-y boy. You're far from fucking perfect. That pristine image you shine with a rag in the mirror used to be just as tarnished as mine and yet you seem to be acceptable for that family of yours."

"You're pathetic," he says. "And at first, I felt sorry for you. For Stavros picking me when you won time and again. But then—then you proved why he did. Over and over. Your MO is what it is. What it's always been, isn't it? Can you blame me for wanting to steer clear of you?"

"And what's that?"

His laugh grates on every nerve I have. "A piece of shit who doesn't give a fuck about anyone other than using them for your own needs. Instead of using them to get back at me."

"Fuck you."

"Fuck me?" He steps into me, finger in my chest and ire in his voice. "You slept with my girlfriend after I got the ride. You reeled her in, you made her think she was important, that you cared, and then you took her fucking virginity before dumping her as a total *fuck you* to me. Because I won a ride I had no more control over than you. That type of shit? That type of man? He's un-fucking-forgivable."

His words assault me. One after another. Jesus. I did that?

But the minute I think the thought, the memory comes back in a torrent of snapshots.

There are so many excuses I can give, ones that are dead truths—she wanted to, she asked me to be her first, she was the one who came on to me—but anything I say, regardless of it being the truth, does nothing to make me look better. In fact, it makes me look even worse.

I'm in a no-win situation here as I should be without a pot to piss in or a window to throw it out of.

The things you do at that age are so very different than what you do as an adult.

"Would you want *that* guy with your sister? Would you want him anywhere fucking near her? And would you wonder every second of every minute since you found out about them, if he's fucking her just to spite you? To get back at you? Would you?" He shoves against me and the fight is fucking gone. "You would. You know it. And the sad fact is you don't even fucking blame me for thinking it."

"She's different," I whisper but it holds no weight. How can it when the things I did in my past, the things I did to try and make me feel worth something, were fucked up too?

"You're goddamn right she is and you're nowhere near good enough for her."

"Tell me something I don't know," I snap at him. "But isn't that for Sofia to decide?"

"Not when you've convinced her that you're a stand-up—"

"I haven't convinced her of shit. She's a grown woman who has her own life, her own goals, her own fucking feelings, but it seems she's so goddamn busy managing everyone else in your family that you seem to forget that."

"I don't forget shit. Don't tell me how to be with my sister."

"Why not? You seem like you do a good job of telling everyone else how to be. When's the last time you asked her how her gallery was going? When was the last time you asked her anything about herself other than where she is to help with your mamá or papá?"

"That's none of your business."

"No? Because I'm the one at the gallery with her, painting and putting displays together. I'm the one trying to help her procure art to showcase. I'm the fucking one there when she's exhausted from your parents and pleasing your grandfather, not-fucking-you." I straighten my shoulders and step back into him. I've found my even footing and I'm goddamn good and well with it. "You talk a good game. You talk about respecting women, about not wronging them, but it doesn't seem you respect the one who deserves it the most."

"You don't know shit—"

"But I do. I know someone needs to stand up for your sister and if it isn't going to be you—like it should be after she's had your back all these years—then it sure as fuck is going to be me."

I take a few steps back.

"Like me. Hate me. I don't give a fuck what you think of me, but your sister, she deserves better than the both of us, and it seems only one of us is trying to fix that."

This time when I walk away, he doesn't follow me.

CHAPTER THIRTY-SIX

Sofia

"You okay?" I ask, the response on the other end of the line slow to come.

"Yeah." A sigh. "I'm fine. You?"

I nod and look around the crowded airport as I wait for the shuttle to take us out to the private jet. "I'm okay. I'm sorry . . . for everything."

And what that *everything* is, I have no idea.

I saw Cruz run after him. I saw the door shut. I heard the muffled shouting between the two. And after that, nothing. Chilled fucking silence.

"Don't be," Rossi says. His voice is a soft rumble through the line that I want to crawl into and wrap around myself. "This is on me. All of it. Cruz knowing. The race. The fight after. Things you don't even know about. This is on me." For a man who just took a podium, he sounds like he just got the shit kicked out of him.

"I don't blame you. At all. Please know that."

There's a pause that eats at me. "I'm a lot of things, Sofia, but perfect isn't one of them. I've made mistakes. When I was younger, when I was first on the circuit, fucking yesterday if it really matters, but this time spent with you? It wasn't one of them. Please know that."

"Ollie . . . why do you sound like . . ." Like you're ending this.

"I don't sound like anything. It's important for me that you know that is all."

"Okay. I hear you. I understand you. I . . ." *I wish you were coming with me.* "I wish I were going back home with you."

"You are going home," he says, referring to my flight home to Spain for our once-a-month family dinner at the villa. "Enjoy your time."

"Rossi."

Don't hang up yet.

I love you.

Just . . . I love you.

"I'm not going anywhere, Bellissima. I'm not leaving you," he says, unknowingly reassuring me over the one thing I've feared my whole life.

Being left.

CHAPTER THIRTY-SEVEN

Sofia

THIS VIEW.

This home.

It used to be my place of comfort. Where I'd go when I needed to feel good again. The only spot where I didn't have to work for anything more than a laugh.

But as I stand here, the fields at my back, and a long line of linking tables sprawled across the travertine patio with lights strung overhead above it, it's the first time in forever I feel like I don't belong.

To everyone else, Cruz's cold shoulder has gone unnoticed. He smiles at me when he needs to. When someone might notice if he doesn't. But other than forced niceties on the jet here and our time at the villa, not a meaningful word has been said between us.

Maddix has tried to bridge that gap—God, has she tried—but either she doesn't know the whole scope of what's going on or she's trying to remain neutral.

"He's reckless. He proved as much this weekend," our father says. "He was told to defend and he didn't. He was told to—"

"He's selfish," el patriarca says in that quiet, unyielding voice of his that makes everyone stop.

"Aren't all racers, though?" I ask, causing every head at the table to turn our way.

"Did you have something to say?" Cruz asks, his voice clipped. His eyebrows are raised in the challenge that's lacking in his tone, but I hear it.

"I did. Yes. I said aren't all racers selfish? Isn't that what makes you good? Your pursuit at all costs of others?" I ask.

"Yes, but—"

"No buts, Cruz. Point made." I lift my glass of wine and take a sip, my smirk hidden behind the glass.

"You're wrong, Sofia," our cousin butts in. "There's a difference and Rossi put that difference on display yesterday for all to see. He didn't heed his race engineer's direction. He defied orders."

"He has no place on the grid," my father states.

"His car was faster." I shrug and then turn to Cruz, welcoming the argument. "Can't blame the guy for wanting to show it."

"There's a decorum you follow. Unwritten expectations," Cruz says. Maddix reaches out and links her fingers with his. I can see her trying to calm him and it only infuriates me more by no fault of her own.

"Humph. Seems to me that pertains to all things on and *off* the track, no?" I ask and he damn well knows about me and my place in this family.

"Unruly and dangerous is what he is," our cousin says.

It's not the first time I've heard these arguments. They're just a repeat of what was said when Rossi signed on with Team Gravitas. A lot of accusations, numerous opinions, and not a single one favorable.

The funny thing? I never stopped before to question my own family's opinions. I simply believed them because that's what this family does—it sticks together. It has each other's backs. It rallies for one another.

And yet it seems Rossi has shown me that support is only if you ascribe to the popular opinion. It taught me I've been following blindly for so long that I fear I might have missed some very important things along the way.

Like my own independence.

"But if you broke those rules, Cruz, we'd all be here celebrating your podium, would we not?" I ask.

"Don't you have more important things to be thinking about?" Cruz asks. "Like your gallery's grand opening?"

You fucker.

There's a shifting of everyone at the table as the elephant in the room is brought up. My defiance of el patriarca's request for me to move my grand opening date. Throats are cleared. Glasses of wine are lifted, and huge sips are taken.

But I just hold my brother's leveled gaze.

"You're right. I've had marketing options literally dropped from the sky."

"Aren't you just the little rebel."

"There's a huge difference between standing up for yourself and rebelling. But you'd never know because you've never had to." I shove up out of my chair and scoot it back. My words almost an attack on behalf of Rossi and Stavros's choice to pick my brother all those years ago. "If you'll excuse me, I need to use the bathroom."

But I don't need to do anything other than to get a fucking break from this table, these people, and all the negative comments being made about Rossi. The ones that have been made here and there all day that I'm so done with.

I glance over my shoulder at the table where my family sits, my whole world, and for the first time in my life, I don't really like them.

I love them, sure. Isn't that how family is? But as far as liking them in this moment as they all do the only thing they've ever been trained to do—support Cruz—I don't want to be here.

So I skip the rest of dinner.

I wander the orchard. I walk through the trestles of grapevines. I think of Rossi and miss him.

"Sof."

I just want to walk away, leave the fight with Cruz and not address it—but I do what I've needed to do since the first night I snuck away with Ollie. I need to be myself—Simply Sofia. I need to stand up for what I believe in. For the person I want to be.

"So you're down here to keep this quiet, right? To make sure no one else in the family knows I'm sleeping with Rossi? That I'm shaming the family name?"

He gives the slightest lift of his shoulders as if to say that's on point. "It would kill el patriarca to know you were with him."

"Right. Just like it killed you and yet here you are. Still standing. Still being a stubborn asshole."

"His health is frail, Sofia."

"So you're saying I have to hide it?"

"The fact that you already were says what you think about being with him. That was all you. Not me. Not el patriarca. All you."

"You're something else, Cruz."

"And it seems you're acting out to get attention." He shrugs.

"Says the king of doing just that," I say, and he smirks. Does he ever do anything that doesn't make me want to throttle him and hug him at the same time?

"See? You always did want to be like me. Now you are."

I appreciate him trying to add some levity to the situation but it's not going to fix it.

"Look." I sigh in exasperation. "I can stand in your garage at the next race or Rossi's garage, so you might want to figure out how far you push me before you open your mouth."

He blows out a long, slow whistle. "How long have you been thinking about that zinger?"

"I've been thinking of a lot worse ones so watch your step." I cross my arms over my chest and face him.

"You always did have to plan your fights in your head ahead of time."

"And you always did take pot shots to provoke me."

"Good to see some things never change," he says and takes a seat on the steps behind him.

"But that's just it. A lot has changed." I had so much anger saved up for him, so much animosity toward him, but I look at my brother now and just want my world back together—but on my terms.

"Like what? Tell me one thing that's changed."

"Me," I shout and throw my hands out. "I've changed. I've changed and no one has stopped to take their eyes off you to notice."

"Sof—"

"You don't get it. I've done this for so fucking long. I've made sure the focus stays on you and on your career. And don't get me wrong, I love supporting you, but we are two siblings who are treated so differently. And I'm just . . . I'm just done with it."

"Come on. You're being dramatic, don't you think?"

"No. I'm not. This has been my life. Prop you up constantly while I get the leftovers. Take care of all the problems so you don't have to. And Cruz, I know you've had it rough—more times than I can count—and I'm glad that I was there to help you and support you and be what you needed—but I don't want to be just that anymore. I don't want to be *just* Cruz Navarro's little sister anymore. You of all people should understand this. Should be proud of me for realizing this. And yet you stand there on your pedestal of superiority and judge me."

He chews the inside of his cheek, his eyes holding mine as he nods ever so slowly. "What does this have to do with Rossi? Because you telling me you want to be this new and improved Sofia is one thing, but you fucking Rossi tells me you just want to lift your middle finger at me and rebel."

"Oh my God, Cruz. Stop. Just stop. You're proving my point."

"How's that? What am I proving exactly?"

"My life. My decisions. And I shouldn't have to care how it affects you or why you'd care."

"So you *are* screwing him to piss me off."

"No."

"Then what is it?" he asks but something in my expression has him straightening up, has him looking a little closer. "No. Absolutely not." He shoves up from his seat and his legs eat up the space as he paces angrily.

"What?"

"You're fucking falling for him?" he shouts and then glances toward the upper villa to make sure no one's overhearing this. "You can't. Christ, Sofia, you can't."

"Why not?"

"Because . . ." He shakes his head. "Because you're lying to yourself if you think that man, that he's good . . ."

"Good enough for the Navarro family?" I chuckle. "That's what you were going to say, wasn't it?" I smile in disbelief and shake my head. "I have rules on who I can and can't date, but it was perfectly okay for you to date and soon marry someone out of the preselected marriage pool. One set of rules for the prized son. Another for me. Got it. Fucking awesome. Do you not see the hypocrisy here?"

My brother's expression tightens. He hears what I'm saying. And by the look on his face, he knows there's merit in my words. That they hold more truth than he wants to admit.

"You don't know the real Oliver Rossi," he says.

"And maybe you no longer know the real me," I whisper.

"Sofia."

I lift my eyebrows and shrug. "You don't. Not anymore."

"Sof. Rossi isn't a good guy. He's—"

"What? Brash? Out of control? Made a shit ton of mistakes during his youth? During his career? Yeah, I know that. But I also know he's kind, intelligent, treats me like a fucking queen, and has been there for me for every step of this damn gallery when you haven't stepped foot in there once. So think what you want, and I'll believe what I've been shown."

"I just want the best for you. Always. He's not it."

"I'll be the judge of that. What you're not understanding is, I'm not asking for your approval, I just need your support."

He shakes his head and sighs, obviously conflicted. "This is hard for me."

I step into my brother, my voice soft but my heart firm in every word. "I idolized you growing up, Cruz. In some ways I still do. I've helped you with Mamá and Papá—something only we can understand. And I've tried to be the person you all wanted me to be. I've struggled between being her and being the person I've grown into. I love you. With all my heart. I love Maddix. I'll never stop wanting the best for you, but it's a two-way street. Being protective is one thing, but clipping my wings is a whole other."

And with that, I kiss him on the cheek, and then I walk away.

There's no discussion between us where I ask him not to say anything about Rossi to the rest of our family. I know he won't.

There's no talk about whatever he and Rossi fought about. I'll find out in time.

This was just a big brother realizing his little sister isn't so little anymore. And it's the little sister realizing he might need some time to adjust to that.

I walk up the pathway toward the patio where el patriarca sits in his wheelchair and lean down to kiss his cheek.

"I love you. I have to get going, but please know that I love you."

"Of course you do. You don't have a choice—you're stuck with me," he teases and pats the side of my cheek. "You forced my hand, mija, with the gallery opening."

All that bravado I just had with Cruz is smothered with the disappointment in my grandfather's voice. I swallow and lick my lips.

"El patriarca—"

"I'm not happy that you did," he says. Is that a hint of pride in his voice? Of resignation? "But I can respect you for it. It means you really want this. Who am I to stand in your way from achieving it?"

"Thank you." I whisper the two words out.

He nods and pats my hand. "Let's not make a habit of it though."

CHAPTER THIRTY-EIGHT

Rossi

"ARE WE GOING TO TALK ABOUT IT OR ARE YOU JUST GOING TO work yourself sick trying to get this place ready for artmontecarlo?" I keep my head down, my hands on my screw gun as I finish building yet another display.

But my question is out there.

It's been two days since she got back from the family dinner at the villa. Two days of her avoiding every possible thing in life but this gallery. Two nights of getting lost in each other—that fiery passion turned quiet, more of a necessity like breathing—almost as if she's using me to forget whatever happened while she was there. Or to solidify her reasons why whatever happened did in fact *happen*.

I don't know the answer because she hasn't talked.

But I've kept my head down and tried to be the person she's needed when I don't know what the fuck it is she needs.

I've sat with her on my balcony in comfortable silence. I've worked side by side with her in this gallery, trying to help her make the vision she has for it come to life. I've done everything in my power to please her, to pleasure her, to be whoever she needs me to be in bed so that she can step into her own with the confidence I see her project daily. Something I don't think she ever lets the world see.

And then after she's fallen asleep, after she's snuggled in my sheets,

I've gotten up and worked in silence to try and help her more. To give her a surprise that's worthy of her.

I glance her way when she doesn't respond—yet again. She's standing in a heap of crates. Each one is a piece of art she's waiting to display. *Her babies.* That's what she's called them. Her hands are on her hips and her lips are twisted in thought.

Even like this—hair piled on her head, fresh-faced and makeup free—I stop and stare. She's stunning. Simply put.

"I'm fine. They're fine. Everything's fine. I told you—I just have a lot to do," she says, distracted. "The local artist contest winner will be picked next week. I have all but five pieces in my possession, which is better than I expected to be at this point. I have caterers lined up, but I still need to pick a wine list for the opening. The guest list. Christ, I still need to deal with that. Or should I leave it as an open house? Pull the public in to mingle with the rich so they feel just as coveted. I don't know. I just don't know." Her entire ramble is more for herself than to me.

I set down my tools, move toward her, slip my arms between hers and her torso, and pull her back against my front. With my chin resting on her shoulder, I breathe her in. I love the way she leans her head back and rests it against me. Almost as if she finds comfort in me.

I brush my lips against her neck. While her silence is worrying, she came back to me. She's here with me. If it were something more, she wouldn't have done that, would she?

"Making this gallery perfect isn't going to make them love you any less or any more, you know. They love you because they love you."

But isn't that the crux of the matter?

She's busting her ass to try and make her family love her more, like her more, approve of her more, as a means to make up for dating me.

That makes me feel like a real winner.

"Cruz won't tell anyone," she murmurs.

At least she finally said something.

"So you talked to Cruz then? About us? About me? About what?"

"Everything. I . . . I stood my ground."

"Huh. And?"

"And I did." She shrugs and moves out of my grasp to slide a crate to yet another position, as if she's mentally imagining them on the walls. "But don't worry, he won't tell anyone about us."

I twist my lips. *How am I supposed to take that?* "And is that what you want?"

"No." A nervous laugh as she flits from one place to the next. "Of course not. It's just . . . wouldn't that make life easier for you? No team drama. No Stavros bullshit to deal with. No anything. Just us living our life how we want."

"Living our life as we want—*behind closed doors.*"

"For now. *Right?*"

I stare at her. At this gorgeous woman who fuck if I haven't fallen for and yet the revelation is tainted. The feeling stained. "Yep. Right," I say, clipped.

They're my words but there's no heart behind them. No conviction.

Just an emptiness that almost matches the way this conversation has made me feel inside.

"Sofia, I . . ."

"What?" She looks up from her clipboard, eyes wide and lips in a pout.

I love you.

Jesus Christ. I almost said it. I almost laid every card on the fucking table and made myself the most vulnerable I've ever been.

Blair accused me of always wanting the limelight, of needing the attention and adoration from my fans—from everyone. And right now I couldn't give a fuck about any of that so long as I have Sofia.

Hers is the only attention I want or need. She fills a void in me that I never really grasped was missing.

She's my anchor. My confidante. *My fucking everything.*

But as she stands across the gallery shutting me out from whatever happened at the villa, telling me *this* is better if it's kept private, I'm wondering if I've ever been those three things for her.

If it's ever even possible.

And that brings a sense of loneliness I've never felt before.

CHAPTER THIRTY-NINE

Rossi

THE KNOCK ON THE DOOR IS AS UNEXPECTED AS THE PERSON standing on the other side of it when I open it.

"Babbo?" I stare at my dad as he shifts awkwardly, clearly uncomfortable, but on my doorstep nonetheless.

He's worrying his ballcap between his hands, his face is clean shaven, but his eyes... his eyes tell me he's nervous.

"Oliver." He clears his throat. "May I come in?"

"Sure. Yes. Of course." But it doesn't matter how many words I speak because I'm still trying to process that he's here, on my doorstep. And suddenly, I'm the one who's nervous. "Come in." I close the door behind him. "Mamma's okay?" I ask.

"Yes. Sorry." He glances over his shoulder quickly before turning back and taking in the extravagance all around him. "She's fine. Didn't mean to scare you." Another step. A hand reaching out to touch and then pulling back. "She wanted to come but I—uh—told her I needed to do this on my own."

A lead weight drops in my stomach. "Do what?"

"Do you—can I have some water, please?"

"Yes." I take a step toward the kitchen and know I'm going to need something more than water right now. "Or would you like something else? A beer? A whiskey? Wine?"

His half-smile is one of gratitude. "I'll have whatever you do. Thanks."

My mind races as I head to the kitchen and try to figure out why my father is here. When I come back out with two glasses of whiskey poured—because I think this might be a *something stronger* type of conversation—he's standing in the same spot.

It's weird. It's not like we're strangers. We talk on the phone. We exchange texts. I visit them occasionally in the offseason—and yet, it feels like we are right now.

"Babbo." I hold out his drink to him and hate that his hand tremors when he takes it. What can be that bad?

"Thanks."

"Come. Sit."

We take a few minutes to settle and then we sit across from each other, our eyes locked and suddenly years of what feels like misunderstood distance rioting between us.

"I—uh—I've done wrong by you, Oliver."

I take a slow sip of my whiskey and look at anything but my father, because I'm the one who did wrong all those years ago. I'm the one who screwed my family up. "Go on."

"Please. Look at me?" he pleads. And I do as he asks. "It wasn't until we talked last that you made me see the error in my ways." He clears his throat and takes a deep breath. "I have failed you so many times, son, and I wanted to come here, to see you and explain, and ask for your forgiveness."

"I don't...understand."

"I've always hated art. It was all your nonna wanted to do—paint, study how to paint, look at paintings. It became her whole life. She was a single mother, and she spent her life so determined to make a living out of her art, that she stopped living. We were dirt poor, Oliver. Many nights we didn't eat because she refused to get a job because *this painting*, the one she was manically working on, was going to be her big break. I was teased. My clothes had holes in them. I ate the school lunches and filled my pockets with anything extra they'd give me because food at home wasn't guaranteed. It was a miserable existence and all because she knew her big break was coming...but it never did."

"I don't understand." I think of how when I stayed with her after being expelled. None of this sounds familiar. In fact, she bought me expensive art kits. She encouraged my appreciation for it by taking me to museums. "When I stayed with her . . ."

"We provided all of that for you. For her."

"But . . ." I stare at him, blinking.

"She was your kindred spirit. She made you laugh and helped you be a kid again after . . . everything. Do you think I was going to badmouth her or let you see the real side of everything? The circus looks beautiful to kids. It's only when you become an adult that you see the threadbare costumes and the scars on the animals."

I lean back and blow out a disbelieving sigh, and as much as I want to hold steadfast to my memories, thinking back, there were chinks in the armor. There were seams that were threadbare.

"I loved your nonna with all my heart, but she was a burden on your mamma and me financially. We sent every scrap of money her way so that she didn't die in poverty and so that you didn't think ill of the one person you idolized."

"But you were also paying for all the problems I caused."

He nods solemnly. "Yes. I was. But I deserved that. That was my fault."

I chuckle more because I don't know how to process any of this yet. "How? I threw the punches."

"And I was the one who was a bad father. I think some part of me let the bullying go on, hoping that they would shame you to stop with the art obsession. But I didn't know how bad it was or how much you suffered. And when you snapped, they deserved it. And, as your father, I deserved the punishment—the endless bills—because of it."

"Whew. I don't even know what to say."

A memory floats back. My father hugging me. Crying. Telling me it would be all right and apologizing for failing me. I didn't understand it at the time. I was too wrapped up in the anger, the pain, the confusion, to care. But it makes sense now.

And I hate that I never wondered about it before.

"You don't have to say anything. I'm proud of you, Oliver. I'm proud of the kid you were, how you stood up for yourself when I didn't. Of the teenage kid who took my badgering to focus on something else you were talented at. Of the man you've become, and how you've handled all the past years have thrown at you."

I hear his words. I feel them. But . . . "You haven't been here. You always have an excuse. How—*fuck*." I hate when my voice breaks. Even worse, I hate the tears that burn in my eyes.

"You're right." He starts to get up to move toward me but then stops himself. And I'm not sure that I want him to stop, but I'm also not sure that I want him not to. Everyone needs their parents, but I've felt alone for so long—alone despite their phone calls and supportive texts—that I'm not sure what it is I want. "There is no excuse for my absence other than to tell you that I keep working, just in case. Just in case this racing thing fails. Just in case my income is needed. Just so that you never feel that I'm a burden to you like I felt my mamma was to me. That's not the place of a child. The place of a child is to spread their wings and soar. It's to surpass everything you've ever done as an adult. It's not to ever worry about paying for their parents because their parents are self-sufficient."

Jesus. Fucking. Christ.

"For years I thought it was me," I whisper. "I thought you were embarrassed of me. What I'd done. The financial hardship I'd put you through. All of that. And then I succeeded. Then I made it to the fucking top and you still didn't come and, I assumed . . ." I swallow over the broken emotion that feels like shards of glass in my throat. Over the years of doubt and the months of loneliness. "I assumed I still wasn't good enough for you."

"No, Oliver. No." He moves to me now. He sits on the edge of the coffee table in front of me and pats me gruffly on the knee. "It was never about you. It was about me. And I thought I was doing right by you. I thought the less pressure you had from me—being there, supporting us, I don't know—that it would be easier for you. But when you called, when you told me you couldn't even fight me face to face, I realized just how bad I had failed you. Even without knowing the why, I know I failed you."

I close my eyes and inhale a shaky breath. *He thinks he failed . . . me?* "I don't know what to say."

"You don't have to say anything." His smile is hesitant. Reticent. "And I don't expect forgiveness. I just hope that you can hear what I've told you. Look at it all for yourself and then maybe find it in you to let us rebuild this relationship. Not right away, of course, but maybe, in time."

So many emotions I never expected when I answered the unexpected knock at my door—anger, surprise, longing, loneliness, *love*—war within me. The little boy needs this more than he could ever know while the grown man in me is more cautious with my emotions.

I meet his eyes. They're still full of kindness, still the man who pushed me into this career, which clearly, I'm positively grateful for.

"So I guess this racing thing wasn't such a bad idea," I say, uncertain how to proceed. His smile is a slow, hesitant crawl across his lips.

"I'd say."

"I'd like to work on us, Babbo. I appreciate you coming here to talk face to face. I know it's hard for a man to admit he's done wrong by someone. But I'd like to try."

"That's more than I could ever ask for." Tears well in his eyes. "Thank you."

CHAPTER FORTY

Sofia

"Ollie. I really don't have the time—"

His lips meet mine in a searing kiss, cutting my words off. "You have time for this. I'm making you make time for this." He links his fingers with mine. "We deserve a break and . . . I have a surprise for you."

I chuckle nervously. "And I've played along, but a girl can only have so much mystery before she starts asking questions."

He tucks a tendril of hair behind my ear, his fingers so gentle for a man so many others see as gruff. "Let me do this for you. Let me take care of you tonight. Let me surprise you. Please."

I lean forward and press my lips to his. It's when I'm here, when the focus of my world narrows to just him, that I feel the most at peace these days.

And the least alone.

I think the feeling is mutual though. There's a lighter air to Rossi these days. I'd like to think I have some part in that, but I sense it's the open dialogue that is happening between him and his parents that is at its heart.

While that whole visit from his father came out of the blue and knocked him astride for a few days, I'm so very proud of him for listening instead of reacting. For contemplating instead of shutting it down. For revisiting old memories to look at them with new eyes instead of relying on decade-old ones.

So when Rossi told me to *get ready*, I assumed it was because he wanted to celebrate an all-around incredible and transformative few weeks. The gallery for me. Working on things with his parents for him. Our relationship getting better and stronger with each passing day.

What I didn't expect was the short jet ride to Rome or the private car meeting us to whisk us away somewhere private.

Let's hope I dressed right for what he has in store for us.

"I don't need fancy date nights, Ollie."

"I know you don't, which is why it's that much more important that I do this. That I show you what you mean to me."

And when the car turns the corner and pulls up in front of a nondescript building, one that I know to be one of the biggest private galleries in Europe, I gasp.

"What are we . . ."

"Taking some time out to enjoy what you love."

"What you love too," I whisper.

His eyes meet mine, and I love the lopsided smile that graces his lips followed by the subtlest of nods. "That I love too."

I'll get him to not be embarrassed by it yet. I'll get him to not feel the stain those bullies left on him all those years ago.

I reach over and squeeze his hand. "I don't even know what to say." Excitement rushes through me. The revered pieces rumored to be kept here, that this mysterious, private owner has procured, is incredible. And a chance to gain entrance to see them is incredibly rare.

Kings. Presidents. Prime Ministers.

"You don't need to say anything. Maybe it'll inspire you to decide on a name for that gallery yet."

I roll my eyes. "Perhaps. But . . . Ollie, how did you get access to this . . . ?"

"It's nice to know that *the* Sofia Navarro, the woman who has the world at her fingertips, can actually be surprised," he says as I lean forward and press my lips to his.

And you, Oliver Rossi, are the biggest surprise of all.

I'm awed the minute we walk into the private reception area. There's a docent waiting, dressed in all black except for the vibrant pink frames of her glasses, with a few pieces of paperwork for us to sign, one of which is a nondisclosure agreement.

No wonder this place is shrouded in such mystery.

"I have so many questions," I murmur against his ear as we take an elevator to the next floor.

"They'll all be answered. I promise." He brings our linked fingers to his mouth and kisses the back of my hand.

And when the doors open, when the docent ushers us out, my eyes and art-loving heart are filled with the most incredible sights.

We're given a guided tour of each remarkable, awe-inspiring piece. We're gifted with the supposed stories behind them. The history of how said pieces came into the collector's possession.

The collection has been curated from new artists and from the classics. There's no rhyme or reason to how they were selected other than they were liked by the collector and no expense was spared for he or she to acquire them.

I'm in awe at every one and am even more impressed at the questions Rossi asks and the depth to those questions.

I think of the little boy poring over art books in secret. The dates and locations handwritten to some of the pictures in the ones in his house. And I love that I now know the deeper story behind them. That he doesn't feel the need to hide from me. That he opened up to me.

"What?" he asks when I study his profile while he contemplates the impressionist piece in front of us.

"I'm just trying to figure you out," I say.

"I assumed that already happened a long time ago." He flashes a smile and pulls me against him by his arm around my shoulders to press a kiss against my head.

"It did. Tell me about the dates in your art books at home. Your nonna's books."

He pauses. I can feel his body stiffen and his fingers in mine tense. It's not easy to erase a lifetime of hiding something. I wait for him to brush off the question like he has in the past, but am overcome when he keeps his lips on my scalp and whispers. "Those dates. Those places. They were my own little personal *fuck you* to everyone who told me I couldn't like it. The bullies. My babbo." He chuckles and twirls me out playfully before pulling me back into him. "Guess that last one seems a little outdated now, doesn't it?" A sharp smile. Another brush of his lips against mine.

"Isn't that what life is though? Think one thing only to find out it's so very different once you stop and hear it for yourself?" It seems we've both been doing a lot of that lately.

Me with my family.

Him with his family. With his original misperceptions of who I was and who I really am.

"Look at us," he says and winks.

"Look at us," I repeat.

"I have many more talents I could show you," he teases.

I lean in and whisper in his ear. "I'm pretty sure I've been on the receiving end of many of them."

"Lucky for you, Bellissima. Lucky for you."

We both laugh, but the contentment remains. That he opened up to me. That we're in a really good place right now. That despite what my brother thinks, this is the real Oliver Rossi. The man, right here, right now. The man giving me this gift—his time, his honesty, his effort—is the real one.

The private tour is followed by a candlelit dinner in one of the museum's private rooms. An oval room with paintings all around and us at its center. The food is decadent and flavorful but the company is the real star of the show.

"How did you even arrange all this?" I ask as he tops my glass off with wine.

"You may be a Navarro, Bellissima, but I'm an F1 driver and that does count for something in this world." He winks and smiles, ever playful but clearly still struggling with our situation.

"Do you worry about the next race? About Cruz and what he'll say or do?" I ask.

"No. If there's a problem with it, it's his. Not mine."

"I know but—"

"No buts." He takes my chair by its seat and abruptly pulls me toward him so that my knees are between his thighs. "Stop talking about your brother. This is about us. You. Me. Tonight." He cups the side of my neck and pulls me into him so that his lips can brush against mine. "And how I'm falling for you and don't know what to do about it."

My breath hitches. My soul jumps with joy.

It's his goofy smile—the one that matches mine—that gives me the confidence needed to respond.

"Well at least we're both on the same page."

CHAPTER FORTY-ONE

Rossi

"A PART OF ME FEELS PRIVILEGED FOR THIS CHANCE—TO SEE ALL this incredible art. The Monet. The Bosch. A freaking van Gogh. I mean . . . every piece in here is like a capsule in time we were privileged to get lost in."

"I know."

"And another part of me feels selfish and slightly ridiculous at this spoil of riches. Art is meant to be seen. Shared. The general public should get a chance to see this too."

"Agreed."

"Agreed?" She turns and looks at me.

"Yes, I agree. Wholeheartedly. There's a lot of stunning things in this gallery, Bellissima, but I assure you the most gorgeous one is you." I slide my hands around her waist from behind and nuzzle her neck.

"You're trying to distract me, Ollie."

"Is it working?" I nip her shoulder. "God, I fucking want you."

"Hmm. There's no shortage there."

"You're talented and gorgeous and funny and—"

"You've already got the girl, Rossi. You can stop trying to impress me."

"Uh-uh. Never." Another kiss to the curve of her shoulder. Our docent has given us privacy to walk around and admire the pieces without her. And while I truly appreciate a second chance to look at the art, all I can think about is getting this fan-fucking-tastic dress off her. "If there weren't cameras covering every inch of this place, I'd do a hell of a lot more than simply impress you."

"Oh?" she murmurs as she shifts and moves to stare at the next painting.

"Mm. I'd start by peeling you out of this sexy-as-fuck dress."

Her head shifts to look up at the camera in the corner. It's the slightest of motions but it makes my balls draw up fucking tight because I know she's gauging—is it feasible?

"It's rather hot in here, isn't it?" she asks as she shifts slightly, but I continue to have my body ghost her. Continue to have my warm breath against her neck where her pulse is fluttering erratically beneath my lips.

"And then I'd drop to my knees, Bellissima. Hook that leg of yours over my shoulder and slide my tongue down your slit."

She emits the softest mewl as I bring my hand up and hold it still on her hip so I can rub my hardened cock against her ass.

"I'd circle your clit. Suck it. Then slide my tongue back down and fuck you with it."

"Ollie." She's fucking breathless and my name has never sounded sexier.

"Mm, that's right, Sof. I'd be on my knees worshipping you like the goddamn royalty that you are." I slide my hands up and down her hips and then span them up her rib cage and over her breasts.

Christ. I'm going to fucking come in my pants if I don't get some relief here. But the pain is worth it. The ache in my balls definitely fucking worth it, knowing how goddamn good and wet she's going to be for me on the jet ride home.

"Would you come for me like that? On my tongue? Riding my face? Or would you wait for me to sink my cock into that dripping pussy of yours? Would you cry out and beg me to fill you as full as I can? Would you dig your nails in my ass and tell me you wanted me even deeper?" I chuckle and I watch the chills chase over her skin. "Baby, I know you. That right now you're dripping for me. I can hear it in your erratic breathing. Can smell how turned on you are for me. Can feel your ass pushing against my cock. Yeah, you want me."

"I always want you," she pants out.

"And I can't wait for you to show me just how bad, but I have one more surprise for you tonight."

Her body stiffens against me. "What are you talking about?" She turns to face me, her eyes narrowed.

And then I chuckle. I realize what she thinks I'm going to do. Propose.

Nope. Not happening. And yet a small part of me stands a little taller at the idea.

"No. Not *that*, Sofia."

She exhales and chuckles. "Just making sure."

I roll my eyes. "You told me it's a shame to hide this art from everyone. That it should be shared."

"Ollie," she says like a warning. "What are you talking about?"

I take her hand and lead her to a closed door, a room sealed off for just this occasion. "I'm talking about this."

CHAPTER FORTY-TWO

Sofia

I GASP.

Midnight Madness is displayed across from where we stand. Its stark colors and dramatic brush strokes are so vibrant, so violent, that I stand there, mouth agape and soul touched.

"This is where it's been," I say, completely transfixed by it. "It's . . . I've admired it so long. Its beauty. Its elegance. The way it commands attention. It's hard to believe it's real. It's hard to believe I get to be graced with its presence."

"I know exactly how that feels," he murmurs but there's something about the way he says it that has me glancing toward him. He's not looking at the painting, he's looking at me.

Oh. *Oh.*

I hold my hand out to him, wanting him to come join me. Needing him at my side.

"For one star to shine to its full potential, it needs to shine alone. For the other stars around it to dim. *Midnight Madness*," I murmur.

"What?"

"The meaning behind the painting. Or at least that's what I've read." I glance his way, overwhelmed and so incredibly grateful for this opportunity.

"For one star to shine to its full potential, it needs to shine alone," Rossi says quietly, as if he's absorbing the words into his very being.

"I can't believe you arranged for me to see this. I knew it existed, have seen pictures of it, but never thought I'd get to be in the same room as it."

"I can do one better than that."

Something drops in my stomach. "Rossi."

"I've gotten Mikah Mastroni to agree to showcase it in your gallery."

I see his lips moving but don't really hear him. "What did you just say?"

"You heard me." He presses a kiss to my cheek. "He's agreed to let it be on display in the gallery."

"What? How? I mean—*what?*"

"I figured, what better way to draw people to your gallery? To give it notoriety from the start? To ensure that you prove to your family that you can and will succeed at this?"

I don't know how to process this. How to fathom the hoops he must have jumped through to get this to happen. "But . . . how?"

His smile is the most genuine I've ever seen. "It took a while." He chuckles and runs a hand through his hair. "I've been plotting behind your back, but I knew that was your dream painting, and I wanted to get it for you. I offered to buy it—which was a hard no. It was a tough negotiation, but I convinced Mastroni that the world needed to see it to appreciate it better. That by showcasing it to the public, it would increase its worth. You name it, I tried to sell it."

I stare at him in awe. Even if Mastroni had said no, this is the most generous thing anyone has tried to do for me. "And it's been here this whole time?"

"It's been on loan to the owner of this gallery, but in two weeks, it'll be on loan, to yours."

My mouth is dry. My hands are trembling. What this would mean to a new gallery. The way it would cement my name, my presence in the art world. The way it would validate me. "I'm still not processing this." I emit a nervous laugh.

"I know. It comes with a long list of restrictions and security and parameters, but I already have that all taken care of. Insurance has been bought, transport has been arranged, contracts have been signed."

"But Oliver."

"No *but anything.*" He steps into me and brushes his lips against mine. "You keep telling me to let everybody see the real me. The only person that matters to me who sees *the real me* is you. It's hard. I'm not an easy man to be with. I have faults and lapses and will never be perfect, but this is me trying to be the man you need. That you deserve. The one who tries to help you achieve your dreams and goals."

"I want you just how you are. Can't you see that?"

"The want between us has never been the hard part, Sof. It's figuring out how to not be me that is. And I'm trying. Bit by bit. Day by day."

"Not to be you?" I reach out and cup his face, bringing my lips to his. "But you are the man I want. You are the man I choose. Just you."

CHAPTER FORTY-THREE

Sofia

"Thank you for tonight. Thank you for my surprise. Thank you for... being you." I pull my hair over my shoulder to give him access to the zipper on the back of my dress.

He presses a kiss to my bare shoulder as he slowly unzips my dress. The fabric falls to the ground with that distinct waterfall of sound so that when I step out of where it's pooled at my ankles, I'm in nothing more than heels and panties.

"Sofia," Rossi groans. "It never ceases to amaze me how stunning you are."

His words glide over my skin like a feather. Soft enough to touch and hard enough to incite a visceral reaction from me.

We meet in the middle. Moonlight streams through the open windows of the room and the cool Mediterranean breeze flutters in, but there's nothing that can distract me from the man before me.

Not his soft kisses nor his hard body.
Not his endless praise nor his dirty mouth.
Not his intense eyes or his demanding hands.

We connect in quiet sighs and unhurried touches. Our lips are languorous, our bodies in constant contact.

"Sofia?" Our eyes meet. He reaches out and rubs his thumb over my bottom lip. "I love you."

Everything stops. My breath. My hand moving on his back. My heart.

And then the biggest smile crawls over my lips as I'm filled with an incredible warmth that isn't from our bodies connecting.

I lift my head up and brush my lips over his. "Took you long enough." I chuckle. "I love you too, Ollie. I've been in love with you for some time."

He leans back and looks at me, his cheeks flush and the cutest smile ever on his lips. Almost as if he can't believe this is happening.

"I'm a little overwhelmed, Sof." Another kiss. Another meeting of our eyes. And then he pushes into me in one steady stroke, our fingers linking and our moans desirous. It's a dance of familiarity. We know each other's bodies. We know what the other likes. And in this murmured silence, we do our best to give to the other.

A lift of my hips here. A brush of his thumb there. The warmth of his mouth on my skin. The scrape of my nails down his jaw.

It's a slow build of pressure. Of pleasure. Of trust. All three things we're used to but after tonight, I feel like have been solidified in a way I've never experienced before.

I'm Oliver Rossi's. Completely.

My body. My heart. My soul.

And the way he makes love to me, the gentle demand, the quiet encouragement, and the murmured sexiness, tells me he feels the same.

And when that slow build can't stay contained, when the coil it's slowly turning snaps, I come undone.

Pulse by blissful pulse around him. Wave after wave of sensation.

It's his lips on mine that encourage, that coax, that overwhelm.

And it's his cry of my name when he comes that tells me all I need to hear.

He loves me.

He. Loves. Me.

CHAPTER FORTY-FOUR

Sofia

"It's not the same," I call out to my phone. It's on the counter and Lilith is on speaker. Leave it to me to forget to charge my AirPods. But we need to catch up and this allows us to do that while I keep my hands free to keep working.

"I don't understand though. You could have hired people to do all this for you, just as easily, so why are you doing it yourself?" she asks.

"Because I want to. Because if this succeeds, I want it to be because of me and—"

"Because your boyfriend is kickass and gave you the best surprise ever."

I know. He did. I glance at the empty space at the back of the gallery. The wall I've dedicated to *Midnight Madness* and where every necessary security requirement has been placed.

"I still can't believe it."

"I can. That man had it bad for you from the first moment he saw you and he hasn't let up since. Don't let that one get away."

I won't. I think the words but don't say them.

"And no name for it yet?"

I open my mouth and close it. "I've narrowed it down some."

"Well at least you're getting somewhere."

I smile even though she can't see it. I've definitely more than narrowed it down. I just need to figure out if I'm ready to take that next step and actually use it.

"Sof?"

The voice at the back of the gallery has me startling. "Lil? Someone's here. I have to go."

"Okay. I'll be there. With bells on."

"Love you. Later."

I push the button on my phone to end the call and look up to see Cruz standing in the back workspace of the gallery.

It's the first time I've seen him since the family dinner at the villa two weeks ago. It pained me to skip the last race, but I needed to for my own sake. I was busy and Cruz needed to understand that I meant what I said about everything—my needs, the woman I've become, and Rossi.

I worried about what might happen between them in my absence. Is it stupid to say I was grateful that Cruz ignored Rossi except for when it was necessary to interact on a professional and very public level?

His whistle is low and drawn-out as he takes in the place. "Whoa."

I struggle with being stubborn and holding firm to my grudge by making a smart-ass comment like "you would have known what it looked like if you'd have stopped by" or simply accepting that he's here and that he took the first step.

Our eyes meet and a lifetime of ups, downs, only having each other to understand, forgiveness, and acceptance passes between us.

He gives the slightest of nods—almost as if he feels that same realization—and walks around the gallery. I track him as he takes in the bay windows overlooking the sea, examines where each piece of art will be displayed, takes in the desk area that has our family story woven into pieces of it that only he'd recognize.

"This is cool," he murmurs as he notices items that were el patriarca's, our father's, and our great-great grandparents' that we never met. "I didn't know you had these." He glances up at me and then back to them.

I nod. "I've had them for some time and wanted to weave that history here, even if it's just for us to know."

I love the look on his face as he takes them in. "I didn't want to stop by for a lot of reasons," he finally says as he continues to move around. "Because we fought. Because it would seem meaningless if I came after the fact that you called me on it." He stops moving and turns to face me for the first time. His eyes plead with me to understand. *This. This is the brother who has always had my back.*

"True to all of the above, but you didn't come before we fought."

"You're right. I didn't. I know you well enough to know that you don't want my name tied to here so you *can* say you did it on your own."

Fuck. He's right on that.

"Well, your silence and absence spoke volumes," I say.

"And what did it say?" he asks.

"That you thought I shouldn't do this. Just like all the other men in our family think I shouldn't."

"I announced it at Maddix's birthday, did I not?"

"True, but then silence after that."

His smile is reticent, almost amused. "I can see why you'd think that, but when have I ever not been supportive of anything you've done? When have I tried to hold you back from the things you want?" He takes a step closer. "In hindsight, I can see and understand why you'd think that, but I'm proud of you. I've always been proud of you. I'm sorry I didn't voice it out loud or tell you sooner."

I hate that his words make stupid tears fill my eyes. I hate that I can be mad at him one second and then miss him and forgive him and realize how much I love him the next. "I didn't need you to come here and say all that. I just needed you here, Cruz," I say.

"I know. And I haven't been here for you. I've been so consumed with myself that—"

"Understandably. It's not like you're not some huge driver or anything."

"That's a bullshit excuse and you know it. Don't let me off the hook that easily." He steps forward and pulls me in for a quick hug. "You've always taken care of and looked out for me. I should have done the same for you and I didn't. I'm sorry."

"You're forgiven." I push at his chest, as this is getting too lovey-dovey. "Don't let it happen again."

He chuckles. "So you're living here now in Monaco? Like full-time?" He raises his eyebrows. It's so weird to me that he doesn't know this when we usually know everything about everything. *Shows our lack of communication.*

"You just realized that, huh?"

"No. Maddix had to point it out for me."

"Of course she did." We laugh.

"I'm proud of you, Sof. I truly am. And this place is going to kick some serious ass." He takes it all in again. "Between the location and your genius marketing idea with the flyers, and some huge painting people are talking about? You seem to have captured the buzz."

"Even if that is when el patriarca was supposed to throw you a party at the villa?"

"He threw out dates around my schedule. I pointed out the ones I could do. How was I to know he was going to use that as leverage to see if you were willing to fight for this?"

"Sneaky bastard," I mutter.

"Yes, he's that too." He chuckles. "This opening is way more important than a party for me. It truly is."

"Delivery," a voice calls through the back door moments before I'm met with a gigantic bouquet of peonies.

"Wow. Okay. Thank you." I laugh in disbelief as I sign for the delivery and then open the card.

> *I see you. I know how hard you're working. I know you're going to kick ass.*
> —Ollie

I must get the goofiest grin on my face because when I look up, Cruz is looking at me with a dubious expression.

"What?" I ask.

He blows out a long, exhaustive breath. "They're from him, aren't they?"

"So what if they are?" I ask because while I appreciate what my brother has said about me and my dreams, this whole Rossi thing is still floating out there between us.

He grimaces. "I don't like thinking about you with any man, let alone him."

I nod. "That genius marketing idea? The flyers blanketing Monaco?

That painting I got on loan that everyone's talking about? A lot of the work done in here to transform it to what it looks like? All that? That was all Rossi. Every single bit of it. For me. Because he believes in me."

"Shit," he grumbles and scrubs a hand over his face.

"Yeah. I know. You might just have to start liking him."

He eyes me. "I'm a work in progress, let's not get ahead of ourselves," he teases.

"I love him, Cruz." The words are out before I can stop them.

"Jesus."

"I do." I smile.

"And el patriarca?"

"I don't know." Jesus. I just fixed shit between us. Can't he be okay with that? "I'll figure it out. It's my life, right?"

He nods. "And it's private for now but it's Rossi—a public figure—how long do you think you'll be able to keep your relationship a secret?"

"I don't know. I'm figuring it all out."

"Uh-huh."

"You were allowed and afforded the grace to change and grow from the disaster you were, why isn't he? You were allowed a redemption story. So is he."

CHAPTER FORTY-FIVE

Sofia

"**O**H, DARLING, SO LOVELY TO SEE YOU." I FREEZE AT THE SOUND OF my mother. At the slur to her voice. At the way she floats into the Gravitas sponsor party like she's never been gone. At the way my stomach flips.

I unclench my jaw. "Hello, Mamá."

"You missed me. I can tell." She smacks a loud kiss on both my cheeks as I glance over to where Cruz is entertaining the sponsors, as is his job to do. *Thank God she hasn't spotted him yet.*

"Yes," I say softly. "Why don't we step over here?"

"Why? I didn't come here to be a shrinking violet in the corner. I'm a goddamn thing of beauty."

Too bad you're not that weird flower who only blooms once a year.

I cringe and try to tug her to the outskirts of the party before she makes the scene she's bound to make. *She's never refrained before.* She then plucks a martini off a passing tray.

"Mamá. I think you've had enough."

"Of course. Of course I've had enough. That's all you ever say while you're busy fucking your way through the driver circuit," she says loudly and earns multiple head turns. "Is he here? Can I rate him? You know your father was a lousy lay—"

"Mamá," I bark as gasps and muffled laughs litter the space around us.

"What?" She waves a hand. "Why hide the truth?"

"Mrs. Navarro." Rossi's voice breaks through the roaring in my head. I swallow back the tears and terror that suddenly own me.

No.

He can't see this.

He can't know this.

He . . . "Please go," I say to him.

"Well, aren't you a tall drink of water. Sexy. I've seen you from afar but hmm, never had the chance to appreciate you up close and personal." She runs a finger down his chest as she tries to concentrate through the alcohol. "You should fuck this one, Sofy," she calls over her shoulder before turning back to Rossi and rubbing her breasts against his chest. "And if you don't, I might want a crack at him." She throws her head back and cackles.

I'm absolutely mortified. Why? Why tonight? Just when my life's starting to become my own am I reminded handily that it's not. That my duty is her and everyone else that I don't want to be responsible for anymore.

And yet duty calls. It's ingrained in me like the blood that runs through my veins.

Rossi meets my eyes. He looks helpless. Confused. In disbelief. And I plead with him to just go. To just leave. To please do as I ask.

He physically steps back and removes her hands from his chest. "Why don't we take a step outside?" he asks as he leads her toward the exit.

With my head down, I follow behind them, humiliated but grateful that she's listening. That more damage hasn't been done . . . yet.

My mother hit on my boyfriend.

My boyfriend now knows the truth about how horrid she is.

I just want to crawl in a hole and die.

But I can't because I'm watching Rossi open the door and, the only thing I need is her to follow him as he ushers us through it. And the minute we are, he turns to me. "Sof—"

"Please. Don't. Just . . . go. I need you to go."

"Let me go get some water for her."

"It won't help. Nothing does." Tears well and a lone one slides down my cheek, killing me with each and every moment of its descent. "I don't want you to see this. To be affected by it. To even know anything about this because . . ." *This is my life.* My ball and chain. "Just . . . please."

CHAPTER FORTY-SIX

Rossi

Don't leave me.
 Every part of me riots at those three words and the woman I just met—the woman who makes Sofia say them when she lets her guard down.

I know what it's like to have a fear of something. To have something chase you and weigh you down your whole life, and I hate that this trainwreck of a woman has done that to Sofia.

Don't leave me.

Sadly, Sofia is probably better off that she did leave, but wounds still happen and scars still break open when scratched.

And Genevieve Navarro did just that. Scratched a wound she caused in public. In front of me.

Then what did I do at the first chance I had to prove to Sofia that I wouldn't leave her? *I left.* I let her redirect me back inside and I took the bait like a fucking idiot.

In my defense, I was trying to think of anything and everything to help. *Water. She needs water.* Like that's going to make someone as inebriated as Sofia's mother sober up some.

But when I return with a glass of it, they're nowhere to be found.

Sofia. Her mother. *Gone.* The patio is empty. The gardens surrounding them are too.

And now she won't answer her goddamn phone.

I scrub a hand over my face and sigh. If only I could get Sofia's expression out of my head. Her mortification. Her shame. Her resignation.

Her mother's behavior is not her fault and yet the look Sofia gave me said she felt it was.

I move through the room again offering polite smiles to everyone who meets my eyes while I search for her.

She's fucking nowhere.

I try her cell again and am greeted with silence.

"Cruz?" I approach him and he looks less than thrilled. Sure, we're cordial in public, but privately there's a lot left unspoken. I'm fine with that. I'm good with it. But right now, I just need his fucking help.

"What do you need?" I tilt my head to the side and lift my chin. He narrows his eyes. "I'm busy."

I step in closer and murmur in his ear. "It's your sister."

The death glare I'm leveled with is how I feel inside. But those three words get him to excuse himself from the conversation he's having and move outside.

"What? What did you do to her?" he snaps the second the door shuts.

I stare at him, blinking—not giving a flying fuck, because she's what matters. "Your mamá was here." The blood drains from his face. "She caused quite the scene—"

"When? How? Where was I?"

"You were talking. She was . . . drunk. Out of control."

"*Fuck.*" And the same expression that was on Sofia's face when she last looked at me is on his. A mirror image. I don't want to feel sorry for him, but I do. And I am. Years of conditioning makes two siblings react the same way. Years of conditioning have worn them down into acceptance, into resignation.

And that's why he cares so much about his sister. And why she has no problem putting herself in front of Cruz if their parents are nearby.

They've been through everything together and are close because of it.

He's just trying to protect her like she does him.

"Sofia redirected her attention so she wouldn't see you. I'm assuming to keep her away from the press." I shrug. I can only guess at this point. "I helped her get your mamá outside. And then . . . she left, and I can't get ahold of her. I don't want her to be alone."

"I think I know where she'll be."

"She needs . . . I don't know what she needs, Cruz, but it's probably you. You're her anchor."

Cruz looks at me and for the first time in all of our interactions, I feel like he truly sees me. He steps forward, puts his hand on my shoulder, and squeezes. "She doesn't need me, Rossi." He sniffs as I look at him confused. "She needs you. You're the man she needs."

Our eyes hold and there's something in that look, something in the resigned nod that tells me he may not like this new development, but that he trusts me with his sister. That he's handing the responsibility over to me.

That I just might be good enough for her.

I move through the darkness, over the wall, and out onto the grass. I'm out of breath and worried as fuck, but all of that dissipates the minute I see Sofia. She's in her formal gown, heels are thrown on the grass behind her, knees are tucked up to her chin, and she's staring at the city's lights before her.

She looks so lonely. Withdrawn. Sad.

She has to know I'm here. It's not like I've been quiet in my approach, but she doesn't turn to face me. She doesn't say a word.

I sit beside her and link my fingers with hers as she rests her head on my shoulder. We don't speak. We don't do anything other than stare at the lights together and listen to the crickets sing.

There's comfort in the silence. In having her at my side and knowing I'm there for her. And a peace to it too.

You're the man she needs.

Let's hope he's right because right now, I don't know what to do or say, other than be here for her and protect her in any way I can.

"I'm embarrassed you saw that," she finally says.

I run my thumb back and forth over the top of her hand. "Don't be. You're not defined by who your parents are. Or by actions you can't control. I know that more than anyone."

I love that she doesn't argue with me on it. I appreciate that she just nods her head where it rests against my shoulder and accepts what I tell her.

"It wasn't always this bad. Her showing up and making a scene has been something more over the past few years. We try to avoid it as much as possible, but we can't prevent event organizers from accepting Mrs. Navarro from wanting to attend. And I can't stop her from showing up drunk and saying such crass things as she did to you tonight."

I press a kiss onto the top of her head. "I can handle myself, Bellissima. It's not the worst thing anyone's said to me by far."

"Yeah, but she said it to me. She said it about you. She said it in a room full of people who matter. Who talk. Who look at Cruz Navarro and revel about how much he's had to overcome to be where he is and then at his little sister, Sofia, and feel sorry for her."

"I assure you no one was thinking that."

"They laugh. And then they pity. I don't want either." Her exhale is shaky and it breaks my heart.

"How old were you when she left?" I finally ask the question that's been on my mind.

Don't leave me.

"Nine? Ten? I don't know. The years run together. Maybe earlier. She'd make huge promises, say we'd do them when she came back from the next trip, the next weekend with friends, but those weekends became longer and longer. My papá was traipsing around the globe, browbeating Cruz into being the next legacy Navarro, while I was sitting at home waiting for someone, anyone to come home."

Jesus. My parents were the exact opposite. I can't imagine how painful that would have been for a little girl.

"I'm sorry you went through that but from my perspective, they're the ones who own the blame. Not you."

"Tell that to nine-year-old me."

"I know." I press another kiss to her head. "I can't imagine."

"I tell myself every time that I'm over it. That I don't care, and then she pops back up and I'm left scrambling to salvage everything she doesn't ruin. It's my status quo. It's how I keep my family whole despite the cavity she caused."

"Scars are scars, Bellissima. The ones you can't see are often the worst." I rest the side of my head on the top of hers. "You're nothing like your mamá. Those scars? The pain they caused? Your reflex to protect your brother at your own expense? Those guarantee that."

"I have a ton of them."

"All I see is beauty in them," I say.

"I love you, but are you sure you want to do this? I mean, you've experienced three of my family members and none of them have been exactly kind to you."

"And yet, I'm still here." I chuckle. "Trying for the first time ever to play by the rules."

"You? Play by the rules?" She scoffs.

"That's how you know I've got it bad for you."

She looks up at me and smiles. "You do, don't you?"

"I do." I shrug. "I might be out of control on the track, but when it comes to us, to you and me, I'm completely under yours."

"You didn't leave," she whispers.

"No. You're stuck with me."

CHAPTER FORTY-SEVEN

Rossi

I'M RIDING A HIGH.

It's been a great week and I have a feeling that today's going to be a good day. My car is on pace. My team is in sync. Sofia snuck into my driver's room and gave me a good luck kiss.

I mean, I'm riding a fucking high.

"So we have the drivers' parade and then a team meeting," Carina says as she waves to someone down the way. "And then—"

"Oliver!"

I hear the voice and stop dead in my tracks, my gaze immediately laser focused in the direction of it.

It takes me a second. My heart is in my throat and the smile I want to smile withheld. *Am I hearing things?*

And then I see them. *My parents.* They're nestled halfway up the friends and family section, their orange and yellow shirts standing out in a sea of them. They wave like lunatics. Like I'm a little boy at my first race and they want to make sure I see them and know they're there.

My chest constricts and all those little-boy feelings I choose to ignore time and again flood me with a vengeance I can't even comprehend.

It's hard to swallow.

I blink a few times behind my sunglasses.

And I finally let that smile come.
They came.
They finally came.
They finally showed up for me.

CHAPTER FORTY-EIGHT

Rossi

"ALEC?" I SAY THROUGH GRITTED TEETH.

It's hot.

The race has been one caution and restart after another.

Everyone's on pace, and it's been dog fight after fucking dog fight with all of us in each other's dirty air, struggling to gain a position and stay there.

Cruz is in front of me.

Riggs is behind me, coming in fast and full of momentum.

Two laps are left.

"Alec?" I ask again. "Free to fight or no?"

I repeat the question I've rarely asked in my career. The checkered flag is within my sights. My car's running at full capacity to push harder, to overtake Cruz and win the race. It would still be a one-two finish for Gravitas if I placed first.

And yet . . . I ask the fucking question no driver wants to ask.

"Defend, Rossi. Defend."

I take those three words like a hit on the chin. They sting and suck but fuck if I'm letting Spencer Riggs in between us.

"I've never been a fan of red anyway," I say, referring to the Moretti team color.

And I fucking defend my ass off.

Each corner. Every chicane. I try to make my car seem larger in the space and anticipate any lane I think Riggs might try to take.

It's a brutal fight. He moves, I move. He hesitates, I try to capitalize on it.

All while trying not to slow us both down so that Cruz has more time to gain.

Riggs tries his hardest to get a wheel in each turn, to use DRS to his advantage, to try a last-ditch attempt on the final straight, but I hold him off.

"Fuck, yeah!" Alec yells into my earpiece as every part of my body that was tight with tension eases. I feel like I can finally breathe. "Great teamwork, Rossi. Mega driving right there."

I've had much more satisfying podiums. Ones where I've taken the overall win. Ones where I did anything possible to get there.

But for some reason, this one hits me hard.

My chest constricts but I blink back the damn tears and pull into the number two spot on the start/finish line.

I climb out of my car to the cheer of the crowd. I stand on its hood for a second and breathe it all in before I jump off and am immediately grabbed into a ferocious hug by Cruz.

"Thanks for having my back. This win is because of you," he says in my ear before he's whisked away by his crew and me by my crew.

But I'm searching for her in the crowd. Those amber eyes and that huge smile and it feels that much more complete once I see her.

Maybe one of these days I'll be able to kiss her when I win.

Maybe . . .

But I do see my parents. And I'm overcome with emotion yet again. We stare at each other for a beat as my babbo raises a fist in celebration before putting an arm around my mamma and hugging her to him.

So strange to see them here.

And so very cool too.

As I turn to walk away, Stavros is in front of me. His usual scowl isn't there, and I'm currently looking at what is probably the closest thing to a smile I've ever seen.

I'm still not in the mood for his shit or for his sharp words to ruin my good day.

"Good job," Stavros says.

"Right."

He nods. "Sometimes fire lights a fuse. Sometimes it destroys all it touches. I lit a fuse all those years ago. I was wrong in how I did it, so I'll give you that."

"If that's an apology, you can suck—"

"It's not. But you've shown you can respect authority and your teammate. That I will applaud."

Okay.

"I have my team to get to," I say and turn without giving him anything more.

Footsteps.

They're at my back, coming closer. Company is the last thing I want right now and yet they keep coming.

And it's not because I'm pissed or grumpy or a surly asshole—I'm usually a bit of all three—but because I just want to soak in this moment.

I have a woman I love and who loves me in return.

I've made some headway with my parents and while I'd love to introduce them to Sofia, I'm content with still taking things slow.

And I did something good today. I thought of we instead of me and who the fuck knew I had it in me?

So is there any doubt that she's coming to find me to acknowledge it? She's known me longer than anyone here.

"Go away, Blair," I say.

"She's not the only one who knows you find the best view of the track before race week starts and after a podium to soak it all in."

I startle at the sound of Cruz's voice.

This is interesting.

"Didn't realize I was that predictable."

Cruz chuckles. "You're anything but predictable, Rossi."

His footsteps stop beside me and I glance up at him. He's holding out a beer to me while he takes a drink of his own. I eye him cautiously.

I've seen a lot of olive branches given to others in my lifetime but not a single one has been outstretched to me.

I'll wait to reserve judgment.

But I accept the beer and wait to see what the fuck this visit is about.

"I'm having a good day, Navarro. Why are you here trying to fuck it up?" If he's not going to talk, then I will.

He stands silently for a beat before taking a seat beside me. *Fucking great.*

"This thing with you and my sister?"

"You mean the thing that's none of your business?"

"Yeah. That." He clears his throat. "I'm not real thrilled with it."

"Just like I'm not real thrilled that you're my girlfriend's brother."

"I can't help that." He shrugs.

"Just like I can't help loving her. You of all people should understand that." I take a sip of my beer.

"Fuck," he mutters.

"Look, you don't have to like me. You don't have to forgive me. I know I screwed up all those years ago. I did some shitty things, things I'm not proud of. I blamed you for something that wasn't your fault. Wisdom comes with age and with meeting someone who pushes you to be a better person each and every day. That person was your sister."

"Quit making sense, Rossi. I think I liked things better when I didn't actually begin to like you."

"Same." I chuckle.

"So where does that leave us because clearly, we're stuck together for the time being?"

"Seems to be the case." I take a sip of my beer and savor the taste. "I don't expect to be best friends, but I hoped that today I proved I can at least be a good teammate."

"Agreed. On all fronts." He holds his hand out for me. I stare at it, then up to his eyes, before shaking it. "Thanks again for the help today."

"No problem."

He shoves up from his seat and starts to walk away. "Oh. And if you hurt my sister, we're going to have a fucking problem."

I chuckle to myself but keep my eyes on the track and grandstands in front of me.

Even footing.

What is it with Navarros and their need for it?

CHAPTER FORTY-NINE

Rossi

"I HEAR THIS IS WHERE ALL THE DRIVERS GO TO GET A BREAK FROM being so incredible," Sofia says when I enter my hotel room.

She's standing in a yellow jumpsuit, her hair thrown up in a messy ponytail, and adoration etched in every line of her expression.

For me.

Whew.

The sight of her after the day I've had—my parents showing up, my podium, my chat with Cruz—is like the reward after a long fucking battle.

For the first time in as long as I can remember, everything in my life is good. Is positive.

I finally belong.

"I don't know about incredible, but I know seeing you here is the best part of my day."

"Is that flattery, Mr. Rossi?" she asks as she moves toward me and slides her hands up my chest to thread through my hair at the back of my neck.

"Maybe." I brush my lips over hers.

Home.

It's my first thought.

I want her, is a close second.

"Good thing flattery gets you everywhere with me." She chuckles and then pulls me in for another kiss.

"Lucky me."

CHAPTER FIFTY

Sofia

"Breathe, Bellissima," Rossi murmurs into the back of my neck. "There's a crowd of people outside the gallery waiting for you to open your doors. To enjoy that incredible space you've created. To revel over the many incredible pieces you've painstakingly curated. You look stunning. You *are* stunning."

"I couldn't have done it without you," I say, turning to face him. The sunset is vibrant against the darkening sky and with all the windows in the Navarro villa, the room is bathed in a soft light.

He winks and smirks. "You can thank me later."

I brush my lips against his. "Promise?"

"I promise." He pats my ass. "Now are you going to tell me what you've named the gallery?"

"I don't officially have one yet."

"You're opening the gallery without one?"

I nod. "Good things take time."

"Like us?"

I grin and brush my lips against his. "Like us."

"Now, let's get to your grand opening. Our car is waiting."

"Wait." I pull him back against me and savor the softness of his kiss and knowing that he's mine. "I love you."

He slides his hand up and down my back and he deepens the kiss.

When the front door opens, we both startle apart. And when I hear the familiar hum of my grandfather's wheelchair, dread drops like a weight into my stomach.

He looks at me, then Rossi, and back to me. His hands shake in their position on the arms of his wheelchair. "Out of my house."

"Sir," Rossi says.

"El patriarca," I say, my voice pleading as I struggle between what's been ingrained in me and what I want.

"I come here to surprise my granddaughter—to celebrate her accomplishments—to find you're trying to ruin her reputation? Trying to sully our name?"

"No. El patriarca." Tears well in my eyes as everything I've battled in my head comes to living color in front of me. "He's not—we're not." I shake my head back and forth.

I swore when the time came for him to find out about us that I'd be strong, that I'd tell him like it is, but now that he's sitting before me, I've been reduced to a little girl still scrambling for approval.

"It's not what you think," I say.

"Sofia," Rossi says evenly as he takes several steps back. The muscle pulses in his jaw and his eyes hold a sadness I can't even begin to understand. "This is your night. Go enjoy it."

"But—"

"It's yours. You deserve everything that happens tonight."

"Ollie." My heart breaks as I take a step forward and he takes a step back.

"Sofia," my grandfather warns like I'm a child.

But it works. I hesitate. I falter. And I'm not proud of it.

"Go. Your customers are waiting for you," Rossi says, his smile as bittersweet as the hurt in his eyes. "Hasn't this been the story all along?" He smiles, but it's his reserved, sad smile.

For one star to shine to its full potential, it needs to shine alone. For the other stars around it to dim. Midnight Madness.

I choke on my protest as he walks out the door and shuts it behind him. I turn to face my grandfather, the man I adore but now don't particularly like.

"El patriarca. I can explain. Oliver is—"

"Enough. I don't want you to speak of him again. *Understood?*" he asks and the veiled threat is clear.

I stare at him with my heart in my throat and a bitterness on my tongue I've never tasted before.

"Come, let's go now."

> It's fine. We're fine. I shouldn't have been there. Don't let this ruin your night. You deserve every ounce of praise you receive tonight.

I reread Rossi's text over and over, trying to fight back the tears that threaten and the urge to look back over my shoulder behind us to see if he's following in his own car.

He's not.

I know he's not.

Hasn't this been the story all along? Rossi's comment repeats over and over.

"It's a good night, Sofia. All I wanted was to celebrate you. None of this other business matters." My grandfather pats my hand and smiles softly. "The art show always did bring out so many tourists," he says absently of the abundance of people milling about the street.

"Hmm," I say, mind occupied with Rossi and how I failed him in so many ways tonight.

"Look at all of them here," he murmurs when we turn the corner to the street the gallery is on. "All waiting for you."

I look to where he's pointing and am staggered by the amount of people lining the streets, waiting for us to open.

Holy shit.

It hits me then. The magnanimity of what I've accomplished. Of what *we've* accomplished. I glance back behind the car again. The opportunity in front of me and the person missing who I'm so used to having behind me.

And I don't think I've ever felt more alone.

He should be here. With me.

"We're here, Mr. Navarro."

"Thank you," my grandfather says to the driver as he pulls in behind the gallery.

A million things run through my head. Mostly what I should say to my grandfather about what an incredible man Rossi is. How tonight wouldn't be possible without him. How he's wrong about him.

A part of me knows there's no changing the mind of a man who's lived almost a century and is set in his ways.

The other part of me fears letting him down even more.

It wasn't like Rossi and I could exactly be a couple tonight anyway. We were more going to be in the same space at the same time.

So does it really matter that we arrive separately?

Chickenshit. My inner voice calls me that over and over at the top of her lungs to add to the shame I'm feeling.

I can't handle this right now. I have to finish tonight and then fix everything else.

But before I can process any of it, the door is opened and my grandfather, his nurse, and myself are ushered out of the car and into the rear entrance of the gallery.

Cruz and Maddix. Lilith and Zach. The few employees I've hired, several other friends, and a few cousins. All cheer as we walk in. By the look on Cruz's face, it seems I'm not the only one surprised by my grandfather's appearance.

I accept the champagne flute handed to me and plaster a smile I don't feel onto my face. Fake it until you make it.

"Everything okay?" Maddix asks as Cruz narrows his eyes at me.

"Yes. Fine." *No. It's not.* I draw in a fortifying breath. "Should we do this?"

Another cheer as I glance back toward *Midnight Madness*. To the painting on the far wall with its stark colors and violent emotions for all to see, much like it seems most of my family makes me feel most days.

Maybe that's why I am so touched by this painting. The anger. The longing. The violence. The dark hope for better.

"You did this, Sof. You really did," I murmur to try and hype myself up as I unlock the door and welcome the public into the gallery. To *my* gallery.

To *our* gallery.

Time passes in a blur of people. Each minute lapsing has me questioning myself and the person I thought I had become. That Rossi had helped me become.

I accept their praise.

And glance around wishing he were here.

I welcome their gratitude for a new gallery that appreciates local artists.

And smile at the memory of us making love on the floor right over there covered in paint.

I listen to stories about how certain pieces have touched them.

And I think of a man who believed enough in me he papered the entire town to make me see it too.

I put sold signs on over half the pieces I have on display.

And I stare at a painting unattainable to everyone else that he made sure to get for me.

It's a good night. Surreal. Astounding.

It's a horrible night. Lonely. Empty.

My gallery is packed. It's so full people are still waiting outside to get in and yet the suffocation I feel is real.

From the rules and parameters of a last name I never had a choice to make.

From a man I owe the world to—my legacy, my history—but that doesn't realistically live in mine.

And from another man, one I love with all my heart, who stepped back tonight so I could step up.

"Cruz." I call to my brother as a sudden sense of panic takes over.

What am I doing?

How can I hurt him like this?

"Yeah?" His eyes cloud when he takes in my face. "What is it? What's wrong?"

"I need you to hold things down for me for a bit."

He barks out a confused laugh. "Why? How? This is your night."

"He deserves to be here."

It's all I have to say. All he has to hear.

He nods and says, "He does."

CHAPTER FIFTY-ONE

Sofia

"Rossi?" I pound on the front of his door like a mad woman. "Ollie. *Please.*"

I've worked myself up into a tizzy by the time I reach his front door. And even more so when he doesn't answer instantly like I'd planned out in my head on the car ride over.

Knock. Knock. Knock.

Why should he open the door?

You didn't defend him.

Knock. Knock. Knock.

You completely disregarded him.

You didn't stand up for him.

Knock. Knock. Knock.

"Sofia?" He yanks the door open. "Is everything okay?" His eyes take me in. I can see the worry in them but there's also a distance there too. His guard's up.

"No. It's not okay."

I wait for the flippant comment, for the snide remark. For the signature Oliver Rossi everyone knows and expects.

"What do you need?" he asks me.

Not *what's wrong* after I blew him off, but *what do you need?*

I don't deserve him.

Not in a million years after the way I treated him in front of my grandfather.

"You," I say. "I need you, Ollie. With me. At my side. At *our* gallery. *I need you.*"

He shakes his head, almost as if he doesn't want to believe me. Almost as if he does, he'll know I'll hurt him again. "No, you don't." A strained smile. "I can't be there. Your grandfather is there and the last thing I want is to cause a rift between you and him . . ."

"That's just it. It will and for the first time in my life I'm okay with it because I love you, and I'm sick of hiding it. I'm sick of pretending to others that I don't." My heart is in my throat as I reach for his hand, fearful that he'll take a step back. But he doesn't. He links his fingers with mine and that symbol of trust, of faith in me, is more than I deserve. "If my grandfather has a problem with us, then he'll just have to learn to deal with it."

"You sure about that?" He chuckles and for a brief second, I see the trace of a smile. And I have hope.

"*So sure*. I'm in the wrong on this. Oddly enough, you're the one who taught me that. Who made me see it. This is me and I'm pretty damn proud of her. And you, Ollie, you're my choice. I can be a Navarro and have you."

"Even footing, huh?"

I bark out laughing but when I lift my chin to the waiting car, he doesn't hesitate.

Just like I never should have in the first place.

He holds my hand all the way back to the gallery. I'm not oblivious to the fact that his palm is clammy or that he's obviously nervous about this.

I don't blame him. Moreover, I totally respect him as a man and as my boyfriend for walking into a room when he knows he's the villain.

Then again, he's used to it.

"And here we are," I say nervously as the car pulls up to the front of the gallery. This big reveal—or rather thumbing of my nose at el patriarca—can go a few ways. I just hope however it unfolds, it doesn't affect the gallery's opening.

"Here we are," he repeats as he opens the door and helps me out of the car.

"You good with awkward, Ollie, because I have a feeling we're about to make this evening exactly that."

"Bellissima, don't you know *trouble* is my middle name." He smirks and pulls me against him so he can brush his lips tenderly to mine.

I'm well aware of the crowd inside my gallery looking out the window at us.

For the first time in my life, I don't fucking care.

It's a glorious feeling.

We walk in the gallery, hand in hand, amid the murmurs our kiss had already started.

There's still a buzz here. Still a crowd waiting patiently to sate their curiosity over seeing the new gallery in town, over laying eyes on *Midnight Madness*, and of hobnobbing with some of the F1 drivers.

But it's the pair of eyes on the far side of the gallery from the man sitting in the wheelchair who owns my attention. I can feel his eyes on me and can sense his disapproval.

And while I care in some respects, I truly don't when it comes to the ones that matter.

"Excuse me. Everyone, may I have your attention?" I say loudly as my assistant hurries across the space with a microphone for me. Rossi's hand is on my back in quiet encouragement. "I just wanted to take a moment to thank you all for taking time out of your Monaco adventures to help me celebrate the grand opening of the gallery. This has been a dream of mine for as long as I can remember. To own one. To run one. To get to talk art with people all day. It just seemed that I lacked courage to actually do it. So in addition to all of you for coming out, I'd like to thank Lilith for always pushing me."

"Love you," she says and blows a kiss to me across the space.

"To my brother for understanding me better than anyone."

Cruz lifts his glass up in the air.

"To my grandfather for understanding that when you love something, you fight for it, even if it's against what everyone else wants."

When I meet el patriarca's eyes across the space, I can see the fire in them, can sense his disapproval, but my comment says it all.

"And most of all, to Oliver Rossi. It was a lot of his hard work and dedication that brought this place to life. Not just with the physical labor but with pushing me to be uncomfortable so that I grew as a person and as a woman."

"Even footing," he murmurs beside me and I smile.

"So thank you all for being here, for making the gallery's first night be beyond my wildest dreams, and for all of your future support."

A round of applause goes up as everyone lifts their glasses in a mock toast.

"You did it," Rossi murmurs in my ear. "Soak it in because this is all you, baby."

I rest my head against his for a moment and hate that while I'm definitely appreciating the moment, I'm also looking around to see if my grandfather is still there.

"He's gone," Cruz says when he realizes what I'm doing. "You don't have to worry anymore."

I glance at my brother. "Thanks. *I guess.*"

"He'll come around, Sof. I know he will. And if he doesn't, then I'll just have to help him along until he does." He smiles and glances at Rossi and then back to me. "I told you. I have your back. Always."

"That makes two of us," Rossi says before pressing a kiss to my cheek, giving me a wink, and then walking away to blend in seamlessly in my life like he's always been there.

Funny how fast life changes from one truth to the next.

From one misconception to the next.

And to one untouchable rival becoming your whole entire world.

CHAPTER FIFTY-TWO

Sofia

"That was... incredible."

"Exhilarating," Rossi adds.

"Unbelievable." I lean back on the lounge chair, my back to his front, and welcome his arms sliding around me.

"Perfection."

"I couldn't have done any of it without you," I say as the moon reflects off the water. The waves and their ripples dance in its shimmer.

"I disagree. You were already doing it and I just helped get you there a little faster."

"Mm." I snuggle into the feel of him. To the notion that I nearly failed to stand up for this—this man, this feeling, this chance at something I've never felt before—and I don't think I'll ever let myself live that down. I have to make it up to him, I just don't know how. "I'm so glad I let you stalk me at the festival, Ollie."

He chuckles and presses a kiss to my shoulder. "And I'm so happy you made me wait."

"What?" I shift so I can look at him.

He nods. "You made me wait. You made me work for you." He brushes his lips against mine. "You made me realize from just a small taste, that you were worth chasing. *Worth trying.*"

"A taste? Is that so?" My grin's wide and my heart's full, but it's the look in his eyes that gives me pause. "What is it?"

He smiles sheepishly. "I don't think I've ever been this happy before."

"Even footing?" I say, as if I'm asking as a quid pro quo.

"Even footing." He nods.

"Neither have I."

And if I never remember another thing in my life, the utter joy and contentment on his face right now will be it.

CHAPTER FIFTY-THREE

Rossi

"I COULD DO THIS ALL DAY." I SMACK A HAND FIRMLY ON SOFIA'S bikini-clad ass, enjoying the sound of the connection and the feel of her sunbathed skin beneath my hand.

"What's that? Smack my ass? Lounge in the sun? Be with me forever and always?" She lifts a lone brow. "Be careful what your answer is, Ollie, because your reward might just hinge on it."

"My reward?"

"Yep."

I narrow my brows and pretend to think. "How about all three? This." I squeeze her butt again. "That." I point to the sun above. "And you."

Jesus. When did I become sappy? But one scrape of her nails down my legs in response says exactly why.

This woman.

Fuck.

She's everything.

"Mm. I *guess* I'll have to accept that answer."

"It's not like you had a choice, Sof. You're stuck with me." I chuckle. "You know you've made it big time, Miss Gallery Owner, when the tabloids already have you breaking up with me and moving on to the next man."

"I believe it was rumored I'd dumped you for the heir to Villanosa Yachts," she says and then squirms when I squeeze her ass.

"Fucker," I mutter playfully.

"Are you already doubting my love for you, Ollie?" she asks sweetly with a bat of her lashes and a wiggle of her hips.

I lean in and kiss her bare shoulder. "I do believe it was your lips wrapped around my cock this morning as a wake-up call so I'm pretty sure I don't give a fuck what the tabloids say."

Christ. Talk about a way to wake up. Her warm mouth. My hard cock. Her fingernails grazing against my balls.

"Good thing, but just in case . . ."

"Just in case?" I look at her, her lifted eyebrows, and her suggestive smirk. "What am I missing?"

Thoughts of her stripping off her bikini and riding me right here on the deck fill my head . . . just about the same time a helicopter flies overhead.

It's a normal sound here in Monaco. Helicopters flying here and there to deliver or deposit their affluent owners in style, but this one in particular hovers over the complex we are in.

And no sooner than I look up do bright blue papers suddenly begin trickling through the air.

It's like a ticker tape parade raining down on us. The closer they get, the bigger the papers become.

What the hell?

This was my gimmick, my kick ass idea. Who the hell's stealing it from me?

"What is it?" Sofia asks.

"Some fucker stole my idea. I hope he gets fined for not jumping through all the goddamn hoops I had to jump through to do it."

"What an asshole," she says as we both look up and wait for the flyers to reach us.

I stand up and grab the first one, prepared to be pissed, but when I do, when I read the words on the page, my heart stutters in my chest. I look over to Sofia whose grin is huge. Her expression's nervous.

"Sofia." I swallow over the lump in my throat. "I can't accept this."

"It's not up for discussion. Aren't you the one who told me if I want something the only way to say it is to speak up?"

"Yeah." I don't know where to look. At the paper or at my woman.

"Well, I'm speaking up."

I look at the paper again. "A huge thank you to everyone for making the grand opening of the *Simply-Just Gallery* a giant success." It goes on to tell the winner of the contest, but it's the words at the bottom that make me smile. "Hope to see you soon. Oliver Rossi and Sofia Navarro. Owners."

"Sofia. You didn't have to do that. I'm not an owner." But God does it feel good for her to see me as one.

"No, but I didn't want anyone to ever doubt how much you are a part of this with me. How much you've done. And I screwed up with el patriarca. I made you feel unwelcome, unwanted, and I hated that. It pushed me into the limelight. It felt empty. Wrong. And so this is my way of showing you and the world ... and the tabloids, how important you are to me. How much you mean to me. That you are a part of my world."

I struggle to speak, the feeling of belonging overwhelming when, for so long, I feel like I never have hits me hard. But rather than say something, I lean forward and take her lips in a slow, grateful kiss that shows her how I feel instead.

When I lean back and look at her, I know the tears in her eyes are from happiness, and it fills me with an immense pride to know I put them there.

"Did you notice?"

"What?"

"I finally gave it a name."

"Oh. Jesus. Yes. You're right. I was a little overwhelmed by everything else." I look at the paper again.

Simply-Just Gallery.

"Sofia," I whisper.

"You get it?"

"I get it."

Simply Sofia. Just Ollie.

Simply-Just.

Chills chase over my skin despite the sun. I blink away tears. She took something that was ours and made it that much more. I can't smile any wider.

"It's only fitting since you stole my flyer idea," I say, needing a break from all this emotion.

"Even footing, huh?"

"Even footing." She grins.

"Oooh, I hope there's hell to pay for it." She holds her hands out in front of me like she's waiting to be handcuffed. "Please, Ollie. Make me pay," she whispers.

And when I launch myself at her, when I slant my lips over hers and deepen the kiss, I know I'm complete.

I didn't need her to make me, but she showed me who the real me was. She taught me to own it.

And with this stunt, she showed me she loves the man I am. The man I became with her help. And the one I will keep striving to be.

Because she deserves nothing less.

EPILOGUE

Sofia

THE MUSIC IS A CONSTANT THROB. THE DUSTY FIELDS. THE COOL night air. The heat emanating off people. The excitement humming through the crowd.

We're brought back to last year. Same place. Different time.

But it feels so right, so real to be back here with Ollie in the space that brought us together—if not tumultuously for a bit—before we realized the fight was worth it. To be the one dancing with him this time around instead of teasing. To be the one snuggling up with him after a night of endless music instead of wondering if he's still thinking of me.

Our trip here is a bit different in some ways. We can't go anywhere without security and the VIP section at the front of the stage has become our new best friend.

"So much for getting lost in the crowd, huh?" were Ollie's first comments when we tried to blend in around the back but were noticed immediately.

It has its perks. F1's newfound popularity in America and its followers' ravenous appetites for all things to do with the sport, including the drivers' wives and girlfriends.

And then there's me with a double whammy—a sister and a girlfriend.

"Hey." He presses a kiss to my shoulder. The whole weekend he's stood at my back, his hands on me, his watchful eye all around us as if he's afraid his celebrity status might hurt me. Mr. Protective is most definitely back. "I'm gonna grab us a new drink before the show starts. Will you be okay by yourself?"

"I'll be fine, Ollie." I turn in his arms and press a searing kiss to his lips as I run my hand down his cheek—*my* tangible reminder of how real and incredible he is.

"You sure?"

"Lilith and Zach are right over there. Dozens of security guards are at each set of railings. I assure you, I'll be fine."

"Okay. Only if you are."

"I am."

He kisses me one more time before walking away, our fingers linked until we can't touch anymore.

It isn't a minute before Lilith's beside me, arm slung around my neck and a kiss plastered to my cheek. "I've gotta admit, being your friend has its perks, Navarro." She stretches her arms out. "Look at all this space around us."

I glance over my shoulder at all the people jam-packed on the other side of the barricade for general admission. "Yeah, I have to admit. It's nice."

"So with this VIP access, do you think Rossi could get us up there to meet the band?" she asks of BENT. This is the first time in the festival's history that they're using a repeat headliner, but the damn band just keeps getting better and more popular. "You know I have a thing for Vincent Jennings. The way he holds that guitar. The grit to his voice. His ass in those jeans."

"I'm right here, you know," Zach says jokingly. "Current boyfriend who is not a hot guitar player."

Lilith smacks a kiss to his lips. It's loud and dramatic and signifies everything she is. "Current boyfriend, you are the best. But if I got the chance, I might ask for a hall pass with Vince."

Before he can respond, there's a tapping on the microphone and the crowd goes wild in anticipation for the hottest band in the world to perform. But then there's a second pause as the crowd tries to figure out who's walking center stage.

But I see him.

I know.

Did you enjoy Sofia and Rossi's story? Do you want to meet the rest of the drivers in the *Full Throttle* world?

Be ready for another lap around the circuit in these upcoming books available now.

Off The Grid – For Spencer Riggs, his team owner's daughter is off-limits. But weren't limits made to be pushed? Available now.

On The Edge – Cruz Navarro needs to be on his best behavior to earn a lifetime branding deal and faking a relationship to the public is the best way to do that. Until faking it becomes making it. And this reformed playboy falls hard. Read Cruz and Maddix's story NOW.

Over the Limit – For Lachlan Evans, Blair Carmichael is everything. Gorgeous, funny, and intelligent she's everything he's ever wanted. Oh, and she's also his teammate's ex-girlfriend—and completely off-limits. But sometimes when you want something bad enough . . . it's worth the risks. You can meet Lachlan and Blair NOW.

Looking for another sexy racecar driver to read until my next one comes out? Have you met Colton Donavan yet in **The Driven Series**? He's a reckless, bad boy with a good guy heart buried underneath. You can meet him in this completed series which is available now..

ABOUT THE AUTHOR

New York Times Bestselling author K. Bromberg writes contemporary romance novels that make you work to get your happily ever after. She likes to write strong heroines and damaged heroes, who we love to hate but can't help but love.

Since publishing her first book on a whim in 2013, Kristy has sold over two million copies of her books across twenty different countries and has landed on the *New York Times*, *USA Today*, and *Wall Street Journal* Bestsellers lists over thirty times. (She still wakes up and asks herself how she got so lucky for all this to happen.)

A mom of three, Kristy finds the only thing harder than finishing the book she's writing is navigating parenthood during the teenage years (send more wine!). She loves dogs, sports, a good book, and is an expert procrastinator. She lives in Southern California with her family.

www.ingramcontent.com/pod-product-compliance
Lightning Source LLC
LaVergne TN
LVHW021051100526
838202LV00083B/5512